# CHILDREN OF EARTH

# CHILDREN OF EARTH

## CHRIS BACHE

*atmosphere press*

# PROLOGUE: 305

Colonel Brenner was sitting at her desk going over the budget for the new Mud Dog program when the receptionist knocked and walked in. "Colonel, Captain Bergstrom is on line one and says he needs to speak with you."

"All right." The colonel thanked the receptionist and turned on her work pad. "Captain, how may I assist you?"

Captain Bergstrom drew a deep breath. His hand had a slight tremble as he wiped the sweat off his forehead. "Good afternoon, ma'am. I have live cargo for sector four."

Brenner looked curiously at him. "You know the procedure, Captain. As soon as your cargo is cleared, you're free to deliver it."

Bergstrom had a nervous look on his face. "I'm sorry, ma'am, but the cargo is marked classified."

"Return it to sender: we don't like secrets at Fort Victory!"

Bergstrom fell silent as an unmistakable look of fear swept across his face. "General Raincheck ordered the cargo, ma'am." He looked around like someone might have appeared in the room to overhear them, then he whispered, somewhat embarrassed, " What if it's a doll of wrath?"

Brenner scoffed; of all the bullshit myths that would win them the war, this was her least favorite.

Being the ex-girlfriend of Alex Raincheck, the captain's eagerness to rid himself of his cargo made Brenner suspicious. "Then it's definitely not coming to this planet. Good day, Captain." She then severed the connection.

Brenner immediately contacted shipping and receiving

and demanded to speak with Captain Scott. "This is Colonel Brenner. Connect me to Captain Scott," she asserted.

After a brief pause, a man with a deep voice answered, "Colonel, what can I help you with?"

"Have we received any unusual or classified cargo in the last month?"

"I'm not aware of any, but I can check," he replied while his fingers pecked away at the keyboard. "It appears we did. One came in last night, then another right before you called. Both of them were cleared by General Raincheck, ma'am."

"Okay, thank you, Captain."

After disconnecting, she was even more suspicious of Raincheck's activities. She stormed to his office and was greeted by his receptionist, Sergeant Monroe. "Good morning, ma'am."

"Good morning, Sergeant. Is General Raincheck in his office?"

The receptionist stood up from her desk and walked over to the counter. "I'm sorry, ma'am, but he is currently in an important meeting," she replied.

Brenner thanked the receptionist and walked into Raincheck's office. "General Raincheck, sir, may I have a word with you?"

Raincheck was in the middle of a meeting with two other senior officers when Colonel Brenner entered the room. All eyes turned toward her before shifting to Raincheck, who calmly addressed her, "Colonel, I'm in a meeting right now. I'll contact you later."

Brenner scowled and gritted her teeth. "Now, Alex!"

Raincheck could tell that something was bothering her. He cleared his throat and stood up from his desk. "Gentlemen, we'll have to continue this discussion later."

The two men wished her a pleasant day.

"You too, sir." She nodded as the two gentlemen left the office. She then turned to face Raincheck. "Okay, Alex, what's going on?"

Raincheck tried to hold back an incriminating smile. "We were just reminiscing."

Brenner placed her hands on her hips and leaned forward. "I'm talking about the secret deliveries!" she barked.

"Diane, it's just a special food order for one of the nonhuman cadets."

Brenner gave him a suspicious frown. "Alex, Evolutions eat the same food as we do!"

She could almost see the red flags fluttering in the wind as Raincheck hesitated to answer her question. "She's not an Evolution."

"Then what is she?" Brenner suddenly had a bad feeling. "Alex, what did you bring on this base?"

Sergeant Monroe opened the door. "Sir, sector four just called. They're bringing 305 in right now."

"Okay, Sergeant, thank you."

Brenner became concerned when she detected fear in Raincheck's tone. "Alex, who is 305?"

"The first Mud Dog candidate."

Brenner took a moment to gather her thoughts. Nothing Raincheck said made any sense. "I'm afraid to ask, but why has she been placed in maximum security?" Brenner asked, anticipating a disappointing response from him.

"It's just to avoid any misunderstanding about her temporary appearances..." Brenner put her hand on his shoulder and checked the bottom of her shoe, interrupting him in mid-sentence. "Diane, what are you doing?"

She responded with an unmistakable tone of sarcasm. "I smell something foul, and I was just wondering if it was coming from the bottom of my shoe or your mouth!"

Raincheck started to speak when Brenner cut him off. "I don't care if you outrank me or you're bigger than me. As base commander, I'm responsible for the welfare of everyone on this base, and if you and your cohorts brought anything remotely dangerous to this base, I will personally kick your shiny little brass." She huffed and gritted her teeth.

Raincheck placed a calming hand on her shoulder and did his best to alleviate her concerns. "Diane. Everything's going to be all right. Trust me."

The tone of her voice shifted as old wounds resurfaced and tears welled in her eyes. "I did once, and we both know how that turned out. Now I want to see 305!"

Raincheck gazed into her eyes. "Okay, but remember, this is only temporary."

As they strolled toward sector four, Brenner inquired about the topic of conversation with the two generals.

"Just old times, that's all."

"You weren't bragging about us again, were you?"

"Diane, I wouldn't do that. Besides, I think Alice would divorce me if I did."

"I hope not, Alex. I don't like it when your friends look at me as another one of your conquests," she stated as they headed to sector four.

⋯⋯◆⋯⋯

They walked down a long, dimly lit corridor until they came to a pair of doors with a large handwritten sign that read "Chowhall". Brenner chuckled, figuring it was the guards having a little fun. Raincheck grabbed the doorknob, reminding her it was only a temporary form. "I know, Alex, you told me already! What is she, a butterfly?"

"Not exactly," he answered, opening the door.

As they entered the cargo bay, they saw a large black crate surrounded by security personnel. Each had their cyberhounds, a lethal combination of machine and dog. The faint scent of black rose perfume lingered in the air. It was the one smell that never failed to send chills down her spine and a cold reminder of why you should never judge a book by its cover.

It was the same perfume her adversary wore; she was

beautiful with long blonde hair and a radiating smile; she was Raincheck's little sister and very protective of her big brother. But something dark and sinister lurked within her. Even after his sister's passing, Brenner would feel her icy stare as a cold chill raced through her as if Half-pint were watching her from the grave.

Brenner nearly jumped out of her skin as her heart pounded against her chest at the sudden sound of alarms and the flashing red lights as the iron doors slowly opened. Chaos ensued as the cyberhounds fought desperately to get away from the enormous black cage being wheeled into the bay; on the side, it was marked "305". Raincheck watched nervously as the guards struggled with all their might to keep the massive beasts under control. "Sergeant, shut those dogs up!" the captain shouted angrily.

"We're trying, sir, but whatever's in that cage is spooking them", he desperately shouted back.

While people were scurrying around trying to bring things back to order, their chaos caught the attention of the cage's occupant.

A sudden, deafening bang erupted from the black box, spreading fear throughout the bay. The central control unit initiated a countdown for protocol procedures, ordering guards and their canines to take cover. Unfortunately, a guard and his dog couldn't reach safety in time and got trapped inside the danger zone. The guard desperately pounded on the iron doors, but the protocol had already been activated, and the doors were locked shut.

Brenner was trembling with fear as the strong scent of black rose filled the air, and a thick black mist escaped through a crack in the box. Everyone behind the safety shield watched helplessly as a giant serpent slithered out of the mist. Its scales were the color of tarnished gold, and the head appeared like a ferocious wolf. Her eyes glowed deep red as she tauntingly made her way toward the man, who was frozen in fear. But her attention was diverted when she saw the dog fleeing in terror. The chase was short-lived as the massive beast caught and devoured the poor creature in one bite. Unsatisfied with the measly morsel, she turned her attention back to the man. Everyone watched, expecting the worst as 305 quickly slithered toward him. However, the floodlights suddenly came on, and she uttered a loud, nightmarish shriek, transformed into mist, and retreated into the box.

Brenner's fear immediately turned to anger, thinking about all the ways things could have gone wrong or the sheer level of stupidity required to concoct such an idiotic plan, let alone to think it would actually work.

Raincheck knew she was about to explode by the look on her face. "Diane, I know what you're gonna say. But just let me..."

Without further thinking, Brenner drew her fist back and delivered a full-blown right hook to his jaw, knocking him unconscious. She turned to the sergeant who had witnessed the entire incident. "Sergeant, when that idiot comes to, tell him I want that hellspawn creature off this planet, or he'll find himself behind bars before the sun goes down."

"Yes, ma'am!" he replied as she stormed off.

✦

# CHAPTER 1

Carl tapped the screen of his media pad and began to read out loud:

*"The war between Humans and Evolution Shifters, our brothers and sisters whom we call Nature's Children, can be traced back to a long-dead planet called Earth. When the Human ancestors, the Children of Earth, left the planet, they took the war with them and continued their battle for generations. With each side growing stronger and wiser in the ways of war, they knew each other well – their strengths, their weaknesses – and it proved them to be an equal force. But on that dark day when the Shezón attacked, the Children of Earth set aside their differences and united to defeat the Shezón and send them back to their own dimension with a warning: 'We are the Children of Earth. Divided, we are strong. United, we are invincible.' These words formed the United Military Alliance, bringing Humans and Evolutions together. And now we are here together again, to welcome you to the new government building and the home of the new and revised Mud Dog program."*

Carl looked over at Raya, sitting in the chair in front of his desk. "Well, what do you think? How is it?"

The tired look on her face and the expression of her pouting lips only added to her appeal. But like the old veterans always say, never judge a woman by her beauty: it could be the last mistake you ever make. He had never really understood the meaning of those words until he met Raya. In her Human form, she was petite, with a smile so beautiful it made you smile back. With all her beauty and charm, you would never know she was one of Nature's Daughters. But in her feline form...

Raya suddenly interrupted his thoughts. She was tired, and he could hear it in her voice. "Carl, I already told you, the speech is good just the way it is."

"Yeah, but how good is it really?" he replied, smiling.

She stood up from her chair and shot him an irritated look. "Good night, Carl. I'm going home now." She snatched her work pad off his desk and headed for the door.

Carl stood up and called out, "Wait, Raya..."

She turned to look at him. "What?"

"I just wanted to thank you for helping me with my speech."

Raya smiled and walked back toward his desk. "It's okay. I don't mind helping. Besides, you're starting to grow on me."

He gave her a questioning smile. "That wasn't a compliment, was it?"

"Sweet dreams, Carl," she answered, waving her hand over her shoulder as she exited through the door.

Carl closed the door and walked to his desk, thinking back to his unforgettable first encounter with her...

He had been waiting in the starport with butterflies in the pit of his stomach, and for good reason. Raya was a college graduate, with multiple degrees, and the youngest daughter of the Space Force general, Goleen, who was known to be quite protective of his little girl. The only reason she wasn't Carl's boss was because she was a civilian. He felt like a peasant being in charge of the princess.

Like all Humans, he knew about Uteakons and their ability to shift from humanoid to feline forms. But he had only met them in person once before. It was aboard an enemy vessel, where the conditions were tense and could have cost him his life. But quick thinking on the Uteakons' part saved him. They were fierce warriors who proved unabashedly loyal to those who earned it, and he welcomed them into the United Military Alliance.

Carl's media pad started to buzz. It was a text announcing the arrival of the Uteakon ship, now safely secured at dock five. Just as he arrived at the dock, the ship's airlock opened, and a ramp descended. It was pitch-black and silent inside. Carl started approaching it when he saw a pair of yellow eyes looking at him from the darkness. He stopped dead in his tracks and his heart leaped into his throat as a thunderous roar came from inside the hull, followed by a deep growling that echoed in his ears.

"It's okay," he said in the bravest voice he could muster. "I'm Captain Winfield. I am here to take you to Fort Victory."

There was a moment of silence between them all, then a young girl, who appeared to be about nine years old, walked out of the transport. She had long, light brown hair and big dimples when she smiled. "Sorry, I forgot Humans don't speak feline. I was just saying my name is Ocean, and I'm glad to meet you." She was well-mannered and maintained good eye contact with him when she spoke.

"Hello, Ocean. My name is Carl Winfield, and I'm glad to meet you, too," he responded, extending his hand. She looked at it, then gave him a puzzled look. Carl pulled his hand away, realizing she didn't understand the gesture. "It's an Earth greeting," he explained. "I thought there were six of you."

"There are. The others are afraid to come out. They're not used to being around Humans."

He smiled. "How come you're not afraid of me?"

She squared her shoulders confidently and said, "Because I'm bigger than you are."

He laughed and put his hand on her shoulder. "I believe you."

She hollered over to the others. "Hey, you cowards, get out here!"

Carl gasped at the apparent insult and slowly backed away from Ocean as thunderous roars came out of the transport. He knew the Uteakons were sensitive about respect and wanted to avoid any misunderstanding. *Do Uteakons joke with insults among themselves like Humans do?* he wondered.

Ocean sensed his discomfort and laughed. "They're coming out now," she said.

His jaw nearly hit the ground when four massive felines casually sauntered out of the craft and down the landing ramp. Calling them large was an understatement. They looked like a Great Dane's worst nightmare.

Carl was even more shocked when Raya, the last of the six, emerged from the shadows. She was the largest of the felines. Her fur was dark brown, almost black, giving her deep yellow eyes a menacing look as the ramp buckled under her weight. Carl was about to introduce himself with a handshake when Ocean grabbed his arm. "You're gonna lose your hand doing that," she said with obvious annoyance.

Once again, he had forgotten the difference in customs.

He was more than a little nervous watching them approach. Intellectually, he knew they weren't vicious and weren't going to hurt him. But when his common sense took one look at their size and appearance, it made a beeline for the back door. Although he was shaking inside, outwardly he kept a calm composure as they slowly approached.

"Ladies," he said with a salute. "I'd like to be the first to welcome you to Fort Victory."

The only one among them who wasn't frightened was Ocean. As they were walking through the terminal, Ocean was in complete awe, seeing the different races of people, Humans and Evolutions, going about their business. She even waved to the kids she recognized from back home.

The last thing Carl wanted to do was make Raya feel intimidated. But that was a little hard for him to avoid, because, at six foot five, he stood out wherever he went. As the son of a drill sergeant, he had been in physical training since childhood, and continued with the Army when they took custody of him after his family was killed by the Shezón. Although his skin was very black, it was really his height, body mass, and military bearing that intimidated people.

When everyone and their belongings were transferred aboard his shuttle, they were given clearance to detach and set off on the eight-hour journey back to Fort Victory.

Carl was piloting the ship, listening to old city jazz, hoping it would ease the tension. Ocean sat in the copilot's seat, preoccupied with studying the operation manuals. He looked over to see four of the cats asleep in the corner as Raya sat ten feet away from him, watching his every movement.

He knew she was frightened, and he didn't blame her. After all, they were the new minorities in the neighborhood, and he knew exactly how that felt. Carl decided to put the ship on autopilot and strike up a conversation to help her relax.

"I know it's not easy moving to a new planet," he began. "Believe me, I've been there, done that. When I transferred to Fort Victory, I was scared. I didn't know anyone. My daughters, Tylee and Zoe, they fit right in, but it took a while for me to feel at home." He smiled at Raya, hoping she understood the gesture as friendly. "What I'm trying to say is, if you ever need anyone, you can always come to me."

Then Carl suddenly sneezed. Raya sprang to her feet faster than his eyes could follow. Before he could react, she was up close and personal, her eyes staring into his. Ocean burst out laughing so hard she fell out of her seat. After a minute of staring him down, Raya turned and walked away from him, ending the conversation.

Carl could feel the long hours of piloting catching up to him. His eyelids were as heavy as steel. He looked around and saw that everyone was asleep. With the shuttle on AI control, he leaned back in his seat to catch a little sleep himself.

A few hours later, Carl awoke and slowly opened his eyes when he felt his chair leaning back. Then he stiffened up, trying not to make any sudden moves because Raya's paws were on the chair's armrest, closing him in. Her jaws were slightly open, exposing dagger-like teeth, while the sound of her sniffing him echoed in his ears.

In that long moment, as she was studying him, his heart was pounding against his chest. He was staring into the eyes of a highly intelligent carnivore with more college degrees than the average doctor. When her curiosity was satisfied, she turned and walked back to the others.

Carl couldn't sleep after that. He'd look over at Raya every now and then, admiring her beauty. She was like living art. Her size, strength, and agility made her one of nature's powerful killing machines. The more he watched her, the more he wanted to know about her.

It wasn't until they had arrived at Fort Victory, when she had seen her sisters approaching, that Raya became comfortable enough to shift into her Human form. There was silence between her and Carl, but as she turned to look back at him, their eyes locked.

She was now a hair over five feet tall and had a strong resemblance to his late wife, Caroline. Her long, dark, reddish-brown hair and olive skin were almost identical. Even her brown eyes were the same shade, but that is where their similarities ended. Caroline was from the Russian colony. She was five foot seven, and her smile never failed to capture his heart. Raya, in spite of the resemblance, was not smiling.

He smiled at Raya again, hoping she would do the same, but her face had no expression. Carl watched her walk away. All he could do for the next few days was ask himself questions about her. *What kind of music does she like? What does she do in her free time?* Back then, he didn't even know her name or which one of his subordinates she was. The only thing he knew for sure was that he couldn't wait to see her again.

——••◆••——

When the first day of construction cleanup began, everyone from the office had volunteered. Some even offered to bring their children to help. With so much to do, he appreciated all the help he could get. Floors had to be swept and mopped. The walls had to be washed. He knew this was going to take more than just a few days.

Carl was in one of the offices with his two daughters, Tylee and Zoe, scrubbing the walls when there was a knock at the door.

"Come in," he called out. A wide smile swept across his face as he looked over to see Raya, who was now in Human form, looking at him with a bashful smile. "Hello, it's good to see you again."

As he walked over to her, Raya's eyes filled with remorse. "I just wanted to apologize for how I acted in the shuttle," she said. "I was just scared."

Carl smiled and nodded his head. "It's okay. As I said, I've been there."

Suddenly, a voice called from down the hallway. "Raya!"

"Coming, Elder," she responded, walking away. Then suddenly she stopped and looked back at him. "I wasn't going to hurt you," she said, then turned and disappeared down the hallway.

When Carl looked at his daughters, they were grinning from ear to ear. "She looks like Mom, doesn't she?" Tylee said. Then she and Zoe started laughing.

"Don't you two start jumping to conclusions," he said rather sternly. "She's a colleague, nothing more. Besides, there are rules against that."

"Yeah, like that's ever stopped anybody," Zoe blurted out.

Later, as everyone was leaving for the day, Carl walked over to Raya, who was talking to Ocean. He wanted to thank her for all the work she put in.

"Oh, hello, I was about to leave," Raya responded. "But if there's something else you need, I can stay." Her face broke into a pleasant smile. She seemed to be mastering that expression rather well.

"No, we're good. I wanted to thank you and your sister for helping out. You did a fine job."

The smile on her face turned hard as Ocean started giggling. "Come on, Ocean. Let's go!" Raya snarled as she grabbed Ocean's hand and stormed out of the office. Carl just stood there dumbfounded.

"What? Did I say something wrong?" he muttered to himself.

"Yes, sir," a timid female voice responded.

He turned to see the receptionist carrying a stack of books. "What did I say wrong?" he asked.

"Well, sir, you assumed that was her sister, and I am pretty sure she took it as if you were calling her childish."

"You mean they aren't sisters?"

"No, sir. That was her daughter. Her youngest. They age differently than we do, and it is constantly pointed out to them by Humans. A Human female would be flattered to think she was younger than her age, but not an Uteakon, sir."

"Just great," Carl muttered as he headed for his office. "She comes halfway across the galaxy, and what's the first thing I do? I insult her."

"Oh, sir?"

He stopped and turned. "Yes, Sergeant?"

"She's also your cultural exchange partner, sir."

He rolled his eyes and smacked the palm of his hand to his forehead. "I swear my luck just gets better and better."

Carl locked up the office and headed for his transport, thinking about Raya. She was all he could think about anymore.

Her smile, the way she spoke, even the way she'd catch him admiring her. He only hoped he hadn't thrown away any chance of getting to know her outside the office.

—◆—

Carl went to her apartment the next day to apologize for the misunderstanding. She was still unpacking the living room decor when he knocked on her door.

"Come in!" she hollered.

He opened the door and walked in to see Raya sitting with her back to him, surrounded by boxes. Her long hair covered some old scars on her back. *I wonder how she got those,* he thought to himself.

"Hello, it's Carl Winfield, your cultural exchange partner." He gasped as she stood up naked. "Oh, I'm sorry. I thought you said to come in." He blushed.

She looked at him, confused. "That's exactly what I said."

"I'm sorry, I wasn't expecting you to be naked."

He could tell by the look on her face that she was becoming irritated with him. "You mean I should be clothed in my own apartment?" she snarled.

He felt himself getting off on the wrong foot again. He had forgotten that Uteakons only wore clothes in public out of respect for Human sensitivities. On their home planet, they went naked, which made sense for a race of shape-shifters. An old image of a giant green cartoon character busting out of its torn clothes crossed his mind...He quickly changed the subject. "I came over to apologize for yesterday and introduce myself to you."

"It's okay. You don't have to apologize. My daughter explained that you meant your remark as a compliment." Her annoyed expression had turned to a smile. "I was just about to have coffee. Would you like some?"

"I would love some, thank you."

Carl followed her to the kitchen, admiring the view, feeling like it was his lucky day. She was beautiful in her humanoid form, but no less dangerous. He enjoyed listening to her talk and seeing her smile when she spoke.

He was helping her unpack when he noticed a military picture of a young man. His skin was as dark as his own. Carl inquired about it.

"My son Remix, that's his graduation picture." She spoke as proudly as any mother would.

"Your son is black. I didn't know that."

He could tell by the look on her face that she had taken offense to his remark. "He's not black. He's Uteakon."

*Now what did she mean by that?* he wondered. *Should I be offended because I am black?*

Carl brought his thoughts to the present as Raya walked back into the office.

"Don't forget to send the Mud Dog files to Sophie," she said

Carl scrunched up his eyebrows. "Who?"

"Second Lieutenant Skyler," she responded with a hint of sarcasm.

"Oh yeah, that's right. Thank you for reminding me."

As Raya prepared to head home, her thoughts turned to the new Mud Dog program, an elite special forces unit in the public limelight. She and four other women had been granted transfers to Fort Victory to work as adjustment counselors and help bring Humans and Evolutions together smoothly. Her father and many other senior officers had laughed whenever they heard about this. The official Mud Dogs were nothing more than glorified actors, controlled by politicians, and the laughing stock of the Armed Forces.

The real Mud Dogs were social misfits who were either

crazy or had problems with authority. Either way, they were the Army's black eye, and were given their own unit. Kept out of public sight, they were forced to do dirty jobs no one else wanted. People laughed and gave them the name Mud Dogs, but they had the last laugh. They did impossible missions and successfully completed them, just not in ways that the Army was willing to brag about.

Her father spoke highly of the old Mud Dogs. Even though they were all Human, he called them real heroes, men with iron balls. When the Human and Uteakon treaty was signed, the Army decided to reactivate the Mud Dog program. This time, they would be armed with the military's most advanced weaponry: and the only ones capable of using them were people born with the Symbian parasite, a NewGen. It was rarely found in males.

On the announcement day, her father and other senior officers passed out cigars and drank Uteakon ale while they bragged about the men who served the actual Mud Dog program and did missions only real men could do.

Raya smiled, remembering the look on their faces and the cigars falling out of their mouths when the Army announced the new Mud Dogs were all females! Mothers, both Humans and Evolutions, covered their children's ears as senior officers verbally expressed their opinions.

Raya's thoughts turned to Carl. He didn't really need her help. It was her attention he wanted. She could see it whenever he looked at her or called her name. She was flattered but confused. She wasn't in heat. And yet he was persistent, which made her even more curious about him. She was playing with fire, and she knew it. His flirtation was subtle but noticeable, especially to the elders.

She wasn't too worried about it; he was her boss, and she enjoyed working with him. Carl knew exactly how difficult it felt to fit into a world that wasn't yours, with people who look and speak as you do but were entirely different from her world. On occasion, he had shown more patience for her than she would've had for herself. She regretted taking her frustrations out on him the first time they met, the awful impression she must have made. She was grateful he was able to look past her rudeness.

The long day was catching up with her. She couldn't wait to shift out of her current form. Every muscle in her body was sore, and her feet felt like she had been wearing shoes made of concrete. Raya stopped off at the guard's desk to check out. She was greeted by Sergeant Williams. He was a tall, young, well-mannered Newtopian soldier who always addressed females by the respectful title of Huntress.

"Good evening, Williams." Raya smiled as she held out her hand. He bowed his head slightly, then took out a clear pad and held it in front of her. Raya pressed the palm of her right hand to it.

"Good evening to you, Huntress. How are you doing?"

"Sore. My whole body feels like I've been wearing a tiny suit all day."

When the pad blinked green, Williams pulled it away. "Too long in Human form. Don't worry, it gets easier," Williams reassured her.

"Easy for you to say. You're young," Raya laughed.

"No, Huntress, just a lot more practice." He smiled and opened the security doors.

Raya thanked Williams and headed out the door into the thick, humid night.

⸺ ••◆•• ⸺

Fort Victory is a place that never sleeps. Even in the late hour, people were going about their way, guided only by dimly lit streetlights and armed guards, while large transports drove down the streets carrying platoons of soldiers.

Raya took out her media pad and called for security. It

seemed silly, calling for an escort when she could easily walk to the front gate, but all civilian employees were required to be escorted for security purposes.

While waiting for security, her friend and neighbor, Marine Lieutenant Sophia Skyler, stopped to talk with her.

"Going home, you lucky girl." Sophie smiled. She was a Newtopian leopard, adopted and raised by Humans, and now a single parent of one child, a daughter named Jasmine Skyler, who was Ocean's best friend.

"You're not going home?" Raya replied.

"No, I'll be in the training center, working out all the glitches in the full virtual machines," Sophie answered, tying her long blonde hair into a ponytail.

"Why can't the technicians work on it?" asked Raya.

"Because it's all blind tech and uses a rhythm only people with ABS can comprehend. Plus, all the technicians are in training right now. That leaves me to do the maintenance. What about you? What are you doing tonight?"

"Finishing a novel Amy gave me."

"Oh, that reminds me, I have a gift for you." Sophie reached into her handbag and pulled out a paperback romance novel called *The Newtopian Rose.* "I got it as an office-warming gift. Although it was sweet, they didn't know that I was blind," Sophie chuckled. "How about you? Any word on your son?"

Raya choked up as tears began forming in her eyes. It had been two weeks and no word from her son. She was worried sick, and the silence was tearing her apart. Raya lowered her head, her tears falling like soft rain. "No...nothing."

Sophie gave Raya a supportive hug and apologized. "I promise you, as soon as we get the soldiers trained in blind tech, the tides will change, and the bugs will run. But they'll have nowhere to go. Even the Shezón can't see in complete darkness. I live in it, I know it well, and when I'm done with the Mud Dogs training, so will they."

The two women talked until security drove up to escort

Raya. "Well, I guess your ride is here. Maybe we'll chat tomorrow," said Sophie.

"Sounds good. Until tomorrow then. Have a good night, Sophie," Raya replied as she got into the transport. She put the book into her handbag, then suddenly remembered she had forgotten to thank Sophie for it. She rolled down the window. "Oh, thanks for the book, by the way," she shouted.

"You wanna thank me, tell me the story behind that T-shirt you're always wearing," Sophie called back as she headed toward the training center.

"You've got a deal," Raya hollered as the transport drove off.

When security dropped her off at the front gate, the driver offered to call her a cab.

"No thanks, I'll walk."

"Very well then, ma'am, have a good night."

Raya walked across the street to the park. She wanted to pick up a copy of the *Uteakon Starr*. Because of communication restrictions, the whole planet was shielded from the outer net. The only information about home came from the newsstands located in the parks.

Behind the counter was a tall, baby-faced young man with long red hair and a pleasant smile. "Good evening, ma'am," he said. "What can I do for you?"

"One copy of the *Uteakon Starr*, please," she answered, placing her work pad on the counter.

"You got it," said the young clerk. He pushed a few buttons on his keyboard, transferring the data onto her work pad. "Okay, you're all set. That'll be one credit, please."

Raya typed five credits into the computer, put her hand on the currency transfer plate, and smiled. "Here, take five," she quipped.

A look of surprise swept across the young man's face. "Thank you very much, ma'am! And have a good night."

Raya put her work pad into her handbag and headed into

the forest. She had always enjoyed the evening walks through the woods. It was the only place that made any sense to her after leaving her planet and the only life she knew behind, but it was a move she was willing to make for the sake of her daughter as she attended the United Military Academy. She was proud of Ocean and wanted to support her in any way she could, and if it meant adapting to a new way of life, she would do it.

Under cover of the forest trees, Raya loosened the straps on her handbag, placed them around her neck, and turned off her digital clothing generator. Now naked, she allowed herself to fall gently forward, appearing as a shadowy blur during the three-second move as her limbs, bones, and organs reshaped themselves, transforming back to her feline birth form.

Raya stretched out the kinks in her body and headed further into the woods. Her fur blended perfectly with the night, allowing her to walk silently in the cover of darkness. When she was close enough to her prey, she would usually take it down with dagger-like claws and a bite force strong enough to break a bone. But tonight, Raya was too tired to hunt and wanted nothing more than relaxation over coffee and a good book.

Her pace quickened when she felt light sprinkles falling from the sky. She didn't mind the drizzle, and even enjoyed the feel of it rolling off her dark fur. It was the heavy downpours she didn't like. It was loud, and the vibrations constantly pounded in her ears as it hit solid objects.

She was relieved to see the large sign: WELCOME TO BRAVO SIX. Bravo Six was like a small city, where most residents were Evolutions, and the businesses catered to Uteakons and Newtopians. There was even a jazz club called the Beastly Swing. It was a home away from home, and the only place since leaving Uteaka where she could stroll down the street in her birth form and not have mothers shield their children from her.

There had always been tension between Evolutions and Humans, but it was more focused on the Uteakons now that they were allies. To the older generation, the Human and Uteakon War was not something either side was willing to forget. For some, there were old wounds that never healed.

To the young, that war was ancient history. Even now, Human boys came to the apartment to visit Ocean. At first, it was out of curiosity, knowing Evolutions weren't accustomed to wearing clothes. But now the young were used to it. Even in the Military Academy, everything was coed and came with severe punishment for anyone breaking the code of conduct.

Raya looked around. The shops were closed for the night, and the only sound of life was the laughter coming from the café across the street. As the rain began to pick up, Raya decided to head over to the café. Inside, it was crowded with young soldiers, Humans, and Evolutions laughing and having a good time. There were even mixed couples among the crowd, openly expressing their feelings. Raya shook the rain from her fur before she entered.

The only seat available was in the corner booth, across from a young Uteakon woman with her nose buried in a book.

"Excuse me, do you mind if I sit here?" Raya asked politely.

The young woman looked over at the empty seat and then at Raya. "It's yours," she said, smiling as she closed her book. "I haven't seen you around here. Are you new?"

"My daughter and I moved here a few weeks ago."

"Then welcome to Fort Victory," the girl replied.

Raya ordered a cup of coffee. Despite its awful taste, the cup was hot and warmed her cold fingers as she listened to the young woman talk about Fort Victory and the friends she had made. She even blushed when she spoke about the boy in her life and how they had talked about marriage and adopting kids, since he wasn't Uteakon. Raya smiled and congratulated her.

Suddenly an argument broke out between a Human boy

and a Newtopian girl who was in tears and walked out of the café. The young soldier quickly followed after her. They argued some more under the heavy downpour until the young man pulled her into his arms. She rejected him at first, pushing him away. Desperate, he pulled her back into his arms, pressing his lips to hers.

Everyone in the café, including Raya, watched with anticipation as the young man pulled a small black box from his pocket and opened it in front of her. Her eyes widened, and her smile almost lit up the rainy night. A moment of heartfelt silence swept throughout the café as a few people wiped tears of joy from their eyes.

When the rain lifted, Raya thanked the Uteakon girl for her kindness and headed home.

$$\text{◆◆◆}$$

# CHAPTER 2

Raya let out a sigh of relief as she stepped into her apartment. "Ocean sweetie, I'm home!" she announced. She expected Ocean to come running from her room and into her arms, but the silence reminded her she was alone. Ocean was visiting her grandmother for the weekend, and her other children were all grown up with their own children. *Where has the time gone?* she asked herself.

Her two-bedroom apartment and all its furniture were an early twenty-first-century Earth design and felt more like a time capsule. But it was charming with just the right ambiance to it. She put her handbag on the kitchen table and headed for the coffee maker. After her long week of getting the training center ready for its grand opening, she was ready for coffee and romance. She chuckled as she thought of the book Amy gave her. Even literary romance was still better than nothing.

While waiting for the coffee to finish perking, she opened her handbag, pulled out her work pad, and logged on to her son's video diary, the 775th Special Operations. The videos let friends and family know how their loved ones were doing.

She always knew her son would follow in his father's footsteps, just like her father. War was in his blood, and when he came of age, Remix joined the military. Even as a kitten, he was never satisfied with staying inside the Kinship and doing things that kittens do, like stalking his mother's tail or roughhousing with his siblings. He was curious about the world outside and wanted to explore it. But he was too young, and his white fur would make him an easy target for flying predators. No matter how often she had told him, she could always picture the gears spinning in his head as he lay sleeping in her paws.

Raya grinned, thinking about all the times he'd get into mischief. He wasn't just clever. He was a fast learner who overcame challenges quickly, testing her alertness and patience. And now he was all grown up, galaxies away. This time, it was her sanity he was trying.

Raya shut down her work pad and headed down the hallway. She wasn't used to the silence in her apartment and didn't realize how empty it would be without her youngest. Before long, her daughter would be ready for her first breeding cycle and off on her own, too.

Raya decided it was time to relax and focus on the romance novel Amy had given her, although she found the Human ideas of romance a little strange and confusing. She loved reading it but wondered why the heroine just didn't take him. That's what she would do. After all, mating was no different from hunting. It was always the strongest who got the best prey.

In the backlands of Uteaka, this was the law of the land and had been for many generations. Survival of a Kinship depended on the physical strength of its members, so females were careful as to whose bloodline came into the Kinship. However, it always came at a price. The largest and most robust males were considered champions and highly sought after by the most vigorous females.

When an Uteakon female goes into heat, her sense of smell is heightened, allowing her to track a mate up to ten miles. And when several females hunt the same male, it becomes a battle of elimination with only one survivor. Eight of her nine children were sired by this law. But nowadays those ways were fading, swept away and soon to be forgotten, as Kinships were torn apart, separating mothers from their children and brothers from their sisters, while the young left for Uteakon cities to answer the military's call for soldiers.

Raya deactivated her uniform badge and headed to her room for the only article of clothing she had that wasn't computer-generated. She kept an old faded brown T-shirt in the nightstand drawer and always wore it on her coffee and romance nights.

Raya took out the shirt, smiling as she thought of Corporal Gill. He was the first Human she had met. Although the color in the shirt may have faded, his scent didn't, nor did the memories she had every time she wore it. Although she didn't find the incident as humorous as her mother did, she disagreed with her father, who wished it had never happened. But it did. She couldn't change the past and wouldn't even if she could.

If it hadn't been for the corporal, Raya never would have found the awakening her sisters talked about, but she wished they had been under different circumstances. Had she not been under the influence of her breeding cycle, her encounter with him could have been as quiet as two strangers whispering in the dark.

Her mother always said, "Change is like the wind. It can come in as calm as a gentle breeze or as fast as a hurricane, affecting the lives of everyone in its path." She sat there, holding the shirt in her lap, as she thought back to the day that had changed everything...

Despite living in the heart of Uteakon City, a bustling place full of educational opportunities and people eager to learn, Raya's life wasn't exciting. Her parents and son were fighting in a galactic war, which made things even more challenging. She had grown accustomed to a predictably comfortable life until a knock on the door from her father, Battle Star Commander General Goleen, changed everything. From that moment on, she found herself walking blindly into a hurricane.

"Dad. What are you doing here?" she had asked suspiciously, then caught herself. "Sorry, Dad... I didn't mean the way it sounded. Come on in."

Her father gave her an awkward smile as he stepped into the apartment, still wearing his military uniform.

"Hello, Kitten. It's good to see you again." He hugged and kissed her on the cheek.

"It's good to see you too, Dad."

Hearing her grandfather's voice, Ocean bolted out of her bedroom, smiling as she ran to him with open arms. "Grandpa!"

"There's my little grand kitten," he boasted, picking her up.

Ocean's smile turned to a frown. "Grandpa, I am not a kitten anymore... I got my Human form. That makes me a child."

"You will always be a kitten to me." He laughed and kissed her cheek.

As Ocean spent time with her grandfather, Raya stepped onto the balcony, wondering about her father's visit. Why was he here? With Uteaka's welfare at stake, her father had no time for anything that wasn't war-related. A surprise family visit was so out of character for him she had an ominous feeling...

Raya took a deep breath and looked down at the people below going about their night activities. Like Fort Victory, Uteakon City had a schedule to follow and never slept. Formerly, most residents were college students. But now it was soldiers passing through. Some returned home for a visit, and others would never return. Raya hated the war and all its misery, but it also had its positive side, the hope of victory. Although small, it was still hope and a lot better than nothing. But she knew it would take more than hope to win a war. It would take trust, something Uteakons and Humans never had, and they never would if the elders had their way. She had tried to stay positive, but the thought of her son Remix fighting alongside Humans and Newtopians—two species who had once been their bitter enemies—rattled her nerves and her sanity.

Raya quickly pulled herself together when she heard her father's shoes walking across the wooden floors. The last thing she wanted was for him to see her crying. He stepped onto the balcony. Raya was afraid and uncertain if she was ready to face him. She continued watching the people below. He stood behind her and wrapped his arms firmly around her shoulders.

"The moon blossom trees are beautiful tonight... When you were a kitten, we would watch them blossom together," he whispered in her ear. His voice was deep and had a soothing tone to it.

Raya was silent, enjoying the security of his embrace. It had been a while since her father had held her like that. Most of the time, he was cold and expressed no emotions. Even his eyes were hard to read. He was a stone soldier and rarely took off his uniform. On those rare occasions he did, it was as if her childhood father was there again and not the cold commander he usually was now.

"When you were a kitten... You would always come running to me during thunderstorms... I would stand over you, protecting you," he whispered in her ear. He tightened his embrace and put his cheek to hers.

"You look troubled...Is there anything wrong?"

Raya spoke softly, gathering all the courage she could. "Remix, is he okay?"

Her father gently turned her around, his hands on her shoulders, smiling as he looked into her eyes.

"Remix is in boot camp, and he's doing fine," he said proudly.

Raya was silent, remembering all the horror stories he'd told her about Humans. Even in her adult years, she'd remember them and shudder. Sometimes, Raya would wake up from a nightmare, crying over the image of a corpse. She was tired of bad dreams, wondering if Remix was alive or dead.

"All my life, you've told me how bad Humans are, how cruel they can be, then you send my son into the heart of it all...and tell me he's fine." Raya looked into his dark green eyes. Her cheeks were red and glistening with tears. "I will never forgive you if they hurt my son, never!"

Goleen held his daughter as her tears pierced the very core of his heart. They were the tears no father wanted to see on his child, let alone be the cause. He stayed silent, torn with guilt. All she knew about Humans was from the bedtime stories. They were just words meant only for entertainment. At the time, he didn't see the harm in portraying Humans as villains and Uteakons as heroes.

Goleen's eyes began to water as his daughter's weeping echoed in his ears. He could still hear her mother warning him about telling stories about Humans when he had never seen or even talked to one. By the time he realized the mistake, the damage was already done, and Remix had already shipped out.

He tightened his embrace. His tone was soft and filled with remorse. " Kitten... I'm sorry... I never meant to hurt you," he whispered in her ear.

Raya felt his stone exterior crumbling as she cried in his arms.

"Your mother told me many times not to tell those stories... She said I didn't know any more about them than they do about us and, entertainment or not, they were still lies." He was silent as Raya continued to cry. "Kitten, if I thought for one moment that those recruits would be in danger from the Humans or the Newtopians... I never would've sent them."

Raya looked up at him. "I know, Dad. It's just that I worry so much." Raya wiped her tears away and gave her father a slight smile, then gently pulled herself out of his arms. Feeling tired and depressed, she shifted into feline form and looked up at the stars in the night sky.

Her father also shifted forms. He was tan with black stripes, making him look like a golden tiger. There was a time when he was a champion amongst champions. Even now, his size and strength are unmatched.

Raya looked over at him as he sat down next to her. He began grooming the side of her cheek like he had when she was a kitten, his large tongue gently pulling on her fur with each swipe he made. It brought back memories of happier times when her life was not so chaotic, and she didn't have all the worries that she did now. Raya sat silently next to her father, watching the stars.

"Kitten, I want you to be the goodwill ambassador at the Fort Victory banquet," he said, breaking the silence.

Raya looked at him, surprised. "Me, why me? I don't know anything about being an ambassador."

"Kitten, you went to college, and look at you now. You're working in a college."

"Yes, Dad. As an information officer. I help college students, not the military," she replied, flicking the end of her tail.

"For as long as I can remember, you've always been the voice for somebody."

"Yes, Dad, and I also remember being kicked out of school and how angry you were every time you had to pick me up. I also remember you taking me by the arm and me having to keep up with your angry pace."

Her father looked back at her. "It's a lot different now. You're not in school. This time, I'm asking you to be Uteaka's voice. If Humans are to know us, I want them to know us as a people, not a military."

Raya was moved by her father's words but wasn't fooled. Even though he meant what he said, he had other motives.

"You just don't want to go to the banquet, do you?"

"You know me, Kitten. I don't do well with speeches or Human interaction, especially with that old bastard, Raincheck, always asking me if I need a booster seat."

Raya burst into laughter. "Sorry, Dad. I don't mean to laugh."

"Laughter is the greatest gift a child can give to a father. You know who taught me that?"

Raya knew the answer. It was the same one she would have for her children.

"Think about it, Kitten. And we'll have lunch tomorrow."

Her father shifted back into Human form and headed back into the apartment and out the door.

"I will," Raya had promised.

As Raya passed by Ocean's bedroom, she stopped to watch. Ocean was sitting at her desk connected to the outer net, laughing and talking with her online friends. Raya's children had learned more about the universe and the people outside of Uteaka than she ever did. Raya had let out a gentle roar, telling Ocean it was time for bed. "Okay, just five more minutes."

"What was that?" inquired one of Ocean's friends.

"Oh, that was my mom. She wants me to cash in and go to bed."

Raya shook her head and chuckled. She barely understood anything Ocean had just said. There were days Raya wished she was more like her children, who were not afraid to step outside their comfort zone and form their own opinions about the universe. But for Uteakons like herself, who had grown up on stories of war, her view about the Human race was based on hate and ill feelings, and she was beginning to realize this, watching Ocean interact with kids from different planets and races.

Raya walked to her room. Wondering if she could make a positive contribution. But anything was better than feeling helpless.

The following morning, her father agreed to meet her at the college. She looked forward to having lunch with him when the war started. It took all his time and left nothing for his daughters. Selfish as it sounded, she wanted a little time for herself. After all, he was her father, not the military's. But war has a way of forcing people to break promises.

Raya was waiting for her father's arrival at 11:45. However, she was greeted not by her father but by one of his infantry sergeants. Sergeant Tank was a tall, muscular young man, standing at five and a half feet—a remarkable height for an Uteakon.

"What are you doing here?" she asked with disappointment.

Sergeant Tank spoke calmly, "Your father has been delayed, and he has sent me to pick you up."

Raya felt let down, tired of her father's broken promises, and was in no mood to talk to him. "Well, you can tell him I don't feel like talking." She pouted.

When her father gives an order, he leaves no room for failure. Sergeant Tank leaned over and gazed intensely into her eyes. The tone of his voice was deep, and his demeanor quickly changed. "My orders are to bring you to your father... So either you walk like a Huntress, or I can carry you like a spoiled child. Either one works for me, Princess!" he said impatiently.

Thinking he was bluffing, Raya started to walk away. Tank picked up Raya and slung her over his shoulder before heading for his transport. They could hear the elders laughing and making comparisons between Raya and her father as she swore and pounded on Tank's back as he carried her down the hallway.

Tank's heart raced as Raya's razor-sharp claws dug into his back.

"Put me down, you troglodyte!" she snarled, tightening her grip.

When he could no longer tolerate the pain, he reached over and delivered a stinging smack to her derrière.

"Ouch!" she cried out, her claws retracting in surprise.

When they got to the transport, Tank put her down and opened the door.

"Have a seat, Huntress," he said calmly and politely.

Raya looked at him sheepishly.

"I can't!" she whispered.

"Why not?"

Raya gritted her teeth as she gave him an angry look. "Because my ass hurts, moron!" she barked, rubbing the stinging area.

Tank opened her door and put his face close to hers. "My back ain't feeling that great either, Karen!" he whispered.

Raya looked up at him. Her anger suddenly turned to guilt, realizing he was a young soldier following orders, and she felt guilty for taking her frustrations out on him. "Sorry about your back. I know you're just following orders... And can we not say anything to my father about this, please?"

He looked at her and smiled. "As you wish, Huntress," he said with a slight bow and then closed her door when she entered.

———••◆••———

When they got to the Army base, Tank escorted her to her father's office.

"Come in," her father shouted through the closed door.

"Your daughter, sir," Tank announced.

"Thank you, Sergeant. You did a fine job."

The sergeant bowed his head gracefully.

"It's been my pleasure, sir." He turned to Raya and bowed his head to her. "Good day, Huntress."

"Good day, Sergeant."

"Please, have a seat, Kitten," her father requested.

She gave him an uncomfortable glance. "I would prefer not to sit if that's all right," Raya replied with a forced grin.

"Very well." He got up from his desk and approached her with open arms.

Raya hugged him and kissed him on the cheek.

"Hi, Dad."

"Kitten, I'm sorry about our lunch. I had an emergency meeting."

"It's okay, Dad. I know you're busy with the war, and yes,

I'll be your ambassador."

"Thank you, Kitten. And I promise we'll have plenty of time together on the ship."

# CHAPTER 3

Raya was on her father's warship studying for her first encounter with humans. Before she left, she had downloaded several romance novels to her media pad, figuring if there would be long hours studying, she would enjoy it, but found human romance excitingly strange. In the stories, the males weren't lured by scent and didn't risk their lives putting their noses where they weren't wanted. And before the male could mate with the female, he'd have to make her laugh, be her friend. This wasn't something Uteakon females were accustomed to. With Uteakon males, it was only a one-night stand on a night she was controlled by biology and wasn't herself. But with a human, would it be a night she would never forget? Raya smiled, thinking about the possibilities.

"You have a visitor," the AI announced.

When the doors opened, her older sister strolled into the room.

"Still at it?" she growled softly.

Albright was a drill sergeant in the Uteakon Army. She was tan with black markings.

"I've been at this all day, and all I got out of it was more questions." Raya stretched out her arms and yawned.

"Come on, time for a break. Follow me."

Raya got up from the desk and shifted forms.

"Where're we going?"

"You'll see."

Raya followed Albright to the observation deck.

"Star watching, Albright. I could've done this from my cabin."

"You know Dad. The rooms have ears." She chuckled.

Albright explained the history of Fort Victory, where Humans and Evolutions lived and trained as one military. It was heavily guarded and the most advanced training facility in the star system. Albright could see how nervous her little sister was and reassured her that everything would be all right.

"Easy for you to say, you live with Humans. I don't even know how to speak their language."

Albright looked at Raya and smiled.

"Yes, you do. We do it every time we're in our Human forms."

"Do we?"

"Yes, they speak Ancient Earth, the same as we do."

Albright fell silent as the doors opened.

"There are my two beautiful daughters," her father announced in a deep roar as he entered the room.

Raya greeted him, touching her nose to his, giving him the father-daughter greeting. Albright did the same.

"I want the two of you to join me for dinner, please."

"Yes, Father." They bowed their heads in acceptance.

Raya and Albright returned to their cabins for their uniform badges and met their father in the general's dining room.

"My beautiful daughters. Come, let's eat," he said as he greeted them with a hug.

He wore blue military casuals, his black hair cut to regulations while his dark green eyes looked into hers.

"Thank you for coming," he said, kissing them both on the cheek.

During dinner, their father talked about the banquet held to honor the beginning of a new alliance, and as ambassador, Raya was expected to give a welcome speech. She was okay with it but rejected the bodyguards he was going to send with her.

"No, Dad, no bodyguards," she demanded.

"This is not a debate, Kitten," he shot back casually.

Raya became annoyed and got up from the table, giving her father an angry look as she shifted forms.

"Fine, but I wouldn't send anyone you're attached to," she threatened as she headed toward the door.

Her father was silent for a moment.

"Wait, Kitten. Come back. Please."

Raya turned and walked back to her father.

"Please, have a seat." Her father had the same look of defeat whenever he gave in to her tantrums.

"I'll grant your request under one condition: you're not to engage in anything with Humans other than conversation and dinner. Do I make myself clear?" He gave her a stern look that demanded an answer.

"Yes, Father, you do." She bowed her head meekly and then headed back to her cabin, trying to develop an idea of what kind of speech she would give. All she knew about Humans was what the old war veterans had told her. Their stories were violent and cruel. But not everything that came from war dealt with such harsh realities. There were stories of forbidden pleasures within the secrets of the sisters' bond.

Raya smiled as she opened the door to her cabin, remembering the stories of her sisters' encounter with the Human soldiers and the forbidden pleasures they had learned from them. But her thoughts of taboo didn't last long as her father's warning echoed in the back of her mind.

Raya felt the frustration building up. There was so much to learn in the short amount of time she had. The Newtopians were pretty much like the Uteakons, and most of them spoke the same dialect of feline.

As for Humans, they were a mystery. By the time Raya's parents' generation had joined the war, the fighting had already fizzled out, leaving nothing but old wounds and harsh feelings between the two races. Even with all the studying, she was still clueless when it came to them.

Raya woke up at 3:30 that Thursday morning, three hours

before meeting her host. Feeling nervous about being alone with the race that was said to be barbaric, she began pacing back and forth, letting out a long, anxious growl as she thought hard about reconsidering her father's offer to send bodyguards. But as a goodwill ambassador, it was her job to establish trust. There had never been any trust between Humans and Uteakons. Raya wanted desperately to change that since they had just as much to lose as she did. She didn't care how selfish her reasons sounded to others. Her son was now a part of that war, and she wanted to give him all the strength that she could.

She quickly gathered her nerves when she heard a knock at the door. It was her father. She knew that if she showed any signs of nervousness, he would send bodyguards with her regardless of her request, losing any hope of earning trust. Raya pulled herself together as much as she could and shifted into her Human form.

"Come in, Dad."

Her father walked into the room and pulled her into his arms. "I figured we could have breakfast before you're taken to the starport." He smiled and brushed the hair away from her eyes.

She gave him a hug and a kiss on the cheek. "Breakfast sounds good, Dad."

Her father looked over at the guard standing in the hallway. "Sergeant. Take my daughter's bags to the shuttle."

"Right away, sir." He bowed his head, then grabbed the luggage sitting by the door.

Raya arrived at the starport around five o'clock that morning. It was quiet, with only a few people waiting for the Fort Victory shuttle. She pulled out her media pad. She had thirty minutes before the port would be filled with military personnel going about their daily routine. Most of them would be young recruits away from home for the first time, carrying nothing but their bravery and the clothes on their backs. It was difficult, as a mother, watching young faces pass by her, knowing they were going off to war. Each individual was a weapon to the military that made the difference between life and extinction. But to the mothers, each son and daughter was a part of themselves they weren't willing to sacrifice, expecting the military to give back what they borrowed. As a Huntress, she knew life didn't work that way. In survival, sacrifices are made.

Raya began reading a novel she had downloaded from the Human Literature Archives. In the story, Human males were passionate about mating and looked into the woman's eyes as he gave her pleasures she never knew were possible and even took pleasure in making the moment last. These were things Uteakon males never did. They didn't even mate in Human form. *Why not?* she asked herself. *What was so wrong with it?* Raya closed the file and began thinking about her sisters' encounter with the Human soldiers and their shared pleasures.

She wanted to know what it would feel like to mate in her other form. And why Humans were so passionate. These were only two of many questions she wanted answers to. When the announcement to Fort Victory was made, Raya grabbed her luggage and boarded the shuttle.

She arrived at Fort Victory and was standing outside the visitor center, admiring the morning view. Fort Victory looked more like a large city than a military base. She was familiar with the sights and sounds, bringing back memories of growing up on an Uteakon Army base. She was even familiar with the sound of soldiers training in the fields while the smell of food and exhaust fumes permeated the air. However, there was one smell she was not familiar with. The scent of Humans was intense and overpowering, making her feel uneasy and a little nervous.

"Ambassador Raya."

"Yes?" Raya looked over to see a tall, pale young soldier approaching her.

"Corporal Gill," he introduced himself with a warm and friendly smile that instantly caught her attention. She watched as he extended his right hand.

"Raya," she answered, mimicking him.

There was a moment of awkward silence before the corporal realized she didn't understand the gesture. He apologized, then explained handshaking customs.

The corporal stood an impressive six foot three, taller than any male she had ever seen. She even had to raise her head just to look into his soft blue eyes and smile, something she'd never had to do before. Although he didn't look any different than an Uteakon male, there were differences. They were subtle but pleasant. The tone of his voice was warm and filled with passion when he spoke to her, unlike the Uteakon male, cold and leaking with testosterone.

The good corporal picked up her traveling bags and escorted her to his transport vehicle. He placed her bags in the back seat and then opened the passenger door for her. As Raya got in, she gave the corporal another appraisal. There was nothing dangerous or barbaric about how he looked or even spoke. If anything, he was the complete opposite of what she was told.

"Thank you!" she said, getting into the vehicle.

"It's my pleasure, ma'am." He smiled and nodded his head as he gently closed her door.

# CHAPTER 4

Raya stopped her daydreaming, picked up the romance novel, and then headed for the kitchen, where she poured herself a cup of coffee. *One more wonderful Human invention*, she thought to herself, blowing into the cup, cooling her first sip... Not only did Raya enjoy the flavor, but it was also the only thing that helped make her breeding cycle a lot more bearable and tasted a hell of a lot better than Roseberry tea.

Raya stepped onto the balcony and set her coffee on the end table next to the sofa, with her legs stretched out across the cushions. She opened the book to the page marked and started reading where she left off, but with thoughts of Corporal Gill still on her mind, she found it challenging to concentrate and closed her book, exchanging it for her cup of coffee as she continued her journey down memory lane.

Corporal Gill had given her a base tour. Their last stop had been the Arctic survival training center. The outside was enormous, with mirrored windows that reflected the sun's light. There were warning signs in big red letters.

(This building is kept at subzero temperatures.)

Inside the building were many rooms that simulated different types of winter terrain. Corporal Gill explained that he was part of an Arctic assault unit specializing in search and rescue. Most of his training was overcoming nature's obstacles, such as mountains and severe winter storms. The last part of the tour was called the testing room. It was a confidence course and the final exam of their training. They stood on the catwalk, looking down on what appeared to be a village knee-deep in snow.

He looked at her, smiling. "What do you see?"

"I don't know, a village?" she responded softly, looking up at him.

"We call it the village of pain." He grinned.

Raya watched him intensely. She was still trying to figure out what part of the corporal was dangerous. He was a boy trapped in the body of a man, well-mannered but innocently naive. Raya listened as he explained about the room.

"It's simple. All you have to do is rescue the people, avoid the traps, and get them across the falling bridge before it falls." He was silent for a moment. His blue eyes looked into hers. "But you only have a certain amount of time to do it."

Raya couldn't help the warm feeling and the laughter that bubbled out of her as he boasted proudly.

After the tour, they returned to the transport, where he took her to a small café, where the two sat out on the patio, shielded from the sun by a large umbrella. After reading the menu, Raya decided she wasn't quite ready to brave the adventures of human cuisine and the two of them agreed on iced tea and conversation.

By the time nine o'clock had come around that morning, the temperatures had reached 85°. Even in the shade, Raya could still feel the humidity, but not nearly as bad as the corporal was feeling. There were beads of sweat running down his forehead, and she could tell he was miserable. Raya pulled a clean handkerchief from her handbag and handed it to him. "Here you go... You can have it," she said, smiling.

He had a surprised, pleasant look on his face. "Thank you, ma'am. I have never gotten used to the temperatures on this planet."

"You're not from this planet?" Raya asked.

"No, ma'am, I'm from a planet called Iglesia... Where the temperatures there never reach above zero."

"Isn't that cold for Humans?"

The corporal looked at her and smiled. "No, ma'am, not for us. We can handle the cold temperatures. It's anything above zero that gets uncomfortable," he said, wiping his forehead.

"So you're not Human?"

"We are, but we evolved to survive the planet. At least that is what they taught us in school," he laughed.

It felt good to hear the corporal laugh. It eased a lot of the nervousness she was feeling.

"I hope you don't mind the questions. It's just that you're the first Human that I have ever met."

"No, ma'am, I don't mind at all." The corporal paused for a moment, taking a drink of his iced tea. "You don't seem to be bothered by the heat."

"Me, no, I'm used to these temperatures," Raya responded.

The corporal smiled and suddenly changed the topic. "And you, ma'am, what's your story?"

Raya picked up her glass and looked over at the corporal. "I'm from the backlands of Uteaka. I moved to the city with my daughter and my son. Now my son is in the military. As for me, I work as an information officer at a college." Raya smiled. "It's not as exciting as your job, I'm afraid." She took another sip of her tea.

The corporal looked into her eyes and grinned. "I'm not so sure about that, ma'am. Intelligence is a lot more exciting than being a snow jockey," he replied with a chuckle.

Raya was looking at the corporal. Something about him was seducing her concentration, her attention focused on his lips as he spoke, his blue eyes never looking away from her. Like the characters in the romance novel, the corporal gave her his undivided attention as if her happiness was his only goal.

After leaving the café, the corporal brought her to a large brick building. Above the doors, it read "Willow Dormitories." The corporal opened her door and held out his hand.

Raya put her hand in his. "Thank you."

"It's nothing fancy, but it keeps the rain off your head." He grabbed her bags from the back seat.

She followed him to the front desk. "Good morning. How can I help you?" asked the clerk, who looked no older than the corporal.

"Ambassador Raya is here to check in." The corporal set her bags down.

"Oh yes, good morning, Ambassador. We've been expecting you." He smiled and pulled out a clear pad, holding it in front of her. Raya placed her hand on the pad until it blinked green.

"Okay, you're all set. Your room is on the third floor, 16 C."

After Raya had checked in, the corporal offered to take her bags to her room. Even though she was still convinced it was the afternoon sun, she respectfully declined his offer and proceeded to her room, carrying her own belongings.

Raya set her bags in the living room and desperately searched through them, looking for her temperature-regulating probe. She knew if she didn't cool her temperature soon, her body would start producing pheromones that would attract the attention of males, and with the banquet on Saturday, there was no way she was going to be in a room full of males while she was in heat. After emptying the last bag, Raya took out a thin silver tube and rolled her eyes, realizing she had grabbed her daughter's toothbrush holder and her regulator was still at home.

"Well, that's just great," she muttered to herself.

Raya called down to the front desk.

"Front desk," said a man's voice.

"Yes, can you send up a regulator?"

"Regulator?"

"Yes, I'm coming into my cycle, and I'm very uncomfortable."

The man paused for a moment as he thought about the

question. "Okay, now I understand... I'll have somebody bring it up right away."

Raya was putting her things away. "I don't know why males can't go through this. Didn't see me standing in line for it," she grumbled.

Raya was in the middle of her ranting when there was a knock at the door. It was one of the dormitory staff. The young woman handed her a small green-colored box on which "TAMPONS" was written in bold black letters.

"Finally, some relief," she said, or so she thought.

Raya opened the box and was surprised when she pulled out a small white cylinder with what appeared to be a cotton bullet attached to a string.

"What the hell is this?"

Raya grew tired of trying to figure out what it was and took the strange device to the front desk and confronted the young man standing behind it.

"Excuse me," she said, trying to keep a calm composure.

"Yes, ma'am."

"I asked for a regulator."

"Well," said the man, "you should've received them by now."

"No. I got this," Raya growled, holding the tampon in front of his face.

"Ma'am, I'm sorry. I guess I don't know what a regulator is."

A woman behind him had overheard the conversation and politely explained to the man that Uteakons don't menstruate. She apologized for the confusion and then went and obtained two ice pads. The woman reassured Raya that the ice would work just as well as a regulator. Although she was curious about what a menstrual cycle was, she wasn't in the mood for a lesson on biology. Raya thanked the woman for her kindness.

"I owe that young man an apology," Raya admitted.

"Don't worry about it," laughed the woman. "It is a woman's dormitory, so he should be used to it by now."

———— ••◆•• ————

When Raya's body temperature had returned to normal, she felt confident that she wouldn't go into an early cycle, removed the ice pads from her forehead and abdomen, and then placed them in the freezer in case she needed them later. Raya was hungry and decided it was time to eat. She stopped at the front desk to make sure it was okay for her to hunt. Behind the desk was an attractive young woman with long green hair that covered her name tag. She had a pleasant smile, and her bare skin was covered in freckles.

"Hello, what can I do for you?"

"Would it be okay for me to hunt in the woods?"

The woman looked puzzled.

"I'm not quite sure about that. Let me find out," the clerk answered, disappearing into the back.

Moments later, when the woman returned, she informed Raya that someone from surveillance was coming to speak with her. As they waited, the two women talked. The desk clerk had never met an Uteakon and was curious. Raya was happy to answer her questions. After about ten minutes, a man from surveillance came over and introduced himself:

"Hello, I'm Captain Parks." He was a tall, gray-haired man with a slightly wrinkled face. "And you must be Ambassador Raya," he declared, extending his right hand.

"I am," she answered.

Raya shot him a curious look. It was the first time she had ever seen anyone that didn't have a youthful appearance. She was impressed and had an impulse to feel his skin. "Do you mind?" Raya inquired as she reached out toward his face.

Captain Parks smiled. "No, I don't mind."

Raya put the palm of her hand on his cheek. The only way she could tell his age was by his scent and the experience reflected in his eyes.

"You are allowed to hunt, but first, I need you to shift into your feline form so I can get you into the system. This way, the security drones won't mistake you for an intruder," he explained, reaching for his scanner.

While Captain Parks was making adjustments. Raya had shifted forms, startling him when he raised his head. Parks froze, his face close to hers as he silently stared into her yellow eyes. Although the experience in his eyes told only half of his story, his scent completed it. The smell of children and another animal she wasn't familiar with lingered on him.

"Holy...! I mean, wow, you are one big girl," he said, breaking the silence. "Ma'am, I need you to hold out your right hand...ah, right leg." The captain stumbled over his words.

Raya knew what he meant and held out her right foot. Parks was comparing his hand to her paw. It looked like a baseball in a catcher's mitt.

Raya gave his hand a gentle squeeze. He looked up at her and smiled, his eyes filled with awe as he watched his hand momentarily disappear.

Raya was becoming the center of attention as the dormitory staff gathered around her. The girl with the long green hair asked if she could feel her fur. Raya nodded her approval. The green-haired girl smiled as she knelt and began running her hands along Raya's side.

"Your beauty is simply incredible."

Raya soon found herself covered in hands. Parks noticed the way her tail was twitching. She was uncomfortable with the attention. Quickly but politely, he broke up the crowd. Before leaving, one woman asked if Raya would roar. As she granted the request, her roar echoed throughout the first floor, startling everyone who heard it. The staff applauded and thanked Raya as they returned to work.

Raya shifted back to her Human form. "Thank you. That was becoming a little awkward."

Captain Parks smiled and shook his head. "That was a wonderful experience. Thank you, ma'am." He turned and began to walk away.

"Captain Parks," Raya called out.

"Yes, ma'am?"

"Do you have grandchildren?"

"I have six, and they can be a handful," he said with a smile.

"I have grand kittens, and I have grandchildren. Inside, I feel very much like a grandmother, but on the outside, I will never know the gift of looking like one. For that, I envy Humans."

"For what it's worth, envy goes both ways. I know grandmothers who would love to look like you." The two of them smiled and then parted ways.

Raya walked over to the information board to look at the map. She agreed on a small, secluded area, away from Humans, then headed out the door. When she got to her destination, Raya looked around before she shifted forms, trying to avoid any misunderstanding of her intentions, then headed silently into the night, her nose to the ground, trying to pick up the scent of prey while the sound of little feet scurried away from her; they were barely a meal and weren't worth the effort. She walked stealthily through the night, listening for sounds of distress as she continued her search.

Raya picked up the smell of musk. Judging by the strength of the odor, the prey wasn't far away. Although the planet and the wildlife were alien to her, she was familiar with the scent, especially when it was left by males searching for a mate.

Raya was tracking the source when the wind suddenly shifted directions, carrying a different but familiar smell. She followed it but wasn't prepared to see the corporal. He was hunched over, trying to catch his breath. He wore gray jogging pants and a white T-shirt, drenched in sweat. Around his head was a jogger's light.

Raya tried to stay focused, but his scent seduced her every thought. Her heart was beating fast, and her temperature was quickly rising. She was going into an early cycle, causing her mind to become clouded as she watched him from the shadows.

Without warning, he took off in a panic. Raya started to follow him, triggering her instinct to pursue when she took her attention off the corporal, realizing why he was running. An enormous sow had picked up his scent and was quickly gaining on him. Enraged, Raya turned, kicking up clouds of dirt as she pursued her rival.

The boar continued her chase, unaware that another hunter was approaching fast. There was a look of fear and panic when the boar realized she had just become the hunted. She turned and tried to flee, but it was too late. Before she knew it, the jaws of death were already locked around her throat, slowly taking her life. Although she was more prominent and outweighed her attacker, she couldn't shake the jaws of the large predator as it quickly brought her to the ground. Within moments blood-curdling squeals echoed as Raya's claws mercilessly tore into her flesh.

Raya ate as much as possible and then headed back to the forest edge, wondering about the corporal.

Raya remembered walking through the lobby, trying to make sense of her body's response. She was positive it wasn't the heat that made her react. *But why?* He was Human. She was Uteakon. Even if he mated with her, conception was biologically impossible. Raya was going into heat, which was taking its toll on her. The green-haired woman noticed something was wrong and ran over to Raya.

"Are you okay?"

As Raya tried to answer, she lost consciousness, causing her uniform badge to deactivate. Before she could shift, the woman caught her and noticed Raya's temperature was high. From their earlier conversation, she suspected Raya was going into heat and quickly rushed her into the shower room, where she stood underneath the cold water holding Raya.

She couldn't believe this small-sized woman was an enormous black cat, now helpless in her arms. Suddenly she gasped, looking at the long, deep scars on Raya's back. "Oh, you poor thing," the green-haired woman whispered compassionately while holding back tears.

Raya was beginning to gain consciousness. "Are you okay?" the green-haired woman asked.

"I am now," Raya responded slowly.

"Good, let's get you dried off," the woman said, turning off the shower.

Raya followed the woman into the locker room, where she was handed a towel. She gave it back to the woman and shifted forms, shaking the water from her body, grateful she wanted to thank her new friend.

Raya shifted back to Human form. "I'm sorry, I don't know your name."

A smile swept across her freckled face. "It's Amy!"

"Thank you, Amy."

"Hey... Just one sister helping another. When you came in, you had a high temperature and were covered in blood," she responded, concerned.

"It wasn't my blood. It was the boar's."

Amy's eyes got wide, and her jaw dropped. "You took down a boar? Remind me not to piss you off," she said jokingly.

Raya didn't know why she found it funny but couldn't help the laughter that bubbled out.

Amy smiled. "I'm glad you're okay. You had a lot of people worried about you."

Raya looked up at her. "Me... Why?"

"Because now that we're one military, that makes you family. What do you say we go on a balcony and have a couple of icy Joe's?"

"Icy Joe's?"

"Cold coffee with an attitude," Amy chuckled.

After Amy changed her clothes, she handed Raya a bath-robe. The two of them sat at a corner table drinking icy Joe's.

"So, if you don't mind me asking, what happened?" Amy asked with genuine concern.

"I started going into heat early. I believe that young man triggered it."

"What young man?" Amy inquired with a concerned look on her face.

Raya picked up her glass, hesitant about answering Amy's question. Her hands were trembling, causing the ice in her glass to rattle, as she remembered the old veterans' stories of females who had broken the code of conduct and were sentenced to death, their corpses left in the open to rot alongside their Human mate, and even thinking about it was taboo.

Amy walked over to Raya. "You're scared." She kneeled and placed her hands on Raya's. "What happened... Did he hurt you?" Amy started to panic.

"No," Raya whispered.

"Are you sure?"

"Of course."

Amy looked into her eyes. "Well, if he did, I'd go down there and beat the snot out of him and then call the MPs!"

"No, it was me. My body started responding to Corporal Gill's."

"What! Corporal Gill?" Amy's startled voice was loud and starting to attract unwanted attention.

Raya was scared. Her heart was pounding. She could feel everyone on the balcony staring. "Please, I'm sorry. I didn't know that would happen," she pleaded softly.

Amy continued holding Raya's trembling hands. "You don't have to be afraid. Being turned on by some hunk isn't a crime. If it were, I would have been locked up long ago." Amy smiled. "Don't worry about it. You're not the only one who's had the hots for somebody outside their race."

"I'm not?"

"No... Humans do it all the time, especially on training days."

"Training day?"

Amy returned to her chair. "Yeah, it's sorta like a holiday for women. Every six months, the Newtopian Marines come to Fort Victory to train right before their PT test." Amy leaned over the table, her brows raised. "And you have never seen so many horny women in one area. It's disgusting!" she responded, trying to hide the look of guilt while remembering their brawny physiques packed into PT uniforms.

"Maybe we're not so different after all. Perhaps it's your Human side that wants the corporal."

As crazy as it sounded, what if Amy was right? Maybe it was her Human side waking up. Raya's sisters had always told her being a feline was only half of who they were. *Whether we like it or not, we have another side we cannot live without*, she thought.

Amy noticed Raya's agitation. "Are you okay?"

"No, I'm not," Raya replied, walking away.

Amy was concerned and escorted Raya back to her dorm room and even stayed with her to ensure she was okay.

She remembered standing in the kitchen, staring into space, feeling confused and unprepared for the physical changes happening, when Amy put her hands on Raya's shoulder, her calm voice breaking through anxious thoughts. "It's okay. I'm right here for you."

Raya turned to face Amy. "What's wrong with me? Am I sick?"

"Nothing is wrong with you." Her voice was reassuring.

She reluctantly looked up at Amy. "I'm sorry I got scared and never felt this way before."

"Let me see if I got this right. Your body has the hots for Corporal Gill," asked Amy.

"Confusingly, yes," Raya admitted.

Raya took a bottle of Uteakon Lacour from the refrigerator and beckoned Amy to join her on the balcony.

"So, are the men on your planet just as confusing as the men on this one?" Amy queried.

"Well, lately, I've had a hard time keeping up with my grandsons," Raya chuckled.

Amy's eyes widened, and her jaw dropped. "Wait a minute,

you're a grandmother?"

"I am."

"I thought you were nineteen or twenty."

"No, I'm forty-eight. When we shift from one form to another, our skin cells regenerate. That's why we don't age as Humans do. Internally, I am forty-eight years old and not as fast as I used to be." Raya chuckled.

Amy looked over at Raya. She had a concerned look on her face and her voice was filled with compassion. "If you don't mind me asking, how did you get those scars?"

"Three males tried to kill me," she responded, taking a sip of her drink.

Amy had a sad look on her face. "That's terrible!"

"Not as bad as it was for them."

"What do you mean?" she asked with a nervous tone.

"They left me for dead," Raya responded chillingly.

Amy went pale for a moment and then turned to nervous laughter. "Well, I'll drink to that. In fact, I'll drink to kids, grandkids, age, men, and friendships. Who cares? Let's just relax and enjoy the moment."

After Amy left, Raya took the ice pads from the freezer and headed off to bed.

CHAPTER 5

Raya was lying on her bed, slapping her tail on the comforter, panting, and hoping for a gust of wind or a slight breeze to find its way through her open window. She was miserably hot and couldn't stop thinking about the corporal. Butterflies would flutter in her stomach whenever he touched her or said her name. But anything beyond conversation was still taboo. The only answers she had came from her sisters, reminding her that there were two sides to every coin.

Raya had always been intrigued by her sisters' stories about rabbits. They talked about how easy it was to catch them and how sweet they tasted when you did. However, Raya found these stories confusing because there were no rabbits on Uteaka, and she had yet to learn what they were. She entered the sisters' bond when Raya had her first breeding cycle and was no longer considered a child. It was then that they revealed the truth about rabbits.

Raya suddenly stopped. Her attention shifted to the soldiers marching in the early morning as the sun was just starting to rise. She lifted her head as a calm, steady breeze rushed through the bedroom window along with the fading scent of Human soldiers, or "rabbits," as her sisters called them, marching to the calling of cadence. She imagined herself luring one of the men away from the platoon, just as her sisters had described. It didn't matter how fast he was. She could always follow his scent; at the right moment, she'd break into a chase and send the rabbit into a panic. Wear him down. And then, when he was trapped, take him down, as her sisters had advised.

The rabbits were Human soldiers who taught them things that could only be described as taboo. Her sisters called it their awakening. She was always envious, listening to them talk about pleasures that could only be felt in Human form. When an Uteakon female is in heat, she's sexually aggressive and easily agitated, making Uteakon males very nervous. But to the Humans, it was a challenge. The risky game was called the Rabbits' Club, but the military called it treason and punishable by death. Military laws have changed since the alliance was formed, but mating with Humans was still unforgivable to her people and brought disgrace to the Kinship.

Raya could already feel the wind of change going from a hurricane to a typhoon. Whether it was bad luck or just rotten timing on nature's part, her female problems couldn't have happened at a worse time. She didn't only represent the military but the people of Uteaka as well, and now, on top of everything, the moment she goes into heat, she'd lose what was left of her sanity and unconsciously pursue the corporal like prey.

"I hate being a female," she muttered as she climbed out of bed and shifted into her Human form.

Raya casually strolled over to the dresser for the Roseberry tea. She hated Roseberry; it was bitter and left an awful taste in her mouth, but it was the only thing she knew that helped with the discomforts of her cycle. Raya looked at her badge and decided to leave it on the dresser as she grabbed the tea and headed for the kitchen.

When her tea was finished, Raya poured a cup and walked onto the balcony. She admired how beautiful Fort Victory was in the morning light. As she looked down, a small crowd of men was gathering below, staring and whistling at her.

"What strange customs Humans have," she muttered.

Raya ignored them and listened to the birds sing as a

cool breeze carried the smell of fresh bread. It was indeed a beautiful morning. Raya enjoyed the novelty of waking up on another planet and seeing Humans and their way of life, which strangely wasn't much different from her own. Except on Uteaka she never had males gathering below her balcony watching her every move; that was annoyingly new. Raya was taking another sip of her tea when she noticed the corporal walking by, holding what looked like a laundry bag. She hollered to him, "Hello, Corporal Gill!"

Gill looked up to see Raya waving to him. His eyes widened as he ran toward the building, yelling something at her. Raya was puzzled by his strange behavior but wouldn't let it ruin her morning as she continued to sip her tea. A minute later, she turned to see Gill bursting through the door, perspiring and out of breath.

"Ma'am, you can't be out there like that!" He paused for a moment to catch his breath. "You need to wear clothes," he said, reaching for her arm.

Raya dropped her cup in surprise as he pulled her off the balcony more forcefully than he intended, sending them on a collision course. The corporal caught her, his hands pressing firmly against the small of her back, a susceptible area during her cycle. Raya lost her breath as a surge of erotic shivers raced through her.

"I'm sorry, that was a bit rough." His voice was deep with a sincere tone, while the scent of Human musk quickly seduced her thoughts. Raya was speechless. Her temperature was rising with each passing second she remained in his arms.

She was feeling the weight of responsibility as she debated her next move. With so much at stake, Raya tried to stay focused, but he wasn't making it easy, as his touch was awakening every sexual nerve in her body.

Gill was innocently naive. He was like easy prey, oblivious to the Huntress in his arms. It took every ounce of strength she had not to conquer and devour the taunting blue-eyed rabbit. Reluctantly, she pulled herself away from him and apologized.

"I'm sorry… I've never had to wear clothes before. All I have is a uniform badge."

He reached into his bag and pulled out the infamous brown T-shirt. "It's an old shirt. You can keep it."

Against her better judgment, she accepted it.

"Thank you."

Raya smiled when he asked her to raise her arms but felt slightly disappointed when he slipped the shirt over her head. Gill noticed her face was flushed.

"Are you okay?"

"Yes, I'm fine. I'm just beginning my cycle, that's all."

"Is there anything I can do to help?" he asked innocently.

Raya smiled and patted him on the chest.

"I'd say you've done quite enough already," Raya responded half-jokingly.

◆◆◆◆◆

It was the night of the banquet, and Raya was at her wit's end with biology. She was beginning her cycle and couldn't stomach Roseberry tea anymore. Raya had minutes. Hours if she was lucky and her body would start producing pheromones, making her a target to every male with a keen sense of smell. Usually, this would be hilarious if it wasn't happening to her.

Raya stopped her thoughts and headed into the kitchen for another cup of coffee. She would always be grateful to Amy for turning her onto it that night. She came to the room with coffee and a curling brush to style Raya's hair and find a ball gown to download. After endless pages of looking at ball gowns, they decided on a silver one. It wasn't fancy and didn't make her stand out. She even loved that it had the feel of silk.

"You look beautiful," Amy told her."

"Thank you for everything you've done for me."

Amy smiled at her and gave her a hug. "Hey, that's what friends do."

When 7:30 came around, Gill was in the lobby waiting for her. He wore black military dress, white cotton gloves, and E4 on the side of his sleeves.

"Go get him, girl," Amy whispered in her ear.

Raya had butterflies in the pit of her stomach. Gill was the first Human she had ever met and the first male who'd ever taken her breath away. Raya took a deep, calming breath and walked over to him.

"Good evening, ma'am. You look lovely tonight." He bowed his head slightly, presenting her with a pink rose necklace. "May I?" The corporal slipped the chain over her head, then kissed her on the cheek.

Raya put her hand to her cheek, trying to catch her breath. It was the first time she felt a blush's warmth or a smile's tingle. Her heart was beating fast, and her temperature was starting to rise. She stood silently, trying to tell herself he was just innocently naive, and it was just a simple gift. But it was his kiss that sealed his fate. Raya pressed her lips to his. "Thank you," she whispered.

Gill blushed as he extended his arm. Raya put her arm in his as he escorted her to a long black luxury transport with solid digital doors that automatically deactivated when you approached it. It was dimly lit with fresh flowers blowing through the air vents. Raya could feel herself sinking into the soft synthetic leather seats as the auto's chauffeur unit greeted her by name.

"Good evening, Ambassador Raya."

"Good evening to you," she responded politely.

"Destination, please?" the unit asked.

Corporal Gill looked over at Raya with a warm grin. "We'll be going to the Grand Hall tonight," he answered.

The Grand Hall was only a short distance away. When they arrived, a long line of luxury transport was waiting to drive up to the red carpet, where security orbs greeted and scanned them. "Good evening, please identify."

"Corporal Gill. And I'll be escorting the Uteakon ambassador, Raya."

"Identity confirmed. Please enjoy the rest of your night."

They walked arm in arm down the red carpet. Raya's thoughts were swirling around in her head. Her biology clock ticking away made her feel like she was racing against time.

Raya rolled her eyes and cursed her luck. With so much at stake, failure was not an option for her. Raya tried desperately to stay focused, but the corporal's scent made it hard. A woman with long red hair talking to the Newtopian ambassador noticed Raya's distress and came over to her.

"Honey, are you okay?" She spoke with a Newtopian accent.

Before Raya could answer, the woman walked her to the powder room. She reached into her handbag and pulled out a small bottle.

"Here, this will help you. It's a vitamin drink. Although it won't stop your cycle, it temporarily prevents you from producing pheromones."

Raya was grateful to the woman and gave her a teary-eyed thank-you. "You're Human. How did you know?" Raya inquired.

"I'm a doctor in Newtopian medicine," she answered, taking a tissue from her purse.

Raya exchanged the empty bottle for the tissue, thanking her once again.

The woman smiled and escorted her back to Corporal Gill. "Here you are, Corporal. She'll be fine now," said the doctor, walking away.

The welcoming ceremony was held in a dining room fit for royalty. On the walls hung the flags of every military branch, Human or Evolution. The tablecloths were pure golden silk, and the glasses were light green crystals.

The first one to give their speech was the ambassador for Newtopia. He stood eight feet tall. He was a broad-shouldered young man with a tan complexion. Even his voice was strong, with a hint of arrogance. He was a champion, and like all champions, his sense of smell was much stronger than the average male and far more aggressive at seeking a mate. Raya was becoming nervous. The Newtopian who was talking to the doctor had picked up her scent. Her only concern now was for the corporal's safety.

When it came time to give her speech, Raya took a deep breath and exhaled as she walked toward the podium, making sure not to make eye contact with the ambassador. "My name is Raya. I'm from Uteaka. My son joined the military because he believes that we are all the Children of Earth. He has often told me how proud he is to fight alongside his brothers- and sisters-in-arms. Just as he has welcomed you, we, the people of Uteaka, also welcome you with open arms." The crowd applauded as Raya bowed and then returned to her seat.

When the welcoming ceremony was finished, elegant meals were wheeled in on fancy carts and served by assistant chefs during dinner.

Gill noticed Raya wasn't eating much and inquired about it.

"You're not eating. Are you okay?"

Raya looked into his eyes. She was momentarily confused. "I'm sorry, what did you say?"

He put a hand on her shoulder, his face close to hers. "I asked if you were okay," he said, concerned.

"I'm fine, just a little warm, that's all." Raya put her hand on his, reassuring him.

He pulled a thin silver tube from his pocket. "Here, this will help you. It's called the temperature shield."

Raya turned her head to the side, trying not to laugh. She didn't have the heart to tell him it was a temperature regulator and wasn't inserted in the pocket. Another example of Uteakon humor. "I'll be okay now," she said, laughing softly.

He laughed with her, then held out his hand, inviting her to the ballroom. Raya thought about her father's warning and didn't see the harm in dancing.

"I would love to." She put her hand in his as he led her to the ballroom. Once again, he made her feel as if her happiness mattered.

Feeling the call of nature, Raya put her thoughts on hold and headed for the bathroom. While washing her hands, a smile swept across her face, remembering how she blushed the whole time they danced to the Vienna Waltz. That night with him left her asking more questions about the Human race. Even now, she still didn't know why they were so taboo. Human or Uteakon, Gill was the only male who made her feel like the princess her father did. She was no longer afraid of the changes happening to her being in his arms and even welcomed the awakening of her Human half. But it was the Human side that was more responsive to him. Her sense of smell was heightened, and her thoughts were focused only on him despite his boyish charm and baby face. He smelled very much like a man. Raya was tired of waiting and moved in for the kill. Like any prey, she had to cut him off from the others.

When the music ended, Raya noticed the women were thanked with a kiss and became confused when he thanked her verbally.

"Did I not do well enough for a kiss?" Raya inquired.

"I'm sorry. I didn't want to be presumptuous." His voice was low, and his smile faded as he moved in for a kiss.

Gill became concerned when he noticed her lips were burning up. "Would you like me to take you home?" he asked innocently.

Raya looked at him and smiled. "Yes, I would like that."

"It would be an honor."

He brought her outside and called for transport. Raya put her hands on his chest and looked up at him. Despite the night's chilly air, her body felt like it would burst into flames at any moment.

"No, please. I'd rather walk if you don't mind?" Raya pleaded softly.

He smiled and put his face close to hers. "Okay, then we can take a shortcut through the park, and if you want, I know a place by the lake. We..."

Raya touched Gill's cheeks before silencing him with a passionate kiss. "Thank you, that would be perfect," she said as Gill placed his hands on the small of her back and pulled her into his arms, pressing his lips closer and harder to hers.

His scent and the warmth of his lips made her body temperature rise, and her heart beat fast and hard, as though the pressure was going to break her ribs at any moment. There was no doubt in her mind how much she wanted him or how much she was willing to kill anyone who got in her way.

Gill slowly released their embrace and smiled. They strolled to the park, which was quiet and dimly lit, with the only sign of activity being a young woman running the concession stand. They settled on a park bench, observing the moon's reflection rippling in the water.

Gill suddenly pointed to the brightest star in the sky. "You see that bright blue star? That's the planet I'm from."

Raya listened silently as his blue eyes twinkled in the moonlight. She studied the movement of his lips, wondering what they would feel like pressed against her neck.

Gill noticed her silence and put his hand on her cheek. "You're burning up!" he said, slightly panicked, taking the temperature shield from his pocket.

Raya put her hands around Gill's. "No, that won't work anymore."

"Then I'll get you something cold to drink."

Before she could respond, Gill got up and headed for the concession stand.

Raya was pacing back and forth, feeling her body temperature rising as she became increasingly agitated waiting for him. Suddenly, she stopped when she felt like someone was watching her from the shadows. She shifted forms as a sizeable Newtopian male came into view. He was orange with black stripes. His large size and boasting attitude made him a champion by breeding standards. He was the kind of male she wouldn't think twice about killing another female over, but tonight, he was in her way.

Raya lowered her head, her ears back, watching his every movement as agitation quickly turned to anger. The hungry look in his eyes and the way he sauntered told her he was confident he'd have no problems dominating her, unaware of the effects of her cycle and the reason why experienced males always approach the female with caution.

She let out a roar, warning him not to come closer. Like the corporal, he was young and naive, oblivious to the warning sign he was not wanted. He ignored her and put his nose to the base of her tail. Raya turned and slapped him with her paw, her large claws pressed against the side of his cheek, keeping him at bay. He was persistent in mounting her and wouldn't tolerate the presence of another male. The longer he stayed, the more he put the corporal in danger.

She gave him one last warning, but his roar was louder and more authoritative, momentarily silencing her as he returned to her tail for another examination. When she felt his wet, cold nose make contact, she exploded into a violent rage. The two big cats rolled on the ground, locked in battle, and the Newtopian's life flashed before his eyes as he tried frantically to keep Raya's jaws from grabbing his throat. He knew it was a losing battle as she brought him to submission when her jaws locked onto his throat. The more he struggled, the tighter her jaws squeezed.

Raya abruptly stopped and let go of her grip when she heard the sound of cups falling on the ground, spilling their contents. She turned around and saw that Gill had arrived on the scene and was running away. Raya immediately pursued him. The large male, relieved to be alive, collected what remained of his dignity and disappeared into the woods.

As he tried to escape, Gill looked back to see a large black cat with piercing yellow eyes closing in on him. At that moment, his adrenaline began to spike. He quickened his pace as he called for help, but with the soldiers training in the fields, his call fell on deaf ears. Desperate, he took a sharp right and headed into the forest, hoping to shake the giant beast from his tail and avoid becoming its next victim.

Gill continued running as far as he could, but his heart beat so fast he had to stop and catch his breath. Gill leaned against an old ironwood tree and breathed so hard that he didn't notice the large cat slowly approaching him. The black beast released a hollow growl as its eyes followed Gill's hands when he went for his sidearm but realized he was unarmed. Gill turned and ran deeper into the woods.

Raya tracked his scent; the only way to catch the rabbit was to wear it down. The longer he panicked, the easier it was to chase him into a trap. As Gill ran north toward the base, Raya circled around and surprised him as she silently walked into his view. Although she made no move toward him, Gill panicked and ran away.

Gill was a well-trained and physically fit soldier. Wearing him down wouldn't be easy, but she was okay with that. Raya was determined to catch him. After all, she had all night, and he wasn't going anywhere. She stayed close enough to keep him in a panic but not far enough away that he could catch his breath. After a while, Gill ran toward an old abandoned building. Raya could hear him breathing heavily, and he was desperate to enter the building. But the doors were chained, and the windows on the first floor had iron bars, making it impossible for him to enter.

Gill turned to see Raya emerging from the shadows, growling softly, letting him know she was ready to mate. Her heart skipped a beat as their eyes locked, imagining her Human side in his arms as he kissed her neck. Her daydreams were short-lived as Gill spotted an old ladder leaning against the building beneath an open window on the second floor. He quickly made a mad dash for it, climbed to the second floor, and then kicked it away, trapping himself inside the building.

She was in a state of sexual frustration. Gill's scent was everywhere, and it was more temptation than she could handle. Raya circled the building, trying desperately to find a way in and collect what was hers. She was hot; her body felt like it was overdosing on hormones and adrenaline. Gill was trapped, and the only thing keeping him from her were the bars on the windows.

Every so often, Gill would poke his head out the window, almost as if he was teasing her. She would look up at him and let out a fierce roar, letting him know she was coming for him. As Raya ripped the bars off the window, falling concrete echoed through the building. She caught his scent and tracked it to the top of the old, rusty stairs. Cautiously, Raya made her way down the long hallway to a wooden door. Behind it, she could hear Gill breathing heavily. His scent was so overwhelming; every cell, every molecule of her wanted this man so much she was drooling just thinking about him. With a deafening roar, she began going through the door using her massive claws and turning it into kindling.

Corporal Gill's blood ran cold, and his life flashed before his eyes as the black beast clawed through the door. He knew it was only a matter of seconds before the relentless creature would claim its prize. Gill looked around the room. The floor was covered in various colors of packing material and empty boxes, but nothing he could use against the beast. Gill felt despair sweep through him. Even if he did find a weapon, with something that big and powerful he didn't stand a chance of coming out unscathed, and whatever this beast wanted, it wouldn't stop until it got what it came for.

Suddenly, Gill spotted an old rusty knife, and the black beast was now inside the room with him. Gill pulled the knife out of the wall and held it before him as he looked the beast in its large yellow eyes.

"I know this knife won't save my life, but it won't save yours either," he said as if he were taking his last stand.

Unfazed by his bold words, the beast continued inching toward him until it stood beneath the pale moonlight shining through the roof's large hole. They stared briefly into each other's eyes before the large black cat turned into a woman.

Gill stood in disbelief as the knife in his hand fell to the floor, breaking the silence between them. "Ambassador!"

She couldn't fight the laws of nature or even expect him to understand she had no control over her body's response. "I'm sorry. I tried to resist. I really did," she pleaded in a soft, gentle tone.

Gill's heart was racing, but not for the same reasons as before. He felt lost in a trance and was at a loss for words. She was an enigma, beautiful and mysterious, as if straight out of a fairy tale. Despite knowing that he should run from her, his feet wouldn't budge, and he was held captive by her essence. Her feminine scent was irresistible and growing stronger by the second. She gently led him to his knees, and though he tried to speak, her pheromones had already begun to affect him. He couldn't help but focus all his attention on her.

As her pheromones began to take effect, Gill's forehead pressed gently against her abdomen as his hands gently caressed her thighs. They were cold as ice but very arousing, and the more he caressed her, the more her temperature rose, causing her to release more pheromones through her sweat.

Raya stopped her thoughts, poured another cup of coffee, and returned to the balcony, blushing over the memories of their moonlight encounter. Even now, she could still picture the steam between them as he stood behind her, holding her burning body to his ice-cold flesh. She woke up feeling pleasures her feline side wasn't capable of. Raya smiled, remembering how he kissed and gently nibbled on her neck while his ice-cold hands explored the rest of her yearning body.

She underestimated the power of the rabbit and let down her guard. Before she knew it, she was under his spell, and the true nature of the rabbit was revealed. All night long, he took his time making love to her in ways she could have never imagined. Raya blew into her cup and took a sip; she would always be grateful to him for making her first experience with a Human unforgettable. In the morning, she woke up in his arms. He was naked and sleeping like a baby; in the distance, Raya could hear the sound of dogs barking and soldiers hollering. She could tell by the sound that they were getting close. She wasn't sure how they would react to her mating with one of their soldiers. She shifted forms and escaped through the hole in the roof.

Raya's thoughts were suddenly interrupted by a knock at the door. She set her coffee down on the table and went to see who it was. She opened the door to see Carl. In his hands were two carryout bags.

"Carl, did you miss me?" she asked jokingly.

He looked at her with a guilty grin. "I ordered takeout and remembered my daughters were gone for the night, so I came over to see if you and Ocean wanna have dinner."

"Dinner sounds good. Come in."

He followed her to the kitchen table, then set the food on the table as Raya walked over to the cupboard. The lighting in her apartment was dim, and it would take a few seconds for his eyes to adjust.

"I hope I'm not intruding."

"You're not. I'm just sitting here going down memory lane."

"Good memories, I hope."

Raya started to blush as she set the plates on the table and then went back for the silverware and glasses.

Carl's eyes had adjusted to the lighting. He looked to see Raya reaching for the top shelf, her shirt lifted, exposing her lower half. Carl shook his head, grinning. "When I ordered this food, I wasn't exactly sure what I was ordering, so I was hoping you could tell me."

"Carl, I don't know anything about Human cuisine."

"Who said it was Human?" He smiled and took out the contents of the bag.

Raya smelled the food. It smelled exactly like the cuisine from the Backlands. "Carl," she said, smiling, "where did you get this?"

"At that new restaurant that just opened up. They serve everything." Carl gave her a puzzled look when she set the table for two. "Only two!"

"Yeah, just you and me. Ocean's visiting her grandmother."

He was serving the food as Raya explained what each entrée was. The first dish was called Sun-berrie. She started to laugh, thinking about the first time she made it.

"What's so funny?" Carl asked.

"The first time I made this was when my oldest daughter went through her Rebirth."

"Rebirth...what is that?"

"It's when we get our Human forms. It was so awful everyone started throwing it at each other."

Raya was laughing so hard that she had tears in her eyes. He couldn't help the warm feeling in his heart, seeing the smile on her face.

When the laughter subsided, he asked about the Backlands. Raya was quiet for a moment. "My mother is actually from the Backlands. I was raised on a military base with my parents. When I came of age, I moved to the Backlands to be with my mother's Kinship."

"When did you move to the city?"

"After Ocean got her Human form, I knew she could never reach her full potential in the Backlands."

⸻ ••◆•• ⸻

Raya was clearing the table as Carl seemed deep in thought. "So who is she, Carl?"

"Who is who?"

"The female you always think about when you look at me."

"What do you mean?" He looked over at her, wondering if she knew the truth.

Raya got up from the table and walked over to the refrigerator. "I'm not an idiot, Carl, and I'd appreciate it if you didn't treat me like one," she said, taking out a bottle of Uteakon Lacour.

Carl nervously looked at the floor, gathering his courage to tell her the truth without giving her the wrong impression. "Her name was Caroline. She was murdered by the Shezón. When she died, I lost my wife and best friend. My daughters lost their mother." The tone of his voice became angry. "They took everything from me." Carl stood up and took a moment to calm down. "When I saw you walk out of that shuttle, your beauty took me by surprise, and then when I saw you in Human form...you look so much like her that all I could think about was getting to know you."

Raya got up and walked over to him. "And what do you know about me, Carl?" Raya inquired playfully.

"You're the woman most men can only dream about, not just your beauty...but who you are, strong but humble, beautiful but not vain."

Raya blushed as she called out his name.

Carl held her hands as he looked into her eyes. "I'll understand if you want a different partner."

His confession aroused more than just her curiosity. "I'm not mad, Carl... I'm impressed, but I want to know what you intend to do with your prey." Raya looked silently back at him, waiting for an answer.

He was silent, feeling guilty; his intentions weren't as earnest as they appeared, and now she knew it.

Raya was familiar with the look in Carl's eyes and gave him a gentle kiss. Carl had the same hungry look Gill had when he turned the tides on her, and she had become the conquered.

Carl pulled her into his arms as he passionately returned her kiss. It was then she began to realize why she was so fascinated with the rabbits. Their robust and passionate nature, desires, and the hunger to pursue what they wanted proved even rabbits have teeth and claws.

Raya was no longer comfortable wearing Gill's shirt, so she decided to change. A smile swept across her face as she walked past Carl. "I will be right back... When I return, I'll expect an answer," Raya said playfully.

Carl watched her disappear down the hallway, asking himself if his actions were proper. He didn't care that she was an alien or his subordinate. He didn't want to lose her friendship over his sexual attraction to her.

Carl felt he was being watched and turned his head toward the hallway to see a pair of deep yellow eyes looking back at him from the shadows.

"Raya... Is that you?" he asked nervously.

Carl was startled when she emerged from the shadows, growling softly as she slowly approached him.

Raya knew by looking at him that he was intimidated by her appearance. She remembered her experience with Gill and that, when it came to Human soldiers, intimidation had a way of bringing out the desire to stand their ground, overcome and conquer. It was the only battle she knew where conquest was not so bad, and the spoils were just as sweet for the conquered as they were for the victor.

Carl started to speak. There was a nervous tone in his voice as Raya approached him, shifting forms and then placing her fingertip to his lips as she whispered, "Don't speak, show me...

and maybe I might let you walk out of here." Raya turned her back to him, trying to contain her laughter.

Carl tried to argue with his morals one last time, but his mind was already made up. He knew he was breaking all the rules and the trouble he would face if they were caught. Carl wrapped his arms around her waist and gently nibbled on her ear. Raya lost her breath as Carl's hands gently pressed against her abdomen. "My dad always said I lacked the sense it took to get out of the rain," he whispered in her ear.

She closed her eyes, feeling a sense of fear and pleasure race through her as Carl's hands slowly followed the curves of her naked body. His warm breath on her neck made every nerve tingle as his hands slowly moved down her stomach. Raya suddenly placed a hand on the back of Carl's, stopping them from going any further. She didn't like disobeying her father's orders any more than she liked bringing shame to the Kinship, but this was her life and her time to live it the way she wanted. Raya released her grip, then moaned with pleasure as Carl slid his hand between her thighs.

Once again, she had given in to the rabbit's seduction. Raya knew what she was doing was taboo but asked herself why it was wrong. Reaching up and pulling him closer to her, Raya was losing herself in Carl's arms as he kissed and gently nibbled on her neck, taking away her second thoughts.

Carl was doing everything right, his touch stimulating every nerve, as his hands left no part of her body unconquered. He was warm and passionate as he gave her his undivided attention. Raya was pleasantly confused. She wasn't in heat. And yet, her body was responding as if it was.

Raya let out a loud gasp as his hand made its way back between her thighs, his fingers gently tickling her, giving her indescribable pleasure. Carl could no longer control his desires and carried Raya into the bedroom, where he laid her on the bed. She looked up at him, smiling innocently. Carl nervously smiled back, realizing he hadn't really thought things through. He regretted not paying better attention to his sexual sensitivity training.

With Evolutions, females were more aggressive and usually wouldn't be a problem for most men, if they weren't stronger than Humans.

Carl removed the rest of his clothing and lay next to her as she reached over and pulled him close, hoping he wouldn't notice her trembling hands. "You look nervous!" he stated.

Raya looked at him. Her voice was soft. "I've never done this outside my cycle, and despite what I look like, I'm not a young female and can't give you the same pleasures."

Carl smiled and kissed her lips. "When Caroline died, that part of me did too. All that changed when I met you."

Once again, she was seduced by the rabbit's passionate nature and determination to bring her to submission. Carl kissed and gently nibbled his way down her stomach until he gently parted her legs, his warm tongue sending rushes of unknown pleasure racing through her. Raya tried desperately to remain calm, but Carl was making it impossible.

Raya never imagined touch could have such a stimulating effect. Every nerve in her body responded to Carl, her thoughts swirling around like a tornado, wondering how much longer she could continue feeding his voracious appetite.

Now wasn't the time to think of that. She decided to give herself to him.

Raya's hips began to quiver without warning as her screams escaped through the open window.

Carl got up from the bed and headed for the bathroom. Raya followed him, her face beet-red, and she was apologizing, looking at the scratches on the sides of his neck.

"Carl, I am so sorry... I don't know what happened... My body's never done that before," she explained with an embarrassed smile.

Carl suddenly burst into laughter.

"It's not funny, Carl," she said, slapping him on the back. Carl flinched but was still laughing.

"Fine, take care of it yourself," Raya said, annoyed, and headed for the kitchen.

Carl gently grabbed her by the arm and apologized.

"Raya, I'm sorry. That was insensitive of me. What you felt was perfectly normal. It's called an orgasm." Carl paused, thinking about the situation. "Wait a minute. You have nine children, and you've never had one before?"

Raya put the palms of her hands on Carl's chest. "No, Carl, I've only mated in this form one other time, and even then, I was in my breeding cycle and not exactly myself," she barked.

Carl pulled her into his arms, looking passionately into her eyes. "Forgive me," he said in a soft, deep tone.

The color of his eyes and the tone of his voice sent warm shivers racing through her. Raya turned her back to him. She wasn't angry with Carl; she just wasn't willing to let him off the hook so fast and wanted to keep him in suspense for a while longer, or at least that was her plan until Carl picked her up and carried her like a princess back into the bedroom.

"Carl, what are you doing?"

"I'm going to make mad passionate love to you until you do forgive me."

"Are you sure about that, Carl? I may never forgive you," she said with a pouting look.

Raya was lying with Carl, her head resting on his chest, preoccupied with his anatomy.

"You having fun?" Carl asked jokingly.

"I've never seen this part of the Human male before."

"You haven't? What about the other guy?"

"I was in heat, Carl, and not paying attention to detail."

After a minute of silence, Raya was even more curious about Human males. "What happened to it? Why is it so small?"

"Small! Ain't that small," Carl instantly shot back.

"Please, Carl. I'm serious," she pleaded.

Carl thought about it for a moment and wasn't sure how to explain it to her without sounding crude. "Well, it worked hard, and now it's just taking a little nap," Carl responded jokingly.

"Carl," she interrupted.

"What?"

"Keep talking to me like that, and I'll bite this off," she said, poking it with her fingers.

Carl wasn't sure whether she was joking and quickly diverted the conversation. "So Uteakons don't do it in their Human forms?"

"No, males won't mate with us in Human form!"

"Why not?" He looked at her, surprised.

"I don't know, Carl. I'm not a male," she said, getting out of bed.

Carl looked up at her. His voice was deep and seductive. "Where are you going?"

"I'm going to take a shower," she responded reluctantly while fighting off the urge to crawl back in bed and make love to him for hours more, but the look in his eyes told her that he was tired and worn out. The smile on his face, however, spoke the loudest as if he was feeling the same way she was, although her stress wasn't gone. It just didn't weigh as much. She leaned over, kissed him on the lips, and headed into the bathroom.

Raya stood underneath the shower, even more confused. If she did wrong, why did it feel so right?

She turned off the shower, wrapped a towel around her, and walked back to the bedroom to see Carl asleep, half-covered in sheets as if he didn't have a care in the world. She smiled as she let her towel fall to the floor, then shifted forms.

Like the corporal, nothing was threatening about him.

When they made love, she was outside her cycle and nervous, yet he was gentle with her.

Carl was the second rabbit she had let down her guard for. The second time she had tasted taboo, it had a much sweeter flavor. But in her Human form, Raya was still vulnerable, a feeling she was most uncomfortable with. She wondered if all the guilty pleasures were worth the risks or the consequences she faced when her father found out.

The only thing influencing her was her hunger for knowledge. However, she was still just as puzzled about Carl as she was with the first rabbit. Carl looked nothing like the corporal. Even though their personalities were different, she was just as attracted to him.

Raya's temperature rose with the morning sun, panting as she watched Carl sleep. Physically, she was stronger than him, and her girth was larger. When she stood on her hind legs, she'd have to look down to look into his eyes. On Uteaka, she'd have no attraction to a male like this and would kill him if he tried to mate with her, but with the rabbits, it was different. What did they have that felines didn't? When her sisters talked about the Human soldiers, they referred to them as rabbits, but the absolute freedom came from what they called the Rabbits' Club, exclusive only to those willing to risk everything.

————— ••◆•• —————

Carl woke up and rolled over to see Raya sleeping. Even as a feline, she was just as beautiful, he thought, running his hand along her soft fur. Carl grinned, thinking how ironic the situation was. As a kid, he was bitten by a dog and developed a fear of them no matter the size or the temperament, and now here he was, lying next to a carnivore who was three hundred pounds plus of pure muscle and a short fuse. Still, he had learned a lot about himself knowing her.

Carl gave her a gentle pat and then got up to use the bathroom. While washing his hands, he looked into the mirror, trying to imagine how Raya must see him. And how confusing it was to see through the many titles Humans gave themselves. He turned off the water, dried his hands, and returned to the bedroom. Raya was still sleeping. Carl decided to make breakfast and order groceries to be delivered.

He was in the kitchen making the same breakfast his mother used to make for him, crispy bacon laying across two sunny-side-up eggs, with wheat toast and grits dripping with real butter.

He had just finished making breakfast when he heard Raya coming out of the bedroom.

"Carl, what are you doing?"

"Making breakfast... You hungry?"

"Breakfast sounds good," she said, coming around the corner.

He froze, seeing Raya wearing his shirt. For a brief moment, she looked like Caroline. Raya noticed his eyes staring at her and looked down at the shirt.

"If it bothers you, I can take it off."

"It doesn't bother me. I was just noticing how sexy you make that shirt look."

Raya looked at him, puzzled. "That had better be a compliment," she muttered, walking past him.

He smiled and pulled her close to him. "It's one of the best compliments I can think of," he said, kissing her lips.

Carl was sitting across the table, watching Raya enjoying her first down-home breakfast. "So, how do you like it?"

Raya looked at him with approval. "It's delicious. I like it."

She picked up the bacon and put it on Carl's plate. He looked at her, surprised. "You don't like bacon?"

"I'm sorry, Carl, cooked meat is an acquired taste," she said with a look of guilt.

"And I take it you've never acquired the taste for it," he said with a grin.

"No, I'm sorry."

He got up from the table and brought over a plate of barely cooked bacon. "I wasn't sure," he said, putting it next to her plate.

"I'm sorry. I don't want you to think I'm ungrateful."

"It's okay. My dad liked his bacon the same way," he said, looking at her warmly.

Raya looked over at Carl. She could tell he was thinking about last night and was now worried about the consequences of the guilty pleasures they had shared.

Carl started to speak. "Raya... About last night."

She put her hand on his, cutting him off.

"Carl, last night we were two people enjoying a well-needed pleasure... You had your reasons... I had mine. So as far as I am concerned, it's just one of the silent benefits to our friendship," she said, emphasizing silence.

Carl got up from the table and walked over to Raya, looking her in the eyes as he held out his hand. "Friends with benefits. I like that," he said in a soft, deep tone.

Raya could feel the warm shivers racing through her once again as she looked up at Carl with a bashful smile. "What?"

"What do you mean what? I'm cashing in on some of those benefits," he said as he picked her up and carried her back into the bedroom. After Carl left, she was still wearing his shirt with nothing to do, and since Ocean wasn't due back until tomorrow, she grabbed the book Sophie had given her and decided to make it a coffee and romance weekend.

# CHAPTER 6

Carl parked his transport in the garage and then walked into the kitchen. Zoe and Tylee were sitting at the table.

Zoe got up to greet him with a hug. "Dad...you're home. I'm glad you're okay. You had us worried."

"Sorry, Baby G. I didn't mean to worry you."

Tylee got up from the table and walked over to him. Her long, dark brown hair was tied into a ponytail, and her taupe-colored eyes were tearing up. "We walk through that door a minute late, and you snap at us. But you can come home anytime you want." Tylee shook her head in frustration and then stormed off to her bedroom.

Carl was silent, drowning in remorse, as he looked over at Zoe, her long black hair hanging above her shoulders and her brown eyes looking into his. "Baby girl, I'm sorry for worrying you," he said, pulling her into his arms.

Zoe gave him an awkward but forgiving smile. Like her mother, she displayed a calm demeanor even though she was upset. "Dad, I know you're a grown man. However, it doesn't change our worry about you."

He put his hands on her cheeks, kissing her on the forehead. "You have my promise. I will always call from now on."

She looked up at him, smiling. "So, who is she?"

"Just a friend, nothing more," Carl muttered.

Zoe looked up at him. Her brown eyes complimented her smile. "You know, Dad, there's nothing wrong with moving on with your life. If Mom could, she would tell you herself. Food for thought, Dad." She spoke with a soft, caring tone.

Carl began to tear up, smiling at her. "You're right. If your mother were here, she'd be very proud of you. I know I am," he whispered.

Carl walked upstairs and stood outside Tylee's closed door. "Ty, can we talk?" After a minute of no answer, Carl knocked firmly on the door. "Ty, I'm coming in."

She was lying on her bed with her face buried in the pillow, muffling the faint sound of sniffling. Carl sat next to her, gently rubbing her back. "Ty, I'm sorry, I was inconsiderate. I know you're angry with me, and you have every right to be."

Tylee kept her face in the pillow and continued to ignore him. "Lord knows I've made many mistakes with you and Zoe since your mother died. The biggest one I'll always regret was not waking you up that night to say goodbye to your mom."

Carl continued rubbing Tylee's back, thinking back to when she was a vibrant little girl who promised to love her daddy forever and ever. But when the girls' mother died, a part of Tylee died too. She was never the same after that. She became quiet, her eyes always sad or resentful whenever she looked at him. Whenever he'd returned from missions, Zoe would come running into his arms, happy to see him. Tylee would look at him and start crying. The longer he was gone, the harder she cried. Carl knew she'd worry so much about losing him, it was hurting her. And when he'd hold her in his arms, trying to calm her down, he'd ask himself the same question with the same tears: "What kind of father does this?"

The only thing he hated more than the Shezón was causing his daughter pain. Carl knew he was beyond duty when it came to the bug's soldiers; it was revenge, and his hunger for it was hurting his family. He had reached his breaking point and retired from the battlefield, where he was transferred to Fort Victory and helped with the construction of the Mud Dog program.

Tylee suddenly sat up. She was still crying. "I thought

something happened to you."

Carl held her close until she calmed down. Her tears ran down the side of his neck. "Ty, I'm sorry for hurting you. I'll call from now on."

She looked up at him. "You promise?"

He gently brushed her tears away with his thumbs and kissed her forehead. "I do."

•••◆•••

Carl was in his training room, working out. Whenever he felt like he was losing control, his father's words would always echo in the back of his mind.

"Boy, that temper of yours is like a beast. Let it work for you and not against you."

There were more days than he could count when he'd give anything to hear one of his father's training speeches or feel his mother's warm embrace after a bad day. She would hold him in her arms, encouraging him to let it all out, and she would dry his tears when he was done crying. "Now, don't you feel better?" she'd say, kissing him on the cheek. Training sergeants always told them, even when he was going to the Military Academy, "Tears are the only thing that reminds us we're still Human."

Carl laughed until he cried, remembering how his mother ruled with an iron hand and a wooden spoon. No matter where she was, Old Faithful was never out of reach. He'd even sell the moon just to see his brother's annoying smile. He turned, startled to see Zoe. She had a worried look on her face. In her hand was a glass of iced tea. "I thought I made it clear not to come in here when I'm training," he barked.

She looked at him meekly. "I thought you might like something cold to drink!" Zoe turned, put the glass on the table, and then headed for the door, feeling hurt.

Carl trusted Zoe. It was himself he questioned. "Zoe, wait.

I'm not mad, just startled," Carl responded, inviting her into his open arms.

Zoe hugged him tightly, her silent tears falling on his shoulder. "Baby girl, I'm sorry. You know how I get when I train. I'm afraid I might accidentally hurt you or Tylee one day."

She spoke to him in Russian. "You're a good poppa. Good poppas don't do that."

They were the words Caroline used when she interrupted him during one of his training sessions while holding Zoe in her arms. He would always try and give her a stern warning, but her smile would always melt his heart as she said those exact words her daughter just did.

Carl slammed down the iced tea and grabbed his shirt off the chair's back as he walked Zoe back to her bedroom. "Good night, baby girl," he said, kissing her on the forehead.

Zoe kissed him on the cheek. "Good night, Dad. I love you."

"I love you too." He watched her close the door, then headed to his room.

◆◆◆◆◆

Carl awoke suddenly from his sleep, sat up gasping for air, and realized it was only a bad dream. Once again, 305 was invading his dreams, its wolf-like head and bloodred eyes staring at him, forcing him to remember Fort Eagle and the day it fell to the Shezón.

He would never forget that day. It was the first time the Army had seen mantis soldiers. They were twice the size of Humans, and their skeletal structure was like mirrored steel, reflecting laser weapons.

Carl was in recess that day, playing dodgeball with the other kids. The playground was filled with children laughing and playing until silence swept throughout the playground as everyone looked up to see thousands of pods falling from the sky. Chaos and panic broke out. Teachers ran out to the playground, gathering all the children. Carl followed them until Half-pint grabbed his arm, forcing him to go the other way.

"Come on, we have to go!" Carl never knew if it was just the dream or if her eyes were bloodred when he looked into them. "Now," she shouted, leading him out of the playground. They were running for the woods when Carl suddenly heard shattering glass, followed by bloodcurdling screams echoing.

"Don't look back. Just keep running," Half-pint shouted, leading him through the thick forest. When they got far enough away from the school, Carl's first thought was his family. "My mom," he shouted, his voice echoing through the woods.

He broke free from Half-pint's grip and ran as fast as possible for his house. Half-pint ran after him. Carl was running toward his house and almost to the back door when she grabbed and tackled him to the ground.

"You can't help them...they're already dead. One day you will have your revenge. I promise, but if you die now, it will never happen."

Carl spent many years trying to get that day out of his head. Even now, the image of bloodied bodies littering the streets still lingered in his mind, and the smell of blood was so strong it made him puke. But hate has a way of changing people. On the battlefield, Carl was used to seeing death and blood. Such things didn't bother him anymore.

There were many times Carl would train until he had no more anger left, and he would fall to his knees wondering what he had become, but the thought of his mother encouraging him to let it all out brought out his tears, reminding him he was still Human.

Carl got out of bed and grabbed his bathrobe, his face pale and his hands trembling.

He walked to the kitchen and grabbed a glass from the

dish strainer and a bottle of cannabis wine from the refrigerator. He sat at the table and tried to steady his hand while pouring the wine.

For as long as he lived, he would always remember that day they found 305. His life had never been the same since. Every night she entered his dreams, forcing him to relive moments of his past, moments he would rather forget. There were nights when the past became too much, and he lay awake trying to convince himself it was just a nightmare. Even in his waking hours, the hellish creature continued to haunt him.

305 looked like something straight out of the deepest part of hell. He questioned the military's actions and the sanity of the top brass. It didn't take a genius to realize when something should be left alone. They were like children, playing with an entity they knew nothing about.

He had been assigned as part of General Raincheck's security and regretted being aboard the Battle Hawk when they got the orders. He was in his office when the general burst through his door. "Carl, meet me on the bridge in five minutes."

"Yes, sir!"

When Carl went to the bridge, Raincheck stood beside Goleen, talking. They were looking at a giant black orb with Shezón warning beacons. "Well, my friend, our search might be over, and hopefully, we can tell the old lady that we found her treasure."

"Treasure? Looks more like Pandora's box. What is it exactly that we are looking at, sir?" Carl interrupted.

Raincheck looked back at him. "I guess I'll find out when you do. Now, have your men fully armed and in the cargo bay."

Carl looked at the two generals as if they were crazy. "If I'm not mistaken, those are Shezón warning beacons, and I'm guessing that whatever is in there is just as bad for us."

Raincheck looked at Carl, unimpressed. His attitude became belligerent. "You might be right, old friend, but I have my orders... And so do you!"

Although his tone was angry, the look in his eyes made Carl's skin crawl. "Yes, sir!" Carl wondered who the bigger fool was, the two generals or himself for following their orders.

Suddenly, someone shouted. "Sir, we're ready."

"Okay, let's open the package," Raincheck responded.

General Goleen's face paled as if he knew what was waiting for them.

Carl started to walk away when his curiosity got the better of him. He turned to see the black orb shattering, sending particles of glowing sand shooting through space.

Inside the sphere were two ships, a large Lansing ship piercing the side of a Shezón battleship. It looked more like a mosquito sucking blood from an arm. Carl started to think he had overreacted and it was just a desperate attempt to take down the enemy.

"Okay, sir, we're ready to scan," someone hollered.

An image of the nightmarish beast appeared inside Carl's head, slowly opening its crimson glowing eyes. A wave of dark energy swept through the ship. There was a momentary feeling of confusion and panic. The bridge crew looked at each other with the same fear, wondering what had just happened. Carl's heart pounded, and his blood ran cold. Whatever was aboard that ship was waiting for them.

He walked to the day room and gathered his team. Everyone was armed and in the cargo bay as ordered. The cold feeling of dread lingered throughout the bay as each soldier stood silently, looking at one another, hoping they'd come out of this one alive. "All right, everyone. Listen up." Carl's loud voice echoed through the room. "Before we begin. Are there any questions?"

Lieutenant Bergstrom raised his hand.

"What is it, Lieutenant?"

"Well, sir, I was wondering why we were taking his weapons. Sir, whatever's on that ship ain't going down with these."

"Protocol, Lieutenant," Carl barked.

"No offense, sir, but the protocol is gonna slow us down. The only weapons we need are the katanas."

Carl knew the lieutenant was right. The katanas were designed to cut through the mantis soldier's exoskeleton, but at close range, it was suicide. The mantis soldiers were slow to draw but lightning-quick at thrusting. "I won't give you the okay to break protocol. You do. It's on your conscience, not mine," Carl said, looking around at the other soldiers.

"Yes, sir," Bergstrom said, laying down his weapon.

Carl watched as the others followed his lead. He drew a deep sigh and then laid his weapon on the ground. "All right, now that we're all on the same page." Carl gave them a quick briefing. "All right, everyone, you know the drill. You know the mission. I want everyone paired up aboard the ship: one Human, one Uteakon. What you miss, they won't. What they miss, you won't. I expect the ship to be cleared quickly and thoroughly. The sooner we do our jobs, the sooner the science team can do theirs, and we can leave this place far behind."

Suddenly, the doors leading to the cargo bay opened up. A science team came through, carrying crates of equipment and wearing hazmat suits.

"All right, soldiers, our dates are here. Let's roll."

"Yes, sir," they hollered in unison as they boarded the cargo carrier bound for the ill-fated battleship.

The ship was dark and covered with dust. There was a bone-chilling silence throughout the enemy vessel. Carl felt his skin crawl while the foul stench of stale death lingered in the air.

As they headed for the rendezvous point, everyone felt like four-year-olds walking through the hallways. Everything from the instrument panels to the door handles was out of reach. The only gratifying thing about the mission were the husks of half-eaten bug soldiers littering the floor and the satisfactory feeling of imagining the pain they suffered as they were being eaten alive. Carl hated the Shezón. They took everything from him, his family, friends. Everyone taken by the bug soldiers. Carl vowed that one day he would take everything from them. *Even if it meant making a deal with the very heart of darkness, so be it*, he had thought to himself, kicking away the husks.

They met up with the Uteakons, who were unarmed and waiting at the end of the hall. He was greeted by the captain. He was about five feet tall, very muscular, and looked like he had just graduated from high school. "Hello, my name is Captain Hook," he announced.

Carl chuckled. "Sorry, it just struck me funny."

"It's okay. I get that a lot from Humans." He handed Carl an earpiece.

Carl looked at it. "What is this?"

"It's a translator. Unless you speak feline."

"No, sorry." He put in the translator as Captain Hook shifted forms. His height and his body mass were no joke. He was light gray and almost the size of a pony. He realized why the Uteakons weren't carrying weapons. They were the weapons.

Hook looked over at his team and then let out several loud roars. "Pair up with the Humans. I want this done quickly. This place curdles my blood... Do not disappoint me... Am I clear?"

"Yes, sir," they roared back.

Each team was assigned a part of the vessel. Carl and Hook took the north end, venturing down what seemed to be the darkest part of the ship. Carl kept a hand on his katana and stayed next to Hook's side.

Hook broke the silence. "You do pretty well for someone who can't see in the dark," he stated with his nose in the air.

"Contact lenses," Carl muttered, looking around.

Hook laughed. "If there is a will, there is a..." He suddenly became silent as the hair on his back stood on end.

Carl felt goosebumps racing up his arm as if they were being watched. "You get the feeling we're about to regret this?" Carl muttered.

"I got that feeling when we boarded this cursed ship," Hook muttered back.

They continued cautiously down the corridor until they came to a pair of giant black metallic doors shielded by a gray mist. Carl began to reach for them when they suddenly opened as if something were inviting them in. The room was almost empty except for an enormous bronze serpent statue in the center. When they approached it, it was covered in dust. Carl was studying the statute when he looked over at the head to see the eyes open and stare at him. The last thing he remembered was the feeling of being pulled out of his body and then waking up aboard the Battle Hawk with the doctor standing over him. Carl never knew what had happened that day. The only thing he knew for sure was he was grateful to the Uteakons for their quick thinking in severing the connection between him and 305.

Carl jumped and nearly fell out of his chair when he felt a hand on his shoulder. He looked over to see Tylee.

"Sorry, Dad. I didn't mean to scare you. I just wanted to know if you were okay," she said, concerned.

"Yeah, I'm fine, baby girl, just a bad dream."

"You wanna talk about it? I'm willing to listen."

Carl looked up, smiling as he put his hand on Tylee's. "I wish I could, baby girl. I really do."

"I know. Top secret, right?" Tylee smiled, grabbed the glass from the strainer, and sat at the table.

Carl watched as she reached for the cannabis wine. "Ah, no, you're too young to drink wine."

"Dad," she said, annoyed. "It's not even alcohol. It's juice."

"I don't care. You're fifteen years old."

"Dad, please, just one glass. It's the only thing that helps with my menstrual cramps," she pleaded.

"What about that stuff I just got for you and Zoe?"

"Dad, I told you, it doesn't work."

"One glass, and that's it."

"That's all I want. Thanks, Dad."

The central control unit started to chime: "You have a

communications request, Captain Winfield."

Carl looked at the clock on the wall. It was 1:45 in the morning. "Who is this calling?" Carl didn't hide his annoyance.

"It's Lieutenant Skyler, sir."

"That's right, Skyler, the Mud Dog candidate files. Let me patch into my office, and I'll send them to you right now," he said in a panic.

"Thank you, sir. I would appreciate that."

Carl could tell by her sarcasm that she was not happy with him for a good reason. It was the third time she had asked for the records on the new Mud Dog program candidates. It was one more reason she found dealing with the Army frustrating.

"Okay, Lieutenant... You should have them now."

"Thank you, sir."

Carl felt bad. He knew she worked hard and long hours to get the training center ready for the grand opening. He was only adding to her workload.

"Lieutenant?"

"Yes, sir?"

"I really feel bad about this. Tell you what. Let me make it up to you. I'll buy your next meal."

"Sir, are you asking me on a date?"

"What? No. Hell no! I would never do that." Carl closed his eyes and cringed, realizing how that had just come across. Before he could correct himself, Lieutenant Skyler responded.

"Oh, really?" There was no mistaking the offense in her words.

"Don't get me wrong, Lieutenant. You're a beautiful young woman. I meant to say, Lieutenant, that I will buy you lunch or anything you want."

There was a long pause before she responded. "Well then, sir, I like Greek."

Carl thought about it for a moment. "They don't have Greek at the cafeteria."

"Yes, sir, I know." With that, she severed the connection.

Carl had a feeling that he had just made a date with the daughter of a Marine base commander whose claws were sharper than most generals'.

# CHAPTER 7

Sophie had finished transferring the mud Dog files to blind tech and was reviewing them with her braille pad. The candidates had all come from different backgrounds. There were those who came from good and financially stable families, while others were surviving any way they could. It didn't matter what part of society you were from. If you were born with the NewGen parasite, you were part of the misunderstood and feared, judged by a common trait they shared: becoming aggressive when provoked. This was okay and even accepted if you were a man, but in a woman, you were considered socially unacceptable and given no breaks. Sophie was all too familiar with it, not because she was NewGen herself, but because she was an Evolution. The only ones who welcomed people with the parasite were the military. They had discovered that the NewGen were biological engineers. For its own protection it altered the hosts' DNA during the gestation, and they were born with the potential to stand against the Shezón both physically and mentally. But like everything else, they had to be trained to become soldiers.

She was grateful to the Army for allowing her to be a part of the new Mud Dogs and train sighted soldiers to use blind tech, giving them the same advantages in combat that she had.

Sophie thought back to the first day reporting for duty. She was standing outside Captain Winfield's office, trying to gather

her nerves. She took a deep breath, exhaled, then knocked.

"Come in."

Sophie could feel butterflies in the pit of her stomach. Captain Winfield was a highly decorated officer and ruled with an iron hand. In the Marine Corps he was well known, and worked with her father to hunt the Shezón.

"Have a seat, Lieutenant," he said with a deep, soothing voice.

"Thank you, sir," she replied nervously.

Captain Winfield noticed her discomfort. "It's okay, Lieutenant. If anyone should be nervous, it should be me," he chuckled in a reassuring tone. "You're the inspiration behind the ABS soldiers."

"Thank you, sir."

Captain Winfield stood up from his desk, looking into the eyes of the lieutenant. "For somebody as young as you, you've accomplished quite a bit to overcome challenges most people would find impossible. The Mud Dog program is lucky to have you, and I want you to know that."

Sophie blushed. With her ABS autolocation, she could hear the rhythm of his heartbeat and knew that he was being honest with her. "Thank you, sir. That means a lot."

"Well, you've earned it. Looking at you, I would never guess that you're blind."

She began to tear up. It felt good to hear those words come from somebody other than her father. The captain walked out from behind the desk and put his hand on Sophie's shoulder. "I'm sorry, Lieutenant. I didn't mean to upset you."

"You didn't, sir. It's just that it's hard to believe it's actually happening."

"Well, Lieutenant, it's happening. Welcome to the Mud Dogs," he said, holding out his hand. He was surprised when Sophie reached out for his hand. "How did you know I was going to shake your hand?" he asked curiously.

"I could feel the vibrations, and I heard your hand coming towards me, sir."

"Advanced BioSonar. Correct?"

"Yes, sir."

"Amazing! Amazing is the only way I can describe you," he replied, giving her hand a firm squeeze. Then he pulled out a clean tissue from his pocket and handed it to Sophie to wipe her tears of happiness as he welcomed her once again into the Mud Dogs. Sophie's thoughts were suddenly interrupted when the security guard opened her door.

"Sorry, ma'am, didn't mean to disturb you, just making my rounds."

"It's okay, Sergeant. I was just leaving." Grabbing her handbag and her cane, she headed for the security desk and then into the rainy night.

◆

Sophie arrived at her apartment a little after 3 AM that night. She was worn out and wanted nothing more than to sink into her soft mattress. When she opened the door, she was greeted by Patty, the apartment's AI control unit.

"Good morning, Lieutenant Skyler."

"Good morning, Patty. Any messages?"

"You have two messages from Jasmine Skyler. Playing first message now:

"'Hello, Mom. I just called to say I love you and I miss you. Dad's taking me out to a fancy restaurant. So I have to go now. I'm waving to you and blowing you kisses.'

"Playing message two: 'Hi Mom, Dad and I had a great time. You should have been there. It was a big fancy restaurant. Dad got to have his own private dining room, mostly because of all the people wanting his autograph. Well, gotta go, Mom. Love you. I'm waving to you and blowing you more kisses.' End of messages."

"I love you too, sweetheart," Sophie whispered to her nine-year-old daughter's voice. She could feel the soreness in her back as she walked to her bedroom. She couldn't remember the last time, other than boot camp, that she had spent so long in Human form. Without thick pads on her feet, they were sore. Sophie undressed, then shifted into her leopard form, letting out a low growl of relief as she completed her transformation.

"Patty, play me some rainy jazz." Sophie leaped up onto her bed and then rolled over on her back, her hind legs stretched out as she folded her front paws over her breasts. *Heaven, I am here*, she thought to herself, sinking into the soft, thick comforter, enjoying the music while the relaxing sound of falling rain played in the background.

Although she could laugh about it now, there was a time when the rain wasn't so tranquil, at least not to a five-year-old caught in a rainstorm for the first time. Back then, it had felt cold and miserable. The harder it rained, the duller her senses became, leaving her feeling helpless and afraid. Sophie would never forget that terrifying day when her world changed. It was a beautiful Saturday morning. Her father decided to take her and her brother Aaron to the park to spend the day. But halfway through the afternoon, storm clouds began to form. Father decided it was time to leave.

"Come on, you two, let's get going before the rain," he yelled to them.

"Okay, coming," they called back.

Aaron ran first, and Sophie ran after him. By the direction of her father's voice, she knew that he was at the top of the long, steep stairs leading up to the parking lot. Sophie ran as fast as possible to keep up with Aaron. When she was halfway up the stairs, soft sprinkles began falling. She stopped to enjoy the moment, with her mouth wide open and her arms stretched out to the side, trying to catch the rain.

Her father was concerned about the weather. "Come on, Sophie, let's go!"

"Coming, Daddy," she hollered.

Without warning, the rain began to come down in sheets, making a deafening roar as it hit the concrete. Sophie covered her ears and screamed desperately for her father. All she could hear and smell was the falling rain, leaving her panic-stricken and with no sense of direction. The sound of the rain was drowning out her echolocation ability. Then she lost her balance, sending her tumbling down the concrete stairs, scraped and bruised. She picked herself up off the ground and continued covering her ears as she screamed desperately for her father. For that brief moment, she was totally alone. It felt like she was trapped in a nightmare. But before Sophie knew it, her father was holding her safely.

Once again, he had come to her rescue when she most needed it, just as he did that day when he had found her abandoned and dying in a trashcan. To his eyes back then, she was just a lost kitten, but that didn't stop him from taking her out of death's hands and giving her a new life on a new planet. Sophie started to laugh when she thought about her father's first words to his granddaughter, Jazzy, the day she was born: "I hope you're a pain in Mommy's ass, just like she was in mine."

Sophie rolled over and drifted off to sleep. And the dream memory started again. She was back in that alley, hearing the sound of a man crying, mourning the death of a loved one:

"How do I move on without you? We both know I'm no good to our son like this. All I have left is my lust for vengeance." His tone became angry and cold. "No matter how many of those bastards I kill, my craving is never satisfied."

Sophie, near death with cold and hunger, called out to him with a plaintive meow as she began to lose consciousness. The next thing she remembered, she was waking up in his hands. They were firm but held her with the gentlest of care. She was safe in the hands of Sam Skyler.

When Sophie arrived at her new home, she was taken out of a box and introduced to Aaron, her rescuer's son and her new playmate.

"Meet the new member of our family," Sam said, holding her gently. Although Sophie understood their speech, she didn't have the vocal cords to respond in a language they could understand. She could not tell her new father that she didn't like being picked up. Sophie began to squirm, digging her back claws into his hand until he gently put her down on the ground.

Aaron put his face to hers. "Hello."

She let out a meow. It wasn't the meow of any house cat he had ever heard. She was different from other kittens. He looked at her, smiled, and welcomed her to the family.

In the eyes of a six-year-old boy, Sophie was a pet, but that didn't stop them from becoming the best of friends. Aaron was gentle and careful not to step on her as she followed him around the house, playfully attacking his leg. After she was done playing, Sophie wandered around the house, calling out for her mom, but there was never an answer.

That night was when her nightmares first started. It was the same nightmare that would always come back to torment her for years: she was trapped in a garbage can, her cries never penetrating the silence as she lay there dying...

Sophie woke up in the kitten box, alone and afraid, crying. This time, however, her cries had not gone unheard. She could hear the sound of bare feet slapping against the wooden stairs, getting louder as he got closer. She knew by his scent that it was Aaron, searching to find the crying's source. Sophie stood on her hind legs, hoping he would notice her.

When Aaron located where the crying was coming from, he went to Sophie and gently picked her up. "It's okay, don't cry," he said, kissing her on the cheek as he carried her to his room. Still scared, Sophie crawled into his pajama shirt and slept comfortably next to his chest, listening to the sound of his beating heart. It was the only sound she knew that made her feel safe, as if her mother was still watching over her.

The next day Aaron and her new father took her to the

vet to register her on the Marine base. All pets had to be registered and given a clean bill of health. When she was checked in, she was registered as a male kitten named Danny. However, when the vet took her out of the cat carrier and examined her, he cooed softly, "Well, well, you're a little Danielle...and far away from your home planet."

The vet called out to his nurse. The door squeaked open, and the nurse poked her head in. "Yes, sir?"

"Bring me a translator."

The nurse paused for a moment. "Sir, those translators don't work on animals." She sounded confused.

"Yes, Sergeant, I am aware of that. Now, if you would please. And tell Commander Skyler to come in here."

"Yes, sir."

When Sam Skyler entered the room, the vet turned to him and said, "Danny is a little Danielle, and we have a big problem."

"What do you mean, problem!? What problem?"

"Sam," he said, dropping rank to speak as an old friend, "this isn't an animal. This is a child, a Newtopian child, leopard to be exact."

"What? She is too small to be a Newtopian."

"They're not born in Human form, Sam. It will be about five years before she will get her Human form." The veterinarian drew a deep breath and then exhaled. "Sam, just having her here could start a war. With the Shezón trying to take us out of existence, we can't afford this."

"Look, John, don't worry about it."

"Don't worry about it!? Sam, next week I retire, and I want to see my grandchildren grow up!"

"All those times I got us in trouble, didn't I get us out?"

The veterinarian chuckled. "Yeah, Sam, that you did."

Her father changed her name to Sophie, his wife's middle name.

———◆◆◆◆◆———

Sophie woke up to the sound of someone walking around in the kitchen and figured it had to be her daughter, Jasmine. Jazzy, she liked to be called now. But what was she doing back in the middle of the night? She was staying with Aaron, and wasn't due home until morning. Sophie got up from the bed and shifted into her Human form. She put on an old flannel shirt that once belonged to Aaron. It was soft and comfortable and always carried his scent. Then she walked to the kitchen to see who was there.

"Jazzy, is everything okay?"

"It's not Jazzy. It's me, Aaron."

Aaron? She was surprised but happy to hear his voice again. Usually he just dropped Jazzy off at the door.

"I hope you don't mind," Aaron said. "I wanted to make some coffee before I headed out."

"Of course. But why are you so early? Is everything okay?"

"Yeah, everything's fine. Jazzy got a little homesick and was pretty tired. She's in her bedroom."

As Sophie went to check on Jazzy, Aaron's thoughts drifted back to his childhood. He was six years old when Dad found Sophie. It was on the morning after the first anniversary of his mother's death that Aaron first met Sophie. His father, the fifth generation of a Marine family and a colonel back then, had just returned from Newtopia, where they had paid tribute to the fallen. Among the names of the deceased was his mother, Major Catherine Sophia Skyler, MD.

It had been a challenging year for them both. His father never smiled. His eyes always had a look of loneliness in them. Many nights, he would sit drinking Scotch in his mother's office. Sometimes, Aaron could hear him crying behind the closed door. It wasn't until Aaron was on his own and living in the streets that he realized that, had it not been for Aunt Julie, his mother's sister, he would have lost his father that year as well. Julie's husband, and friend to his father, was one of the first Marines to lose his life defending the Human race from the Shezón. Julie had lost more than anyone but still found the courage to raise her children, heal the wounded, and help her brother-in-law get through the bad times. Aaron had always admired her strength.

Sophie was near death when his father found her. In one last attempt to save the kitten, Dad had administered CPR, saving not only her life but his own life as well. It didn't take long for Aaron and his father to bond with the kitten, and the healing process began for all three of them. As they would soon find out, raising a Newtopian child wasn't going to be easy, especially one that was traumatized and plagued by nightmares. Aaron spent many nights holding Sophie after a bad dream. It was the only thing that helped her sleep comfortably.

Aaron was having nightmares himself after his mother died. He was only five years old when his mother lost her life. All he had left of her were pictures in a photo album and stories told by his Aunt Julie. His mother and Julie had grown up as children in the Irish colony on Newtopia. Julie was five foot four, with long red hair and a quick temper. She was also a specialist in xenobiology, the study of alien life. Like most of the colonists and Newtopians, she spoke with a thick Irish accent. And never talked about Newtopia, keeping those memories private.

Aaron never realized how much he took for granted until he asked himself what would have happened had he lost his father. His life would have taken a whole new path, and he wouldn't be the person he was now. He was very much like his father, keeping his feelings bottled up until the pressure got too much, and then he would explode. All that changed when Aaron met Sophie. She had more reason than anyone he knew to complain about the hand she was dealt. But Sophie never did. Whether she knew it or not, Sophie had become his mentor.

Aaron was in his room when his father called for him to meet the kitten. "Okay, coming," he shouted back. He ran downstairs to see his father standing in the kitchen, holding a green box with holes in the sides. On his face was the biggest smile Aaron had seen in a year.

"Meet the newest member of our family," his father said.

A tiny, tan-colored kitten was in the box. Her fur was covered in brown spots. Aaron looked into her green eyes for the first time, unaware of how much she would change his life. He named her Danny, unaware as yet that she was a female.

That first night, things started to get strange. Aaron remembered waking up to the sound of a baby crying. It was so soft that he could barely hear it. He grabbed the flashlight he always kept under his pillow and followed the sound to its source. It was coming from downstairs in the living room. Standing at the top of the stairs, shining his flashlight into the darkness, Aaron felt a little scared. To a six-year-old boy, things always seemed scarier at night. He debated whether he should continue. But the sound of the baby crying tugged at his heart.

Guided by his flashlight, Aaron headed down into the darkness, his bare feet slapping against the wooden steps. He looked around but couldn't see any sign of an infant. The only one in the living room was the kitten, who was in a box in the corner. When he shined his light into the box, the kitten stood on her hind legs. There were tears in her eyes, and she was crying like a Human baby.

Aaron's eyes got wide. His heart pounded so fast it felt as if it were going to burst out of his chest. He dropped the flashlight and made a beeline for the stairs, thinking the kitten was possessed. But then the crying got louder and more desperate. Aaron stopped, feeling guilty for running away. *The kitten must be having a nightmare,* he thought. When Aaron had nightmares, waking up alone and scared, he always had his father to help him through the bad times. But the poor kitten was alone.

Brushing away his fear, Aaron returned and took the bundle of fur out of the box. "It's okay, don't cry," he said as he kissed her cheek and brought her upstairs with him. For the rest of that night, the kitten slept soundly, curled up inside the safety of his pajama shirt, next to his heart.

The following morning, Aaron woke up and started to panic. The kitten was gone. He looked around his room but couldn't find her. He ran downstairs and was relieved to see his dad feeding the little cat. After getting a lecture about how a kitten was too small to sleep with him, Aaron told his father how she was crying like a Human baby. His father was skeptical.

"You were probably just dreaming, little man. Kittens don't sound like Humans."

Later, when Aaron was tickling Sophie's belly in the living room, she started giggling. He knew his father wouldn't believe him and continued playing with her. But the boy knew Sophie wasn't an ordinary house cat. There was something different about the kitten. However, he never imagined that Danny would turn out to be a Newtopian child.

His father was angry and wanted to know why she was abandoned and left to die in the trash. He contacted one of the colonels of the Newtopian Marines. When the Marines arrived, a gunnery sergeant, in Human form, knocked on the door. He was over eight feet tall. Aaron's father looked up at the sergeant. "What will happen to her?" he asked, with a tone of sadness in his voice.

"She'll be given to a Kinship that will accept her as their own, sir."

"All right, I'll go get Sophie," he reluctantly replied.

Aaron tried to plead with his father but to no avail. He knew his father was right. Sophie needed to be with her own people. Sam returned with Sophie and they said their goodbyes before handing her over to the sergeant. Aaron saw a momentary look of fear in the soldier's eyes when he saw Sophie. Then the soldier backed away from her.

"I'm sorry, I can't help her," he said in a deep voice with a thick Irish accent.

Aaron's father gave the gunnery sergeant an angry look and demanded an answer. The expression on the sergeant's face was as cold as the tone in his voice. "Because on Newtopia, no one will take her, and she will die. You are the one she was meant for." He turned and started walking toward the door.

"How do you know this?" Sam asked.

The sergeant stopped and turned around. Aaron would never forget the look in his eyes as the tall Newtopian stared back at his father. "Because you and your son...are still alive."

With that, he went out the door and headed for his transport. Aaron's father knew that the sergeant was done talking and would not explain further.

It was only years later, when Aaron was on Newtopia, researching Sophie's origins for his next novel, that he found answers that only led to more questions. Sophie's majestic green eyes traced her to the Children of the Sand. They were feared warriors from a land called Nomale. Even the mention of their name drew a look of fear. They were the last free kingdom on Newtopia and ruled only by females. The land of Nomale was said to be cursed until the queen returned. Aaron never knew if it was just a legend or real, but the only thing he was sure of was that Sophie's background was as mysterious as the land itself.

Aaron's father legally adopted her, and her name became Sophia Danielle Skyler.

It was complicated and confusing, seeing her as his little sister. Aaron thought of her more like a best friend. They enjoyed fun times together.

Sophie didn't stay little for long. Within six months, she was the size of a large dog. When she spoke, her language came out as a roar to the untrained ear. Sophie still slept with Aaron, like a big kitten. Sometimes she curled up at the foot of the bed. Other times, she would lie on her side with a giant paw resting on his chest. Sophie was a far cry from that tiny furball who slept in a shoebox.

While Aaron was at school, Sophie had her own things to

do. Every morning, she would play with the next-door neighbor's dog, a blue Rottweiler named Booter, who stood outside the back door and barked until Sophie came out. She and Booter would immediately start to roughhouse. Sophie had more in common with Booter than she did with Aaron, but that would soon change.

A week after Sophie's fifth birthday, Aaron woke up to Booter's constant barking. Aaron became alarmed. It was almost as if Booter was trying to warn him of something. Aaron tried to wake Sophie, but there was no response. Fearing the worst, he ran into his father's room in a panic, his eyes filled with tears.

"Dad, Dad! Something's wrong with Sophie."

Sam jumped up and ran to find Sophie lying on the bed with a high temperature. She was barely moving. Wearing nothing but a bathrobe and boxer shorts, he picked Sophie up, rushed her to the transport, and broke every traffic law on the way to the hospital. There, he placed her on one of the gurneys and called out for help. A medical team responded immediately, rushing her into the emergency room.

Sophie was in a comatose state. Her cells were beginning to divide as her body prepared for transformation, a process the Newtopians called Rebirth. Aaron and his father spent the next three days by Sophie's side, watching and talking to her unconscious body, hoping she could hear them.

The third day was the hardest. Sophie was in the final stages of her Rebirth. Aaron remembered the doctor coming into the room, briefing them on what was about to occur, and even suggesting Aaron leave the room.

"No, Dad, I wanna stay...please!"

His father knelt, putting his hands on Aaron's shoulders. "You sure about this, son?"

"Yes," Aaron replied.

They watched together in horror as Sophie went into convulsions. A gray, thick, slimy liquid seeped through her pores.

Aaron stood helpless, wishing someone could make it stop. His father remained unfazed throughout the process, having seen much worse in combat. Aaron buried his face in his dad's chest and cried himself to sleep. He was awakened by the nurse shouting for the doctor.

"Doctor Lars, it's happening!"

Aaron looked over to see that the gray liquid had hardened, forming a cocoon around Sophie. It momentarily pulsated and then crumbled, revealing a beautiful, pale, shivering little girl. She had long, wet blonde hair, and her olive skin was covered in brown leopard spots. Aaron couldn't believe how beautiful Sophie looked, even though she now seemed a stranger. He approached cautiously and reached for her, but jumped back when she opened her eyes. They were now an even more majestic green. He was speechless and overcome by her beauty as the rhythm of his heartbeat changed. Although he didn't know it then, that was the day he fell in love with her. But what does an eleven-year-old boy know about love?

<hr>

Aaron started to laugh at the memory of how his father cried like a schoolgirl when Sophie called out his name in Human speech for the first time. His thoughts returned to the present as Sophie came back into the kitchen.

"What's so funny?" she asked.

"I was just thinking about Dad and the time he cried the first time you called out his name."

"He's not made of stone... He does have a sensitive side."

"I know, but with Dad... You rarely see it."

"I don't know... Dad cried when Jazzy was born."

"He did?" Aaron said, genuinely surprised.

"Yeah, we both did. Dad's were tears of joy, and mine were because it hurt like hell." She reached for a glass and poured some milk to take to Jazzy's room.

Aaron remained in the kitchen, remembering how he had sat in the back seat with Sophie in her new Human form, silently staring at her. He was confused and unsure how he felt about the new Sophie. After about twenty minutes, Dad turned his head.

"Boy, stop staring at your sister and say something to her," he scolded.

Aaron reluctantly said, "Hi, Sophie," in a sarcastic tone.

Sophie turned her head and smiled at him. "Hi, Aaron."

It was the first time he heard her call his name in his own language. He remembered turning his head away from her and ignoring her the rest of the way home.

That first night back from the hospital, he had climbed into his bed to go to sleep when Sophie came into the room in her Human form. Smiling, her tiny fingers clutching the blanket as she lifted herself up, she tried to climb in with him.

"What are you doing?" he asked her, alarmed.

"Going to bed," she said simply, trying to climb up.

"Dad said you can't sleep with me anymore, now that you got your Human form."

It was the lie he would regret. As he looked into Sophie's eyes, she looked confused, and her majestic green eyes were filled with tears.

"Please, Aaron, I want to sleep with you," Sophie pleaded.

Her tears were tugging at his heart. "I'm sorry, Sophie," he said, getting out of bed to give her a hug. "I didn't mean to make you cry." Little did he know that those were the first of many tears she would shed because of him.

Aaron walked over to the balcony door and stared aimlessly through the glass, wishing he could rewrite Sophie's story. As he watched, it started to rain. Even after all these years, he could still feel the guilt eating away at him, making him cringe every time he thought about his insensitive words and the tears she would shed. He drew a deep breath and sighed.

Aaron knew there was a vast difference between the characters in the novels he wrote and the real people in his life. People with real feelings that cannot be rewritten or undone. Because if he could, he would have rewritten that chapter long ago, sparing her from all the pain he caused her. Then her tears would've been of joy and not heartbreak. But no matter how many novels he wrote or how many bottles of Scotch he went through, the past always came back to torment him.

Sophie had spent five years of her life in the animal kingdom. For a Newtopian, that was a long time. Then, one day, she woke up in a new body, afraid and confused. She realized she was now a part of the Human race, and when she most needed him, he turned his back on her. But that wouldn't be his last act of betrayal. Back then, Aaron wasn't used to seeing or talking to Sophie in Human form. Physically, she was now a stranger to him, even though her personality hadn't changed. She still followed him around, wanting to do the things they always did, but it wasn't the same anymore. He felt as if his best friend was gone and began to withdraw from Sophie's Human side. And she could feel it.

"What's wrong, Aaron?" she asked one day. "Don't you wanna play?"

He knew by the look in her eyes that she was just as confused about the whole thing as he was. In the heat of anger, he screamed those words he would later long to take back. "No! I don't want to play with you! I hate you!"

Sophie had stood silently facing him. There were no tears in her eyes, only the look of pain and confusion. She turned and shifted into her feline form and headed to her room, his words affecting her like slow-acting poison.

Over the next two days, Sophie began to reject her Human body and remained in her feline form. Her body was still healing from her Rebirth, and without shape-shifting, she was starting to get sick. Three days later, she collapsed on the kitchen floor. By the time the ambulance got her to the hospital, she was already in a coma.

Aaron remembered sitting in the waiting room with his father as the medical staff rushed Sophie into the emergency room. Minutes seemed like hours as they waited for word of her condition. Aaron was standing, looking out the window, when the doctor came into the room with the bad news. They had tried everything to get Sophie back into her Human form, so her body could continue the healing process, but no matter what they did, they couldn't stop her body from shutting down. Dad fell to his knees in shock, tears falling to the floor. The doctor apologized and headed for the door. His last words would haunt Aaron for life.

"If I didn't know any better," the doctor said, "I'd say she was dying from a broken heart."

Aaron remembered running into the hospital room and seeing Sophie's unconscious body lying in bed, connected to monitors. He ran to her side. Sophie was dying, and he knew why. His whole body felt numb, his vision blurry with tears. He tried to shake her awake, but to no avail.

"Sophie, I am sorry... I didn't mean what I said," Aaron cried. "I was just lying... You're the most beautiful girl I've ever seen... And I don't even like girls that much."

When his father came into the room, Aaron ran to him, crying, "It's my fault, Dad."

There were still tears in his father's eyes as he knelt and hugged Aaron.

"No, son, we're both to blame."

No sooner had his father said that, alarms went off in the room. A team of doctors rushed in. Sophie had flatlined, and they were trying to revive her.

"Get those people out of here!" one doctor shouted.

Aaron cried out for Sophie as they were rushed out of the room.

He and Dad were sitting together in the waiting room

when his Aunt Julie, the xenobiologist, ran into Sophie's room. An hour later, she came out, fuming in anger.

"All right, you two! In my office now!" she shouted, grabbing Aaron by the earlobe and swearing in Irish the whole time as she painfully led them down the hallway to her office.

"Sit down, both of you," she barked, pointing to the seats in front of her desk.

Without hesitation, they did as they were told, feeling her wrath.

"What is the matter with you two? Sophie just gets her Human form, and what do you idiots do?" She turned her head, angrily staring at Sam. "Did I not...tell you to take it easy with her...when introducing her to Human things?"

"Yes, ma'am, you did," Sam answered, looking like a guilty child.

"Then why the bloody hell...didn't you listen to me?" she shouted, slamming the palm of her hand on her desk, then angrily turning toward Aaron. "And you treating your sister like a stranger. The two of you are damn lucky that Sophie is a NewGen."

Julie could see the look of confusion on their faces. "It's a parasitical life-form that lives in the brain of females because it's symbiotic with its host. It wouldn't allow Sophie to die. Otherwise, you idiots would be preparing to give her a funeral and not a bloody good apology."

Although Sophie recovered from her close brush with death, Aaron never forgave himself for what he did. Even years later he could still see her lying in the hospital bed, fighting for her life.

⎯⎯⎯•◆•⎯⎯⎯

As Aaron continued to look out Sophie's balcony window, the rain began to pour. He listened as it hit hard against the side of the building, followed by the balcony doors rattling as the wind shook them. He still hated the rain, ever since that day at the park. There was nothing tranquil about it... It was disruptive, and the storms always dragged out memories...

After the fall down the stairs, they had rushed Sophie to the hospital. An hour later, the doctor entered the waiting room. It was just a little head bump, she said. Nothing serious.

His father was skeptical because the doctor looked so young.

"That's because I'm Newtopian," she explained. "And judging by your voice, I'm old enough to be your grandmother."

Aaron noticed that she never looked into his father's eyes when she spoke, same as Sophie. Her name was Doctor Alicia. She was an Advanced BioSonar specialist, and despite being born without sight, she was the Marines' number one surgeon. What vision was to the sighted, sound waves were to people with ABS. His father took the news hard when the doctor explained about Sophie's condition.

"I don't know what to say," he said sadly. "My own daughter is blind, and I didn't know."

"Listen to me, young man," the doctor replied, "sight is not always a gift. In your daughter's case, she has an upgrade to vision."

His father had looked even more confused. "How is being blind better?"

"Okay, look at it like this. You use sight to process information about the world around you. We use sound to process that same information except with a deeper understanding."

The news didn't faze Sophie in the slightest. She was still the same vibrant Sophie that he knew. But now he himself had a better understanding of her world. Aaron helped her as much as he could, at least until she got tired of it, and reminded him she wasn't helpless.

"Yes, Aaron, I know, I'm not stupid," she would say with a thunderous roar. That would be followed by Dad yelling at him to stop teasing his sister.

Aaron drew a deep sigh and took a sip of his coffee as he continued staring into the rainy night, thinking about Sophie.

Even before she got her Human form, Aaron was used to helping her and did so willingly. In the shower, he would scrub her down. With Sophie's large feline size, there was barely any room for both of them, but it was always fun. Sometimes he would sit on her back, pretending they were on a safari, and she was his trusty steed. Whenever Sophie got tired of it, she would sit down with him sliding down her back and onto the floor, letting him know she was done playing.

Aaron never gave it a thought, showering with her. But Sophie was starting to curve out, and it was becoming evident that the flat-chested little girl was quickly fading away.

After writing his first novel, Aaron spent many hours researching Newtopian biology.

From the day they're born, Newtopians are hardwired for survival, and part of their survival entails bringing new life into the world. It was here that nature gave her daughters an unfair advantage over the competition. During his research, Aaron spoke to Newtopian males and was told the same thing by all of them: when the Huntress goes into her breeding cycle, she is like the Venus flytrap, sending out a scent that is strong and alluring. She sweats a pheromone called the Nectar of Desire. Harmless to females, but to the males, it's her most effective weapon, impossible to resist.

That year, their innocence faded, and the reality was quickly moving in for both of them. Her moods would change. One minute she could be delighted, the next, angry. Aaron remembered sitting in the kitchen eating breakfast when Sophie came into the room. She was wearing a pink tank top and a pair of matching shorts as she passed by him. On her face was an angry look. The kind that said, *I'm not in the mood.* Had he listened to his conscience telling him to keep his mouth shut, things would have turned out differently that day.

"What's wrong with you? Are you okay?" he asked, concerned. As she walked over to the refrigerator, Sophie remained silent and took out a carton of milk. Then she walked past him again, still angry and ignoring him. She opened the cupboard and paused for a moment before letting him have it.

"You! You are the problem. Last night I had a nightmare... and you didn't even hold me." Sophie took a glass out of the cupboard, and then turned toward him with an angry look and continued, "You never hold me anymore. The only time you do is when I'm in my leopard form. Why is that?"

She slammed the cupboard door shut. As she was walking away, Aaron had the feeling she didn't expect or even want an answer. At the same time, he didn't feel right just letting her walk away angry and without an explanation. By now, it wasn't just his conscience shouting at him to leave it alone. It was common sense. But rather than listen, he tried to make her feel better.

"I just like to feel your soft fur, that's all."

Sophie suddenly stopped and turned around. "I'm not a pet, asshole," she snarled.

Aaron smiled as he remembered her throwing the carton of milk and how it exploded as it hit the table, covering him with milk. But his smile soon vanished when the rest of the story played out in his mind.

Sophie started to sleep in her Human form more often. In her leopard form, she had never worn clothing when she slept. He thought nothing of it for years, but now Sophie was built like a teenage girl. There were many nights when Aaron wanted nothing more than to hold her, but the longer he kept that secret, the more it was hurting Sophie. She was like a rose that was starting to bloom, and every morning it was becoming more apparent. A rose, a beautiful Newtopian rose. Aaron was scared and didn't know how to tell her that his feelings for her were not the kind that a brother should have for a sister. Sophie hadn't changed. He had, and he felt guilty about it. Not only would acting on his feelings affect Sophie, but his whole family, too. Aaron knew he wasn't good at keeping secrets from her. Sooner or later, it would all come out.

And then, that day, it did. Aaron tried to undo his damage, got up from the table, and started walking toward her. "Wait, Sophie, please," he said. "I didn't mean it like that."

He'd never forget the look on her face when she stood there, silently holding a glass of milk. It was almost as if he had plunged a serrated knife into her heart. Aaron apologized and started walking up the stairs when he heard the sound of shattering glass. He turned to see Sophie leaping over the banister in her leopard form, chasing him up the stairs, her large claws digging into the wood as she quickly closed in on him. Aaron was frightened as he reached the top of the stairs, rolled over on his back, and saw Sophie standing over him. Although he knew she wouldn't hurt him, it was still intimidating, lying beneath such a large cat. At any moment, he expected to hear her roar, exposing her large canines and telling him how angry she felt. But it was the silent tears rolling down her cheeks that he wasn't prepared for. After a moment, she turned and walked into her own bedroom.

The next morning, Aaron woke up to see Sophie lying next to him in Human form, wearing an old white T-shirt that Dad had given her. Aaron moved the hair away from her eyes. On her face was a tranquil look, the kind that said, *I forgive you.*

◆◆◆◆◆

Aaron had woken up to see her lying on her back on top of the comforter, her long white T-shirt hanging above her knees but keeping no secrets about her curves.

Aaron got up and headed to the bathroom for a cold

shower. As he was washing the shampoo from his hair, Sophie came up behind him.

"Why didn't you tell me you were going to take a shower? I would've joined you."

"All right, my turn," Sophie said, switching sides with him. Aaron stood there, watching Sophie, thinking about how much he loved looking into her mesmerizing green eyes as she talked to him, or the way her lips moved when she called his name. Sophie turned her back and waited for him. Aaron grabbed the shampoo as he brushed her hair.

Even though they weren't biologically related, they were still brother and sister to the many people who knew them. With boundaries he wasn't willing to cross. Aaron finished rinsing the shampoo out of her hair and was going to wash her back. He was reaching around Sophie to exchange the brush for the washcloth when Sophie grabbed his wrist.

"Please, Aaron," Sophie asked in a soft, pleading tone.

Feeling guilty, Aaron stopped.

"I'm sorry, Sophie, I can't do this. It's wrong."

Sophie turned around angrily. Aaron could feel the frustrations building up. He stood silently, looking at her, thinking about his answer. He remembered being bullied in school because he was different, and was afraid of what they would do to him if they found out. Not to mention what the bullies would do to Sophie. "I'm sorry," he said, handing the washcloth back to her.

Sophie slapped it out of his hand and started walking away from him.

"Sophie, wait," Aaron pleaded.

"No, I'm sick of listening to your cowardly excuses. And stop comparing me to Human girls because it's pissing me off. I am not Human!"

Sophie stormed off to her room and tried to slam the door shut. Aaron angrily followed her and held out the palm of his hand, stopping the door from closing.

"Sophie, just listen to me, please!" he shouted, pushing the door with such force that it slammed against the wall, making her flinch. Sophie stood there with a surprised look, facing Aaron, his face close enough to hers that their lips were almost touching.

"You know how hard it is laying next to you?" Aaron said, angrily gritting his teeth. "Every time I see you lying next to me, I think about how much I want you, but I can't."

"Why not? I want you to..." Sophie started to cry, her tears falling like raindrops as she struggled to finish her sentence. "At least that way, I would know that I'm more than just a pet to you."

Aaron tried to put his arms around her and comfort her, but she gently pushed him away.

"Please, Aaron, leave me alone. Just go away. Please..." Sophie bawled.

Aaron didn't just hear or see the pain in her tears; he felt it in his heart. He tried one more time to comfort her. Firmly but gently, she pushed him out of her room, then closed the door. Aaron stood helplessly, listening to her crying. It was the worst he had ever felt. She was in pain, and it was his fault. He opened her door and tried one more time to comfort her but was asked again to leave her room, this time in a loud roar that rattled the glass in the window...

Aaron's thoughts were suddenly interrupted, dragging his mind back to the present.

"You're pretty quiet," Sophie said, coming up behind him.

"Just thinking, that's all," Aaron answered.

Sophie knew by the rhythm of his heartbeat what he was thinking. With her gift of ABS, she could read a heartbeat as easily as the sighted could read a look on a face.

"Why are you still thinking about that?" she replied, her voice soft and caring. "I told you, I was going into my breeding cycle and wasn't myself that day. It's sort of like the feline version of PDS."

Aaron chuckled, "You mean PMS."

Sophie playfully slapped him on the back. "Whatever. You know what I mean. Anyway, I'm going to spend a little more time with Jazzy. Why don't you stay tonight? I'm sure Jazzy would like to see you when she wakes up."

"Okay, I will."

Aaron watched as Sophie headed back to Jazzy's bedroom. It had been nine years since he had walked out of Sophie's life, and not a day went by that he didn't regret leaving her as he did. Back then, he was only sixteen and confused. Even in her Human form, she was still technically a feline. Aaron remembered the time their father took them to a wedding. Aaron described the bride to Sophie, her white wedding dress, and the white veil covering her face. Then Sophie told him she wanted to be a bride someday. Aaron looked at her and jokingly asked who she was going to marry. Sophie answered without a second thought.

"I'm going to marry you," she said, smiling.

"Me? You can't marry me. I'm Human," Aaron said insensitively.

"I don't care, Aaron. I'll still marry you anyway," she replied, reaching for his hand.

Sophie would've followed him to the end of the universe and enrolled in the same school of hard knocks as he did. Aaron loved her and didn't want that for Sophie. She deserved a better life than that. At sixteen, he could barely take care of himself, and the only road map he had was his dream of becoming a writer. The road to success was not an easy one.

When he wasn't doing shitty jobs or trying to find a place to sleep, he would work on his novel. There, he could relive the happier times and even create better ones through his writing. Sophie had always been the inspiration behind his novels and the reason he put so much thought into the characters. It was the morning after Sophie's birthday that he got the idea for his first novel, *The Newtopian Rose*. Sophie was sleeping on her back, her arms above her head and her legs spread slightly apart. Aaron studied her. Sophie looked like an angel basking in the sun, her long golden hair spread out on the sky-blue comforter, while her white T-shirt pressed lightly against the curves of her body as the morning sun welcomed her to another day.

Every morning when he woke up, he would watch Sophie sleep, gathering new ideas for his book. There were many mornings he'd put his face close to Sophie's as she slept, thinking how easy it would be to steal a kiss from her. As romantic as that sounded, his morals wouldn't allow him to do that. She was his sister, and there were still boundaries not to be crossed. But to Newtopian biology, those boundaries did not exist.

It wasn't until his first novel was published and on the bestsellers list that he realized what true love really was. With his success and fame, Aaron soon realized that the universe was filled with pretty blondes just as beautiful as Sophie. He even slept with a few of them. But in the morning, the girl was just another pretty face, a groupie looking to be in the limelight. Aaron grew to hate one-night stands and empty relationships. Sex was nothing more than glorified masturbation without love. Yes, his true love for Sophie was the inspiration behind all his novels, but at the end of the day, they were still just fantasy.

Aaron had always planned on going back to get Sophie and give her the life she deserved. But by the time he was ready and could afford to provide her with everything, Sophie had grown up and moved on with her life. For whatever reason, he felt as if Sophie was doing so much better without him. So Aaron never went back and remained in solitude, writing his novels.

Aaron took another sip of his coffee. He wasn't sure if it was the steam coming from the cup or his last memories of Sophie that was making his eyes water. He thought about that fateful morning when everything had changed. He was looking over at Sophie. Her eyes were closed, and a blissful look was on her face. Aaron was lying on his side, watching her sleep, thinking how much he wanted to kiss her. To his surprise, Sophie reached over and pulled him toward her as she playfully kissed his lips.

"Good morning, Aaron," she said, smiling.

It was then he noticed the change in Sophie's voice. It was happy and had a mature tone to it, and the smile on her face radiated like the morning sun. She looked like he felt. Right or wrong, he was in love with her, and she had always been in love with him. And like all fairy-tale romances, somewhere in the pages, there always has to be heartbreak.

When he and Sophie came down to breakfast before school that day, his father was standing in the kitchen holding a letter. He looked over at them, smiling, almost jumping for joy when he told him the news.

"My boy, you are going to be a Marine. The Academy has accepted you!"

It was the happiest he had ever seen his father. Aaron gave his father a fake smile as he promised to take them out for a family celebration after school. Aaron dreaded celebrating. He didn't know how to tell his father he didn't want to go into the military. He disliked war and wanted no part of it. War took his mother and uncle away and turned his father into a blood soldier. Aaron hated that terminology and the way people glamorized them in the entertainment world, making blood soldiers into heroes who saved the universe. In reality, they were ordinary people, living with the pain of losing a loved one until their only purpose for living was vengeance. When his mother died, a part of his father died with her. He kept his suffering silent, but he never stopped being a soldier. Aaron wanted more than anything to become a writer and not a Marine like his father wanted.

When he and Sophie got back from school, there was a note on the kitchen table. His father had been called away, and the celebration was postponed. He would be back sometime tomorrow.

Aaron spent many years thinking about what happened next. Their father was gone, and the air conditioner unit had picked the worst time to break down. Sophie was going into her breeding cycle. She was hot and refused to wear clothing. Aaron became frustrated, watching her go about her daily routine. He wanted to say something to her but knew Sophie was in no mood to be reminded of their father's rules. So he remained silent.

Neither he nor Sophie knew that she was already secreting pheromones that were starting to affect his thinking. But with a fresh scent of caramel rolls filling the house, her pheromones went undetected. Sophie was in the kitchen making dinner when Aaron walked up behind her. She wore nothing but an apron that exposed her back. He leaned over her shoulder to get a whiff of the rolls she was pulling out of the oven. They were golden brown with a light coating of caramel and the alluring scent of cinnamon danced in his nostrils.

"Smells good. No one makes caramel rolls like you," he said.

Sophie put the baking pan on top of the stove, then turned her head to face him. Before he even knew what was happening, her lips were pressed against his. His body responded as his hand quickly made its way under her apron. Then the doorbell rang. Aaron jumped away while Sophie rolled her eyes and exhaled.

"I'll get it," she said, storming off to answer the door.

"Aaron, your idiot friends are here," she hollered into the kitchen with obvious annoyance.

Aaron walked into the living room as Sophie was walking back to the kitchen. At the door was Melvin, a tall, nerdy kid with short red hair. Next to him was Dexter, a chubby, five-foot-seven joker who took pride in making people laugh.

"Sorry guys, can't go out tonight. My dad's gone and I don't want to leave Sophie by herself."

Aaron could see the gears spinning in Dexter's head as he

watched Sophie setting the table for dinner. No doubt he was about to say something that would piss her off. It was sort of like a game between them, to see who would get to the other first. Dexter always knew how to get to Sophie and took pride in doing so.

"Don't blame you. If my dad were gone for the night, I wouldn't leave her alone either," he said with a wink.

"Dude, she's a cat," Melvin quickly interrupted.

Dexter shot Melvin an irritated look. "So, if my cat looked like that, I'd be chasing it every night," he laughed. Sophie gave him the finger as she walked up the stairs.

"And you wonder why she doesn't like you," said Aaron, shaking his head.

Sophie was miserable and shifted forms and began pacing back and forth in the upstairs hallway. The sound of her claws on the wood caught Melvin's attention. As she let out long, slow growls, Melvin turned a pale shade of white and then ran out the door. Dexter had a concerned look on his face; it was a tone they had never heard before, and for the first time they felt nervous being around her. Dexter was silent for a moment, then nodded his head. "I'll see you in school tomorrow." He turned and ran to catch up with Melvin.

Aaron turned to see Sophie slowly coming down the stairs, her growls of frustration echoing in his ears. She had never behaved in this manner before, and he was becoming nervous the closer she got. Aaron walked to the kitchen to grab his media pad. He was concerned for her and was going to call the hospital. She let out a loud roar, warning him not to touch it. He pulled back his hand and then called out her name, unsure as to what she was going to do next. "Sophie, please. You're scaring me," he begged as she continued approaching him.

She shifted forms and then stood in front of him. "Do you want me?"

He stood thinking about his answer. He had no doubts about her beauty or how sexy she looked. His only problem was that she was still his sister and in a vulnerable state. He tried to speak, but she cut him off with a kiss. "Make love to me, Aaron. I wanna know what a Human girl feels when someone she adores becomes her first," she pleaded as sweat glistened on her naked body. Aaron was speechless. All he could do was stare at her, silently arguing with his morals. There were a hundred and one reasons why he shouldn't and only one reason why he should. But like any good mother, nature made sure her daughters would not be ignored.

Aaron's body started to feel as if he were on fire. The pheromones from her sweat had a powerful, stimulating effect that brought him to his knees. He felt lightheaded, his thoughts only on Sophie as she stood in front of him. His sense of smell was heightened, along with the rhythm of his heartbeat as she stood before him. She had the scent of a woman, and he could no longer resist temptation, or the urge to put his nose to the source. Sophie gasped for air as she felt the warmth of his breath. The sound of her moaning encouraged him not to stop as she responded to the pleasure. Neither he nor Sophie understood what was happening to him that night. All they knew was what their hearts felt.

———••◆••———

The next morning, Sophie woke up to Aaron packing a suitcase.

"Aaron, what are you doing?"

"I'm sorry. I gotta leave."

Sophie jumped out of bed, pleading, "Aaron, wait, let me come with you!"

But by the time she got dressed, Aaron was already heading down the road. Sophie was still feeling the effects of the previous night. She was disoriented, and her emotions were swirling around inside her head. She followed Aaron's scent until it started to rain, and her echolocation ability was drowned out by the noise. She fell helplessly to the ground, her knees crushing against the gravel, sobbing heavily as Aaron vanished into the heavy downpour.

————◆◆◆————

For many years, Aaron had tried to understand what happened that night, when he and Sophie gave up their innocence. Why was his will so easily broken? Not that it would've taken much to break it. But it was the way Aaron broke it that always left him asking questions about himself. It wasn't until years later he found the answers in an unlikely place and from a person he would least expect.

He was staying in a hotel, attending a two-day lecture on non-Human authors and how their literature affected the way we see the universe. After the speech, Aaron was walking back to his room when he passed by the cocktail lounge and stopped in for a drink. The lounge was quiet, with only a few people there. He walked over to the bar and ordered a Scotch on the rocks. As he waited for his drink, an old man with a short, thick white beard and neatly trimmed gray hair approached. The man sat down on the stool next to him.

"You're him... You're that writer," the old man said, looking intensely into his eyes. "Your book, *The Newtopian Rose?* I read it."

"Yeah, I did write that book." The last thing he needed right now was another groupie.

"Don't toy with me, boy," the old man snapped back. Aaron could tell by his demeanor and the tattoos on his arm that he was a veteran. "I bet you're still asking yourself what really happened."

"I'm sorry, what?" Aaron replied, giving him a peculiar look.

"In your book. People don't write like that without experience. You see, boy, you're a member now."

"A member of what?" Aaron replied, now intrigued to hear the old man's story.

"The Rabbits' Club. You see, when they go into heat, their instincts take over. And that's when they start hunting rabbits."

"What do you mean?"

"Us, boy. To them, we are nothing more than rabbits, like prey, when they're in heat. They have a strong taste for rabbits. So, like I said, I'll bet you're still asking yourself what happened, ain't you? Well, you see this on my arm?" the old man asked, pointing to a tattoo of a rabbit in military uniform.

"Yeah, I see it."

"Tell you what, Mr. Famous Author. You buy me a drink, keep that smart mouth of yours shut, and by the time I am done, you'll know exactly what happened to you."

Aaron gestured for the bartender. "One for him, too, please."

The bartender nodded and turned to get the drinks. The old man pointed again to his tattoo and told his story.

"You see this rabbit? I got it when I was stationed on Outpost Five on the border planet, Uteakons on one side, Humans on the other. I was eighteen and fresh out of AIT. We were there to watch the Uteakons, and they were there to watch us. It was the tail end of the war, no fighting going on, just young, curious minds playing a dangerous game."

The old man took a sip of his drink and fell silent as if he were deep in thought, then continued, "My first night on guard duty, I was patrolling along the border of the outpost when I heard a noise. I followed it. By the time I realized I was being lured deeper into the woods, I was on enemy territory. I knew if they caught me, I'd be shit outta luck."

The bartender returned with their drinks. Aaron watched as the old man slammed down his in one breath, then slid the empty glass back to the bartender.

"So I take it they didn't find you," Aaron said.

"Oh no, she was watching me the whole time. And I walked right into her trap. Damn near shit my pants when I saw a large cat coming out of the shadows." The old man paused and reached for his second drink.

"A large cat?" Aaron shivered as a strange chill ran up his spine.

The old man stared, his brown eyes wide. "Yep. She made a Great Dane look like a lapdog. All I could do was stand there, staring into her deep yellow eyes, thinking my snow-white ass was done for." He took another sip of his drink, then grinned. "But she had other plans for me... Oh yeah!" The old man continued to grin, nodding his head. "You see," he went on, "the Huntress was in heat and rabbit was on her menu. She circled around me, sizing me up. Then she started doing this low, soft growling, toying with me, breaking me down right before she moved in for the kill." The old man fell silent.

"So what happened next?"

"Next? Well, I watched this large cat turn into a beautiful woman, and I'm talking the kind of beauty that brings a tear to a man's eye. The only thing sharper than her claws was her curves." He paused again, looking down at his drink. "And then she started coming towards me. Her essence was strong and beginning to affect my thinking."

"Essence? What essence?"

The old man shot him a look of disbelief. "The scent of a woman! What are you, a dumb virgin?"

Aaron blushed a deep red, then smiled sheepishly. "Sorry," he said, "that was a stupid question."

The old man stared into his glass again, his voice becoming more serious. "You know, son, from the day we're born, we are told that as Humans, we are better than animals. And then one of nature's daughters comes along and gives us a taste of humility, reminding us where we come from." He shook his head as if still in disbelief. "There I was, on my knees. She was standing there, silent, watching me sniffing her as if I were a dog sniffing its master's crotch. And when I touched the sweat on her body, it felt cold at first. Then it started to get warm until my whole body felt as if I had hot lava flowing through my veins. I tried to get away, but she lifted me to my knees with one hand. Uteakons aren't very tall in their Human form, but they're stronger than we are."

"How did you feel, kneeling there like that?" Aaron interrupted.

"I was confused. I didn't know where I was. All I could think about was the Huntress and what I wanted. But I was a virgin, and the only naked woman I had ever seen was my mother or sisters when I was a child. But eventually, I got over it."

The old man chuckled. Aaron laughed as he suddenly caught the punchline. The old man went on. "Where we lacked inexperience, our instincts took over. And there we were, two people beneath the pale moonlight, doing what nature intended us to do."

The old man guzzled down what was left of his drink. "Well, kid, gotta go," he said. "The Missus needs her medication."

Aaron watched as the old man disappeared out the door, lost in his memories. The bartender came over, smiling as she brought him another drink. Aaron looked up at her, confused.

"It's okay," she said in a soft whisper, "this one's on me. I never get tired of hearing that story. However, his wife's version of it is much sweeter. It just goes to show you, love has no boundaries."

"He married the Uteakon cat woman?"

"Indeed he did," the bartender replied. "They've been married over sixty years now." With that, she left to wait on another customer.

Aaron would always be grateful for the bartender's parting words and the old man's story, which opened his eyes to what really mattered. That in love, there are no boundaries.

Whether it was right or wrong, he and Sophie had ventured outside of innocence together, and what they lacked in experience, they were guided by love.

Aaron's mind came back to the present as a flash of lightning lit up the sky outside the window, followed by a loud explosion of thunder. He still hated stormy nights and the way they always brought back that awful memory of Sophie standing in the rain. It was as if he were frozen in time, with the image of Sophie, tears in her eyes, begging him to come back.

Sophie came into the living room and put her hands on Aaron's shoulders. "Your daughter would like to talk to you," she said.

"Okay, I'll be right there." He hardly knew his daughter. The beautiful child who was conceived on that night they lost their innocence.

Sophie listened as Aaron headed into Jazzy's room.

"Dad," Jazzy said to him.

"Hello, Jazz, er, sorry, I mean Jazzy."

"It's okay, Dad. You can call me Jazz."

Aaron was silent, gathering words to tell her how he felt. And why he left. Jazzy looked into her father's eyes. "Dad, are you okay?"

"Yeah, Jazz, I know we haven't known each other very long," Aaron swallowed hard, "but I want you to know I love you more than life itself, and if I would've known about you, I would have stayed and become the Marine that Grandpa wanted me to be."

Jazzy could see the sadness in his eyes and gave her father a hug. "Then you wouldn't be who you are now. Mom and me, we love who you are. Mom is the soldier. You're the writer."

Sophie was pouring a cup of coffee in the kitchen as she thought about her favorite poem. "The Joker and a Fool." "Once there was a queen in love with a joker and a fool; one made her laugh while the other made her cry, but in the queen's heart, they kept an even balance."

Although he was Aaron's best friend, Dexter was the joker in her life, who always had a way of making her laugh, sometimes when she most needed it.

She was nine years old when he and Aaron became friends. Every day, he would come over after school with Melvin and hang out. Dexter always made it a point to get on her nerves. She'd be in the kitchen doing her homework at the table. Dexter would always make a grand entrance. "Hey, squirt, what are you doing?" he'd ask in the same loud, annoying tone he knew got on her nerves.

"Looking at pictures of birds!" she'd respond sarcastically.

Dexter would chuckle. "What are you all chapped up about?"

"Some asshole keeps asking me stupid questions when I'm trying to do my homework."

Dexter was silent for a moment and hollered down the hallway as he walked out of the kitchen. "Hey Aaron, your sister wants you to leave her alone when she's doing her homework!"

"What?" Aaron responded, confused.

Sophic laughed. Even though he got on her nerves most of the time, there was something cute about his humor.

The year she turned, Dexter's attitude began to change along with the rhythm of his heartbeat whenever he spoke to her. She was all too familiar with the rhythm. It was the same beat Aaron's heart made when he was with her, and the same beat hers made whenever she spoke to either one of them. That year the friendship between Aaron and Dexter began to sour as Sophie was quickly reaching maturity. But the final straw was when Aaron walked out of her life. She was devastated, sobbing heavily when Dexter helped her out of the rain, and vowed he would kick Aaron's ass the next time he saw him.

As for Aaron, he was the one the joker called a fool. She never knew whether to agree or disagree with Dexter and preferred to keep her opinion silent.

The first time she met Aaron, he opened his heart to her, welcoming her to the family. When the night terrors started, he would hold her in his arms, turning nightmares into dreams.

Sophie always loved the time they spent together. Aaron would gently roll her on her back and tickle her as she playfully kicked his hand away with her back feet. Sophie never gave the relationship a name and accepted it for what it was. Things changed, however, when she got her Human form, becoming a stranger to him and even herself.

She'd never forgotten the day they returned from the hospital. Sophie was strapped to her booster seat, confused about her new Human form while feeling Aaron's icy stare. It was the first time she had ever felt it.

Before her Rebirth, she knew instinctively something was about to change in her, but all she could do was wait for it to happen. She never imagined waking up in a new body with new emotions.

Aaron was never the same after that day. The only tears she kept in her memories were the tears of joy she shed the night he confessed his love to her. "Sophie, why are you crying?" he whispered.

"Because I know I'm not a pet to you anymore."

Aaron kissed her. "Sophie, you were never a pet to me. When Dad took you out of that box, he took out my best friend. And when I saw you come out of that cocoon, I fell in love with you, but I was eleven and didn't know what love was. Until you taught me."

Sophie kissed him passionately as Aaron's hand parted her thighs. Once again, her body responded to Aaron's massaging fingers, sending surges of pleasure rushing through her. They made love throughout the night and into the early morning until they rolled over, exhausted, and before she knew it, Aaron had been swallowed up by the heavy rain.

Once again, her Achilles' heel had returned, and her life had taken another drastic turn. Sophie never forgave herself for the pain and confusion Aaron felt. She always believed the fault was hers for not being Human and foolishly falling in love with one. She had always hoped that he would find it in his heart to forgive her, maybe one day come back and meet the child biology allowed them to conceive.

Sophie walked back to the living room and turned on the rain shield before stepping onto the balcony, where she listened to the falling rain while the rolling thunder echoed in the night. When Aaron left, she had to learn how to be Human again. This time there would be no one shielding her from the realities of how Humans felt about Evolutions.

◆

Sophie took another sip of her coffee, smirking as she remembered the rest of the poem. "Just as the fool had walked out of the queen's life, along came the joker, exchanging her tears for laughter."

Dexter never shielded Sophie from the world but helped her become part of it and take the good with the bad. He always said, "You can't force people to change their thinking, but you can certainly laugh at their ignorance."

Hanging around with Dexter, Sophie realized what Aaron underwent, having an Evolution as a sister and the painful realities he had always been shielding her from.

Dexter welcomed the negativity and the snide remarks Aaron would have received when they saw she was pregnant, although not all responses were negative. Most people congratulated the couple, while others would respond to Dexter with disgust when he confessed to being the father. Not only did Dexter teach her to see the funnier side of life. He also helped her to become independent. And when he graduated from high school, Dexter asked her to the graduation ball and even got into a fight protecting her honor.

His name was Woodmen. He was the school bully and Aaron's worst nightmare. Every day he would look for Aaron after school, tormenting and humiliating him in front of the other kids. Sophie was five years old when she first encountered him. She and Aaron were in the park. He was pushing her on the swing. When Woodmen walked by with his entourage, which was made up of kids who hung around him in fear of being his victim if they didn't, Sophie knew by the sound of his footsteps and the way sound waves bounced off him. He was heavier and much taller than Aaron, but it was his scent she would never forget.

Sophie listened as Woodmen's hand slapped Aaron's chest. She immediately jumped off the swing, ran over, and pushed Woodmen away from Aaron. It was the first time Sophie learned the strength difference between Humans and Evolution shifters. Woodmen flew back and fell to the ground as Sophie shifted forms, slowly approaching him as she let out a loud roar, warning Woodmen to leave Aaron alone. All the kids burst into laughter as Sophie suddenly caught the scent of fresh urine emanating from his direction. Woodmen never bothered Aaron after that day, nor did he forget about their encounter. It was apparent that day he recognized her at the graduation ball.

It was the end of the night and they were walking to Dexter's transport when Woodmen hollered out a slur. "Hey Dexter, you into bestiality now?" Woodmen started laughing along with his entourage.

Dexter stopped. Sophie was worried for the safety of her unborn child and begged Dexter to forget about it. "Dexter, please. It doesn't bother me!" she begged frantically.

"It bothers me," he told her in a soft but firm tone.

As Dexter confronted Woodmen, his entourage started teasing Sophie, calling her as if she were an animal.

"Here, kitty kitty kitty," they shouted mockingly.

From the crowd of students, two Evolution boys jumped out, shifting forms, letting out thunderous roars as their transformation was complete. The crowd laughed hysterically as Woodmen's crew ran away in fear, leaving the bully on his own. Dexter had gotten the better of Woodmen and was sitting on top of him, demanding he apologize to his date. "So Dickwood, you gonna apologize, or do I just keep kicking your ass? Either way is good for me. How about you?" Dexter asked mockingly.

Woodmen gave her a half-hearted apology as one of the kids yelled, "Military police!" Everyone scattered. Dexter held her hand as he walked her back to his transport. Sophie was impressed with Dexter and thanked him for standing up for her. "You didn't have to do that. But I'm glad you did."

"Yes, I did. Nobody talks about my date like that and gets away with it." Dexter was silent for a moment. "Besides, my dad would kick my ass if he found out I didn't defend my date's honor." He chuckled and opened the door for her.

When Dexter drove her home, her father was waiting on the front stairs. She could hear the smile in his voice as he called out Dexter's name. "Dexter, why haven't you told anybody you could fight?"

"I don't know, sir...doesn't seem like something to brag about unless you wanna sound like a dick. No offense, sir."

"None taken." Her father laughed.

Sophie grinned, thinking about the end of their night as they stood on the front stairs. She was facing Dexter, waiting for his next move. Her dad was behind the door, eavesdropping. "What are you waiting for? Kiss her, you idiot," he shouted impatiently.

She could hear the rhythm of his heartbeat. Dexter was nervous. "Well, I better do what your father says." Dexter pressed his lips to hers.

She put her arms around him and returned the gesture with a French kiss. "Thank you. I had a great time."

"Sophie, I should be thanking you... I got to take the hottest girl on base to the graduation ball, me... The funny fat kid... Shit like that doesn't happen to guys like me. We end up taking our cousins, and she's just as annoying as my sister."

Sophie was laughing so hard she had tears in her eyes. Dexter gave her another kiss. "I better get going. My dad gets anal when it comes to curfew." He turned and headed for his transport.

The next day, Dexter left for the Army Academy. Once again, Sophie found herself alone but far from helpless. Two years after Jazzy was born, Sophie joined the Marines Academy, not because they were the only military set up for ABS, but because she wanted to continue family traditions. But keeping those traditions wasn't going to be easy for her, as Sophie would soon realize that being a blind female in a man's world wouldn't be easy or appreciated.

Not long after, she arrived at Fort Victory. She had met up with Dexter in the cafeteria. Sophie was stressed out and frustrated that day. She had been working all day long trying to get the blind tech, AI, to communicate with the military's universal AI, but without success. It was like two people sitting in a room trying to converse, but neither spoke the same language. Sophie had thrown up her hands, decided it was time for lunch, and headed to the cafeteria.

She was ready to pay for her lunch when a voice behind her told the cashier to put it on his military account. Her body began to tingle. She didn't recognize the voice. It was his scent, she remembered. "Dexter?"

She could hear the smile in his voice. "Hello, Sophie. It's good to see you again."

Sophie was overcome with delight. "I didn't know you were stationed here?" she inquired.

The tone of his voice became serious. "I'm not. Just dropped off some cargo, and since I was in the neighborhood, I decided to say hi to an old friend. Then I saw somebody standing before me, and it occurred to me... I know that ass."

Sophie burst into laughter. She didn't care that it was attracting attention. After dealing with computers all morning, she was ready for a good laugh.

They sat in the corner booth and talked about old times until careers came up.

"So, what made you join the Army?" Sophie inquired.

"Ever since I was a kid, I always wanted to be a planeteer, so I became a star ranger."

"Do you still want to travel the stars?" she asked jokingly.

"Not anymore. Now all I can think about is just getting through to the next mission."

"What do you mean?"

He had a tone of seriousness she had never heard before. "The bugs, they're getting stronger by the week. Even day. Doesn't matter how many of them we kill. All they're doing is sending workers, wearing us down until the real soldiers step in. Even our katanas don't work anymore. Half my unit found out the hard way."

Dexter took a bite of his cheeseburger and doused his fries with ketchup. "Enough of me. What about you?"

"Me? I went into infantry."

Dexter laughed.

"What's so funny?" Sophie inquired.

"Never pictured you as the badass Marine."

"That's because you were too busy picturing me in other positions," Sophie joked.

Dexter let out a hearty laugh. "Can't argue with that."

Sophie laughed with him. She hadn't laughed like that since the summer of her pregnancy, when she got to know the

Dexter he always kept hidden behind his humor. He'd pick her up from school every day, as Aaron did, and instead of going home, they hung out at the mall. Even though he wasn't the father, Dexter was just as excited about her pregnancy as she was.

When they got bored, they would go around to different shops checking out baby items. Sometimes, she'd have to remind him the baby wouldn't be born in Human form, attracting the attention of other shoppers. They were used to it and didn't care about the staring or the snide whispers.

"So, what brings you to Fort Victory?"

"Jazzy got accepted into the Academy, and I went into the Mud Dog program."

"So, how's that working out for you?"

Sophie let out a sigh. "It's not... I can't get the two AIs to communicate. Long story short," she said, laughing in frustration, "they hate each other. What about you? How long are you in town for?"

"Not long. I leave at zero-four-hundred tomorrow."

Sophie walked Dexter back to the visitors' quarters and gladly accepted his invitation into his room. Dexter reached around her, his face close to hers. "Sorry, I still can't see in the dark." Dexter laughed and then kissed her passionately on the lips.

Sophie locked her arms around him, pressing her mouth harder to his, giving him a long-awaited kiss he should have gotten when he pulled her out of the rain.

Dexter unbuttoned her shirt, his soft lips kissing her bare flesh with each button he undid. Sophie tried to catch her breath as Dexter's mustache lightly brushed against her skin, tickling her as he made his way down her stomach, one button at a time. When the last button was undone, Sophie let her blouse fall to the floor, then removed her bra while Dexter relieved her from the rest of her clothing.

Even during their lovemaking, he never failed to make

her happy, whether by trying to make her laugh during sex or whispering words of heated passion in her ear. He never stopped being the joker who pulled her out of the rain, not even during war. The only time her smile faded was when she felt the rush of pleasure sweep through her like a bursting dam.

Dexter rolled over on his back, laughing.

Sophie playfully slapped him on the chest, inquiring about his laughter. "What's so funny?"

"I never knew you were such a wildcat in bed," Dexter responded.

"Must be my animal magnetism." Sophie straddled him once again.

Dexter chuckled and put his hands around her hips. "Round five coming up," he said with a sudden thrust.

Sophie suddenly stopped her thoughts as the door to her apartment opened.

"Just me," Raya announced.

"You're just in time. Fresh coffee in the pot, and creamer in the back of the refrigerator."

Raya grabbed a cup and then opened the refrigerator for the creamer when she heard somebody walking into the kitchen.

"Good morning, you gorgeous feline." Followed by a pat on the ass.

Raya quickly took her head out of the refrigerator and saw a tall man with light brown hair smiling. "Where I am from, we just say good morning," Raya responded, annoyed.

The man's face suddenly turned a bright shade of red as he apologized frantically. Raya looked over at Sophie as she was coming into the kitchen. "I don't care what you say. There is nothing normal about Human behavior," Raya barked, heading to the balcony.

Sophie laughed as Aaron explained what had happened. "Don't worry, I'll explain to her you thought it was me," Sophie reassured him as she headed to join Raya.

Sophie and Raya were sitting, talking, and listening to the heavy downpour while the sounds of training soldiers echoed in the early morning.

Sophie laughed. "I remember those days," she said, thinking back to boot camp.

"Was it tough?" Raya interrupted.

Sophie was silent, thinking about her answer. She didn't want to lie and say it was the best time of her life, but she didn't want to sound negative. After all, the Marines gave her the strength and the confidence to meet life's challenges. "It was okay," Sophie responded, trying to sound convincing.

Raya looked at her and laughed. "Liar."

Sophie started laughing. "All right, fine, it was the worst time of my life. My drill instructor was a real prick. My dad always tells me. No pain, no gain. I gained quite a bit in a short amount of time. When I was a kitten, my dad would always bring me with him. I would listen to them train, learning their every movement. By the time I got my Human form, I already knew what to do. My dad trained me along with his officers. Sometimes, I would fall, and my dad would come over screaming in my ear, treating me like one of the soldiers.

"'Get your ass up off my ground, Private Skyler,' he would shout.

"'Okay, Daddy,' I'd say. My father and all the men would burst into laughter. They were fun times until my aunt put a stop to it."

Raya looked at Sophie, puzzled. "Really, why'd she do that?"

"She didn't like the language I was using and said it wasn't the language for a five-year-old." Sophie and Raya burst into laughter.

When she finished her coffee, Sophie took off her flannel shirt and shifted forms. Raya followed her lead. They sat silently, listening to the soldiers training in the heavy downpour. Raya noticed Sophie was deep in thought and inquired about it.

"I was thinking about my first day at boot camp, drill instructor Presley was doing a headcount. I didn't answer fast enough, so he got right up in my face, screaming at the top of his lungs.

"'According to my records, it says you're blind, not deaf. Do I need to call your name in sign language now?'" Sophie quoted mockingly.

"'No, sir,' I hollered back.

"Before I left for boot camp, the other soldiers gave me advice on what not to do, and one of them was standing out, but that was a little impossible since there were only two females in the platoon, another girl and me; she was Human, and also had ABS. Her name was Private English. She was headstrong and needed no help from anyone, especially men."

"I don't blame her," Raya said jokingly.

"From day one, Private English stood out. She had a bad attitude and didn't work well with others. She said they slowed her down, and she was right. With ABS, we process information faster than sighted people. That's why our response time is much quicker. Even if we don't know how to fight, we can still avoid the punches or prevent them from sneaking up on us. But she made two mistakes. She was female and bruised a lot of egos."

Raya knew exactly how that felt. The scars on her back reminded her every day.

"I remember one day she refused to take a shower with men and demanded to shower with females. Sergeant Presley had a relaxed tone in his voice. 'Okay,' Sergeant Presley told her. And for the rest of that week, Private English was showering with the female K9 unit."

There was a sudden tone of remorse in Sophie's voice. "She didn't last long after that. They recycled her. Put her in another starting platoon." Sophie started grinning. Her voice had a happier tone to it. "When she left, she left behind a lot of men with bruised egos," Sophie said, laughing.

"Were they hard on you?" Raya asked, concerned.

"No, they didn't say or do anything. They were afraid of me." There was sadness in her voice.

Raya looked at Sophie with surprise. "You, why? You're like the sweetest person I know."

"None of them had ever seen an Evolution or a cat the size of a Great Dane."

"A what?"

"A Great Dane. It's a breed of dog," Sophie answered.

Raya was silent for a moment, trying to picture what a Great Dane would look like. "Are they good to eat?" Raya inquired jokingly.

"I don't know, never tried one." They laughed.

They sat quietly, watching and listening to the storm, enjoying the tranquility before Sophie finished her story.

"As time passed, they were less afraid and more curious about me. It puzzled them because I didn't look any different than a Human girl. Even in the shower, I could feel their eyes watching me, studying me, wondering why I looked so Human. Then when they did start talking to me, the first question they asked was about Newtopia and the people. I told them I was raised by Humans and didn't know anything about my planet or the people. Then, when they realized I wasn't any different than they were, their questions changed, asking me about my blindness and how Advanced BioSonar works. The only thing I didn't tell them was my fear of the rain. I was afraid they would laugh and think I was weak. But some secrets never stay hidden."

Raya looked at Sophie with a puzzled glance. "How'd they find out about yours?"

"I was halfway through boot camp, and we were coming into the rainy season, and one day it started, it rained harder and louder than I had ever felt. I was terrified. The vibrations pounded so hard in my ears. I was in pain, and I had lost all sense of direction and didn't know where I was. People were laughing as I covered my ears, screaming for my father. But they stopped laughing when I shifted. I began pacing back and forth, calling out for my dad. I was so scared I didn't realize that the Humans took it as a threat. One of the drill instructors had his hand on his sidearm, ready to tranquilize me. But my platoon shielded me. One of the guys came towards me, reassuring me everything was going to be okay. He screamed at the top of his lungs, and I could hear him. I went towards him, and I could feel his hands. 'It's okay, Skyler. I got you.' His voice was calm and gentle. "I put my paws on his shoulders and my cheek to his. I could feel his fingers gently scratching my back. I began to calm down. That's when the lieutenant came walking by. I could hear him complaining to Sergeant Presley:

"'What's the meaning of this, Sergeant? Why is that soldier in the arms of another soldier?'

"'The rain, sir. Private Skyler is afraid. It's common in people with ABS, sir.'

"There was a tone of annoyance in the lieutenant's voice. 'So what does that mean? She can do whatever she wants?'

"Sergeant Presley became irritated. 'Do you know what happens when a 300-pound leopard panics, sir?'

"The lieutenant got quiet. 'No, Sergeant, I don't.'

"'Neither do I, and I'd like to keep it that way, sir.'

"That night, the storm was so strong the thunder and the lightning constantly shook the windows. I was so afraid and began pacing back and forth, panting hard while my heart pounded as the thunder and the lightning came again." Sophie started to laugh. "I remember climbing to this guy's bed. I was practically on top of this poor guy, panting hard. That's how scared I was. At first, I thought he would be angry and push me off, but I could hear a smile in his voice.

"'Don't worry, Skyler, I got your back.'

"Even though he could have gotten in trouble. He still held me." Sophie suddenly burst into laughter. "Of course, he thought of me more as a big kitty."

"Men are just boys that never mature!" Raya said, laughing.

They sat silently, listening to the rainfall while rolling thunder echoed in the night. Raya started laughing. "I remember when I was a kitten. I was afraid of thunderstorms. I would always run to my father. He would stand over me, protecting me. Sometimes he would roar so loud it would drown out the thunder. Of course, I couldn't hear much after that," Raya said jokingly.

Sophie was silent, thinking about the rainy days she would spend with her father. "I wasn't always afraid of the rain. In fact, I even looked forward to rainy days. My father called it our daddy-daughter time. We would sit in the living room listening to jazz. His favorite was BB King." Sophie started to chuckle. "I remember what he always used to say. 'Nobody, nobody plays better than BB,'" she joked. "When I got my Human form, I was caught in a rainstorm for the first time. I was five years old; it felt cold and angry, and the vibrations pounded so hard in my ears that it gave me a headache. After that, I was terrified of the rain. It's the only time I feel blind."

"So, how'd you overcome the rain?" Raya inquired.

"I didn't. I learned not to fear the rain. It will always be my Achilles' heel. But even your Achilles' heel can be used to your advantage."

There was a tone of malevolence in Sophie's voice as cold, dark energy momentarily emanated from her. It was the same energy that 305 gave off, but with a much stronger and darker feeling. Raya felt chills running down her spine.

"You almost sounded like a different person then," Raya stated with concern.

"I did? Must be stress." Sophie laughed.

# CHAPTER 8

On Monday morning, the new Mud Dog candidates were set to arrive from Uteaka. When Raya heard the apartment control unit chime, she got out of bed and shifted into Human form.

The unit announced a communications request from Sergeant Teel, which Raya agreed to answer.

"You have a communications request from Sergeant Teel," the unit announced.

"I'll answer," Raya growled, shifting into Human form.

"Good morning, Teel. It's good to hear your voice again."

"Yours too, little sister. So how's that beautiful niece of mine?"

"Ocean, she's fine. It's her mother that's losing it," Raya joked.

"Raya...you're gonna do fine. You always do, just like in Uteakon City."

"I know, but it was a lot easier with other Uteakons."

Teel could hear the defeat in her sister's voice and tried to comfort her as best she could. "I know it's not easy living in a new world. But you are not alone. You got my connection code, and you got Albright's!"

"Thanks, Teel, but you're busy, and so is Albright!"

"I'm never too busy for my little sister, and neither is Albright. So call me!"

"I will, I promise!" Raya smiled.

"Raya, before I forget, I wanted to tell you the recruits have just arrived."

"All right, get them fitted and processed, and I'll be down there later."

"All right, sounds good. See you later, little sister."

Teel severed their connection. She headed over to inspect the barracks one last time, her hand breaking the silence as she slapped the metallic plate on the wall, turning on the barrack lights. Each bed was perfectly made. She bounced the coin she held in her right hand while her index finger slid across the hard surface, looking for dust. The floors were polished and smelled of floor wax, and her reflection looked up at her. Everything was dressed right and ready for the recruits. Teel placed her hands on the small of her back, then stood at ease, enjoying the silence. It felt lifeless and empty, like the war was over and everybody had gone home. Teel walked back to the door. She knew the morning would start as it always did. The air permeated with the smell of breakfast while the sounds of marching soldiers echoed in the early morning.

When the transport arrived and came to a stop, Sergeant Lisa and Sergeant Brenda stepped out of the cab and opened the doors, calling for the recruits. Their voices were loud and firm but compassionate. The girls were now on an alien planet filled with unfamiliar smells and sounds, and even more confusing were the Humans and Newtopians, who looked like them but didn't have the same scent.

The first one to walk out was a large calico feline named Moonlight. She was the size of an Uteakon male and just as strong.

The girls cautiously followed Moonlight out the door, their noses in the air, trying to pick up any familiar scent.

As the cattle transport was empty, Teel faced a group of twenty large NewGen females. They stood in front of the barracks, scared and confused. However, they realized they were not in danger and shifted into their Human forms. Despite their petite size, all of them under five feet tall, they had battle scars from previous encounters with hunters, indicating their experience in the game of survival. Teel knew life was difficult in the Backlands, where only the strong survived. These girls were no strangers to the challenges of life on their planet. Soon, they would have to face the Shezón, who were far stronger than anything they had ever encountered.

Teel faced the new recruits. She was a stone soldier and showed no emotion on the outside as she looked down at the row of young recruits forced into a war they didn't start. She could feel her heart break inside as the girls shivered and their teeth chattered.

"My name is Sergeant Teel, and I would like to be the first one to welcome you to Fort Victory," she said and began her speech that was given to all new recruits.

◆

Teel was reviewing the daily roster when she noticed that the girls were scheduled to shower at the same time as an infantry unit.

"I just love the communication around here!" Teel grumbled.

Sergeant Gomez inquired what was wrong. Teel showed her the schedule and explained the situation. Gomez was surprised and quickly got up from her desk to investigate. She was sure there must have been some mistake because having the girls and the infantry showering together would be disastrous. "I'll be right back," she said.

Teel replied, "Where are you going?"

Gomez answered, "I'm going to straighten this mess out. It would be like throwing those men into a lion's den... No offense."

Teel laughed. "It's okay. I'm not a lioness."

Gomez left the room and went to Lieutenant Iversen's office to inform him of the mistake. When she entered, he greeted her with a snarl. Gomez explained that there had been a mix-up with the shower schedule and that the Uteakon girls were scheduled to shower at the same time as Bravo Company.

Iversen glared at her. "So what's the problem, Sergeant? This is the military. They're going to have to get used to showering with men," he shot back sarcastically.

"Sir, you don't understand. These girls have never seen or smelled a Human man."

Iversen refused to listen. "Sergeant, I assure you these men will not hurt the girls."

"Sir, you don't understand," Gomez tried to explain.

Iversen gave her an angry look. "No... Sergeant, it's you who is not understanding; these men are heroes...and if they want to take a shower, we're going to let them," he barked.

Gomez shot him a sarcastic look. "You've never met an Uteakon, have you, sir?" She grinned.

"No, Sergeant, and I don't care to. Now get out of my office."

"Yes, sir." Gomez turned and headed toward the door, trying desperately not to burst into laughter as she pictured the chaos that was going to occur.

When she got to her office, Teel stood at the window watching a crowd gather around the barracks, waiting to see the new Mud Dogs.

"What's so interesting?" Gomez asked.

Teel pointed to the crowd of people outside.

"So much for secrecy," Gomez responded.

"I don't understand. What's the big deal?"

"You don't see the irony of it. Cats becoming Mud Dogs," Gomez joked.

Teel looked at her, confused.

"Never mind. Inside joke." Gomez chuckled.

"So what did he say?"

Gomez shook her head and rolled her eyes in frustration.

"Apparently, he wants the girls to see what real men look like."

"So what are we going to do?"

"Follow the schedule, of course," she responded, grinning ear to ear.

Teel laughed. "You got a real mean streak in you."

Gomez raised a brow. "Damn right I do. It comes from working with the clueless," she responded, heading back to her desk.

# CHAPTER 9

Sergeant Gomez announced over the intercom that it was time for the ladies to take showers. "All right, ladies, grab your towels and head to the shower room in single-file formation."

Leading the way was Whisper, the second largest feline, who had gray fur with black markings. Following her was Moonlight, the largest of the felines. Soldiers pointed and recorded their movements as the large cats walked down the hallway carrying towels in their jaws that looked like folded washcloths. Onlookers whispered, sending their family and friends messages about the new Mud Dogs.

One of the sergeants behind the front desk started shouting when the girls turned the corner. However, she fell nervously silent when she had the twenty massive felines' undivided attention. The sergeant behind her joked, "What now, genius?"

Teel and Gomez then turned the corner and ordered the girls to return to Human form. "Two legs, ladies."

The girls did as they were ordered, easing the nervousness of onlookers. Teel and Gomez smiled as an unfamiliar scent suddenly caught the girls' attention. The girls followed the smell coming from the shower room. Their curiosity piqued as they spotted a group of men heading toward the locker rooms. The men were six feet tall and over, with broad shoulders and rippling stomachs. The girls watched with intense curiosity, their heads turning as the men walked by. Suddenly, Whisper stepped before the last man, looking curiously at him. It was her first time seeing anyone tower over her, and his scent was unusual.

The other girls followed Whisper's lead. A mixture of uneasiness and amusement swept through the crowd as all eyes focused on the smiling young man surrounded by naked girls, oblivious of their true nature.

"I'm sorry. Can I help you ladies?" he asked, slightly annoyed.

Whisper looked up at him and locked her eyes on his. "So, what's the weather like up there for you?" she inquired as the other girls laughed.

The crowd became silent as the girls gathered around him.

Whisper smiled and put her nose to his face. "Why don't you smell like an Uteakon?"

"Because I'm Human," he replied with a sarcastic tone.

Unfazed by his sarcasm, she continued her investigation. "Are all Humans like you? I've never seen one before," she asked as she reached to touch his chest.

"No, we're all built differently," he responded with obvious annoyance as he gently brushed her hand away.

"Show me!" Whisper demanded, her eyes focused on his towel.

The man was shocked and offended by her request. "Excuse me?" he responded.

Impatiently, Moonlight asked Whisper, "What in the hell are you waiting for?" Without waiting for a response, Moonlight snatched the towel off of him.

As his friends laughed and cheered, the man attempted to push away the curious hands of the girls reaching for him. The laughter stopped abruptly when two girls started arguing and shifted into big cats. Startled, the men quickly ran out the back door.

Glitter's heart raced, and her voice was filled with excitement. She was surprised at how much fun they were to be with and realized that the elders had been wrong about Humans being dangerous. The only thing scary about them was having too much fun. Glitter pointed to the exit. "Hey, the others are getting away!" The floor became littered with towels as the cadets dropped them to pursue the fleeing men, unaware of the crowd waiting outside.

Moonlight was the first out the door and the first to break into a chase with Glitter following behind her; instinctively, Moonlight zeroed in on the largest man while Glitter ran ahead, waiting to ambush him as Moonlight chased him toward her direction. The crowd cheered as the girls knocked the men to the ground. One girl would hold the man while the other reached for his towel. The crowd went wild, chanting, "Rip it off, rip it off."

The crowd erupted into uncontrollable cheering when the girls ripped the towels off the men, then tossed them aside while female spectators collected them as souvenirs. The cheering ended when the military police came storming down, grabbing the girls off the men. The crowd laughed as the girls refused to let go of their prey. One man screamed as one of the girls caught his manhood while the military police pulled her away.

◆◆◆

# CHAPTER 10

Carl was walking to Raya's office, carrying a breakfast tray with coffee and donuts; Raya was reviewing the Mud Dog files when he stepped in.

"I didn't see you come in," Carl stated, setting the tray on her desk.

"I got here an hour ago; I wanted to review the files before assigning them."

"If you want, I can help you with that," Carl offered.

"Thanks, Carl, but this is a one-person job."

"Well, if you change your mind. I'll be in my office."

She was looking at the envelope in her hand. "Carl, what is this?"

"It's your new badge. You've been moved up to level four security."

Raya noticed Carl's agitation and walked over to him. "Carl, what's wrong?"

"Oh, nothing, just thinking, that's all."

Carl had a horrible feeling about why she was given level four clearance and wanted to check into it before he let her go any further on the case.

"Carl, what's wrong? You're starting to scare me."

Carl put his hands on her shoulders. "Until further notice. I want you to stay away from the level four sector."

"Carl, whatever it is, I can handle it."

"That wasn't a question. Do I make myself clear?" he barked.

"Yes," Raya responded meekly.

She walked back to her desk, concerned about Carl. She could tell something was bothering him, and whatever it was clearly had to do with one of the Mud Dog candidates.

Carl was walking back to his office, feeling he was a little hard on her, but it was for her own good. He didn't want Raya or anyone else in the same room with 305. If he had to, he'd take the case on himself.

Carl was beside himself, wondering if his childhood friend had lost his mind. He knew as well as Raincheck that 305 was a very dangerous entity and should've never been disturbed. *Little good it does now*, he thought to himself.

"Sir, General Raincheck would like to see you ASAP."

He turned to see Epstein. "All right, Sergeant. Thank you."

Carl walked over to Raincheck's office.

"Have a seat, Carl." Raincheck was sitting behind his desk, pulling out a bottle of bourbon with two shot glasses.

Carl looked at him suspiciously. "Either you're going to ask me for a date or tell me something I don't want to hear."

"You're definitely not my type," Raincheck joked.

Carl noticed Raincheck's hand tremble slightly as he poured the bourbon. Raincheck wasn't a man easily frightened, even when faced with death. "Alex, what's going on?"

Raincheck looked into Carl's eyes, the tone of his voice serious. "The day we found 305. It was in a state of suspended animation."

"Yes, Alex, I'm aware of that. What I don't know is why that thing is here."

"We may not have a choice anymore."

Carl scrunched up his eyebrows. "What do you mean?"

"All the nests we've been taking out... It's all been for nothing."

He looked tensely into Raincheck's eyes. "What are you talking about, Alex?" His tone mixed with anger and concern.

"We didn't look deep enough. The real nests were a hundred miles below the surface." Raincheck was silent, deep in thought.

Carl gave Raincheck an angry look. "Alex, I can't even begin to tell you how reckless and foolish this is, even for you." He paused for a moment. "I don't know what you're thinking, but 305 is not the hero you think it is. You wake that thing up, and the Shezón will be the least of our worries."

Raincheck looked pale. He didn't like it any more than Carl. "These are not my orders. If it were up to me, I would have left that thing where we found it, and so would Goleen. These orders come straight from the old lady."

Carl knew there was nothing they could do. The orders came straight from the top, the last general herself. "So, how are we to communicate with this thing? Convince it not to kill us?"

"We don't... You need a dream walker for that."

"Dream walker. What's that?" Carl asked.

"It's someone who communicates through dreams."

Carl shot Raincheck an angry look. "Is this a joke to you, Alex?"

Raincheck grinned. "I'm serious. Your girlfriend is a dream walker."

"My girlfriend?"

"Come on, Carl, we both know who Raya looks like."

The two men sat silently, looking at one another before Raincheck broke the silence. "Word to the wise, be cautious with her. She is not Caroline."

"Alex, it was just a one-time thing."

"Listen, my stubborn friend. You don't want to be on the wrong side of a Huntress. You'll find they're not as cute and cuddly as they appear."

"Alex, I appreciate your advice. I really do."

"That advice came from her father," Raincheck interrupted.

Carl suddenly became nervous. "He knows about us?"

"You don't hide things from men like Goleen, especially when it comes to his daughter... My advice is to stick to the Human race."

Carl slammed down the bourbon and then stood up. "Thank you, Alex," Carl responded with obvious sarcasm as he walked out of the office.

Carl stood at the door, greeting the women as they came to work. The first group of women was from the Human government. "Good morning, ladies."

"Good morning, sir," they said in unison as they walked past him.

Carl waved to the Uteakon women coming down the hallway, followed by the Newtopians. "Good morning, ladies," he said with a smile.

The first to walk through the door was Grace. Despite her youthful appearance, she was the oldest of the Evolutions and was always addressed as "Elder" by the other women. Carl smiled as Grace walked by. "Good morning, Elder... I mean Grace."

Grace stopped and smiled at him. "It's okay. You can call me Elder," she responded, putting her nose close to Carl's face. "Somebody smells like a fat rabbit."

Carl was shocked. "Excuse me, that was very inappropriate."

"You're right, sir. I apologize." Grace turned, laughing as she walked away.

He watched as the rest of the women walked by with the same reaction. Feeling self-conscious, he quickly did an underarm and a breath check. Smelling only his deodorant and mouthwash, Carl was puzzled and decided to knock on Raya's door.

"Come in," Raya said. Carl opened the door as Raya was taking a drink of her coffee.

"What's a fat rabbit?"

Raya choked, spraying everything on her desk. "Carl, what makes you think I would know?" she responded, adding to the list of reasons why Uteakon women should mind their own business.

"Call it a hunch," Carl responded sarcastically.

She got up from her desk and walked over to the window. "Isn't that a little Earth creature?" she whispered bashfully.

Carl walked over, putting his face close to hers as she tried to hide her look of guilt. She was hiding something from him, and he would get the truth out of her. "You know, I got ways to make people talk," he said casually.

Carl noticed the closer he put his face to Raya's, the harder she tried not to laugh.

"So you're telling me I smell like a little Earth creature."

"No." Raya turned her back to him.

"Then what's so damn funny?" Carl asked. "Do they know about us?"

"They do now."

"How? I must have taken two showers since then."

"Our sense of smell is stronger than Humans'."

"Can they smell through my uniform?"

"No."

Carl put his face even closer to hers and repeated his question.

"Then how do they know?" Carl pressured.

Raya started laughing as she pointed to his mouth.

Carl tried to look serious as he let out a slight chuckle. "And you didn't think I should know this?"

Raya looked up at him bashfully. "I'm sorry, Carl, I was going to tell you, but it felt so good, I forgot." Raya was flustered with embarrassment and shifted forms, towering over him as her large paws covered Carl's broad shoulders, licking his face.

"No, no, kisses ain't getting you out of this one," he responded, looking up at her.

As Carl looked into Raya's eyes, he saw her remorse and realized his joking had gone too far. He gave her a heartfelt apology. "I'm sorry... I'm just messing with you."

Raya shifted back and looked up at Carl. "I'm sorry, Carl," she said humbly.

Carl smiled, thinking how innocent she looked. "Don't be. I wouldn't have stopped even if you had told me." He gave her a warm hug and apologized.

She couldn't help but melt into his arms, enjoying the moment before her office control started to chime.

"You have a communications request," the AI announced.

"I better let you get back to work."

Raya returned to her desk and answered the video call on her work pad. It was from the sergeant of surveillance.

"Good morning, ma'am." He smiled.

"Good morning to you too, Sergeant. What can I do for you?"

"Well, ma'am. There's been an incident down at the processing station."

Raya looked at her work pad, surprised. "Is everything okay?"

"It's fine. It just got a little chaotic, and I don't know how to explain it, so I'll show you the video."

Raya watched the video. It showed a group of men running out of a building wearing only towels. Raya needed clarification as to why the sergeant was showing her the video. Seconds later, a group of young Uteakon girls was closing in on the men, catching them off guard as they were tackled to the ground. Raya rolled her eyes in disbelief as the girls proceeded to rip the towels off the men. Raya stopped the video.

"I'm sorry, Sergeant. The girls have just arrived here from Uteaka and have never seen or smelled a Human male. I promise you they meant no harm. Are they okay?"

The sergeant shook his head and laughed. "They're fine. A little shaken up."

Raya apologized again and promised she would look into the incident.

The sergeant smiled. "Well, don't be too hard on them. After all, it's a new world for them." The smile on his face vanished. "And besides, it's the first time anybody has had something to laugh about in a long time," he said with a sincere look.

Raya thanked the sergeant, severed their connection, and walked to Carl's office. "Carl, gotta head over to the processing station."

He got up from his desk and walked over to Raya. "I'll come with you."

"No, Carl, that's not a good idea."

"Why, what's wrong?"

She told him about the sergeant's call and the video. Carl let out a slight chuckle and noticed she didn't. "What, you don't see the humor in that?"

"No, I don't," she said calmly and then walked out of his office.

———••◆••———

Security drove her to the processing station, where she spoke to Sergeant Gomez, who explained the conversation with the lieutenant. Raya was furious and ordered a full report on her desk by noon.

"Yes, ma'am," Gomez replied.

Raya walked over to the girls to hear their side of the story. Whisper looked confused as she explained what happened and the game Humans were teaching them. "Did we do something wrong?" Whisper asked.

Raya put a hand on Whisper's cheek and smiled. "No, you didn't," she reassured her.

Something caught the girl's attention. Raya turned to see a woman with the captain's insignia on her field uniform angrily pushing her way through the crowd. She was over six feet tall and physically fit.

"You had better put these animals on a tight leash, or I will," she threatened, putting her face inches away from Raya's.

Raya became angry and responded with a right cross to

the jaw, knocking the woman off her feet. The crowd was going wild. She felt her heart pumping hard as the adrenaline rushed through her.

The captain looked up. "You're about to regret that." She jumped to her feet.

She was as solid as a tank and hit just as hard, bearing her right fist into Raya's left eye, sending her flying back about five feet. She had bitten off more than she could chew as reality approached fast. There was one chance to take her down; if she failed, the musclebound bruiser would make short work of her petite frame.

Raya got up and ran toward her, slamming her head into the woman's stomach and dropping her to the ground. Raya rolled her on her back, then repeatedly punched her until she was unconscious. The crowd started booing as the military police ran to break up the fight. One of the officers, a large man, grabbed Raya by the arm before she could land another punch. Raya turned and punched him in the face with her left fist, knocking him back. The crowd fell silent when it took four MPs to pull Raya off the unconscious woman.

General Raincheck was coming onto the scene as the MPs had Raya in restraints. "So, what happened here? Sergeant Gomez?" Raincheck inquired.

Gomez was explaining the situation when Raincheck exploded. "He said what!"

Raincheck took a deep breath and calmed down as the crowd dispersed. "Tell me something, Sergeant. How do we, as the Human race, invent all this technology and still make a box of rocks look like a social gathering of geniuses? Because I really wanna know!" he said, shaking his head in disbelief.

Raincheck was talking to one of the MPs when the medics passed by, carrying a large woman on a stretcher. "Was that Captain Masterson?"

"Yes, sir," the sergeant answered.

Raincheck looked at the sergeant, confused.

"The Uteakon woman, sir."

Raincheck looked over to see Raya in restraints, talking with an MP. "Great, one more thing that old bastard's gonna rub in my face!" Raincheck muttered sarcastically.

"Sir, what should I do about the Uteakon woman?"

"Let her go and give her the army's sincerest apologies, Sergeant."

"Yes, sir?"

"I want the video from this incident. And I'd like two copies made, one for me and one for the press."

"The press, sir. Why?"

Raincheck took off his sunglasses. "Because I'm tired of seeing the Marines on the front of my newspaper; they may have their blind soldiers, but the Army has the Mud Dogs, and I want the whole damn universe to know it."

After the MPs released her, Raya walked back to the government building. She was furious and in no mood to talk to anybody.

"Raya, can I talk to you?" Carl hollered as she passed by his office.

Everyone watched as Raya ignored him and continued walking. Carl became annoyed and followed her.

"I'd give her time to cool off if I were you, sir," Sergeant Epstein warned.

Carl looked back at her and then at all the ladies in the office. "Last time I checked, I was in charge here, and I seriously doubt anything has changed. Do I make myself clear?" he barked.

"Yes, sir," everyone responded in unison.

Carl walked to Raya's office and opened her door to see a pair of piercing yellow eyes staring into his as she exposed her enormous canines, followed by a deafening roar. Carl closed the door as quickly as he could. He turned to see Sergeant Epstein looking at him. "One word and you'll be scrubbing these floors with a toothbrush," he blurted out jokingly.

"Yes, sir," she muttered, trying not to laugh.

Raya sat down at her desk, holding an ice pack over her left eye, feeling as if she had gotten her ass kicked by a transport carrier. The woman was as big as one, and her knuckles felt like steel. She would feel this one for a while. Despite the pain, it was a good fight and relieved a lot of tension.

She was still disappointed and angry with the lieutenant. Things were supposed to be different for NewGen once they got to Fort Victory, but no matter what planet you worked on or what species you were with, attitudes about NewGen were always the same.

Raya felt terrible for the girls. She never asked to be born with a parasite like the new recruits. She didn't like standing out from other females or being challenged by males, nor did she appreciate being told how her large size threatened the beauty of the Huntress. Raya was often reminded of the consequences and the males that tried to carry them out. The scars on her back refused to let her forget. Had it not been for the NewGen parasite, they would have succeeded. Raya quickly pulled herself together when she heard the knock at the door.

"Come in," she answered.

Carl walked into her office and shut the door behind him. "Raya, can we talk now?"

"Yeah." She got up and walked over to Carl, who was holding out his arms for her. After the day she had, Raya welcomed the comforts of Carl's embrace.

"I talked to Captain Masterson of Bravo Company... She feels bad about what she said. The captain had no idea the girls were Uteakon or never would have phrased it the way she did."

"It's not just that. It's the way those girls were treated. You should've seen the looks on their faces. You don't know what it's like being a big female and just as strong as a male," she said, looking into Carl's eyes.

"There's nothing wrong with being big," Carl shot back.

"Not if you're feline, Carl. It doesn't fit into the male equation of what we should look like," Raya snarled.

"This is Fort Victory, the melting pot of life-forms, so if a woman wants to man up, ain't nothing wrong with that," Carl said, looking into her eyes with a warm smile.

Raya started to bawl. "Carl, I don't wanna be a man."

Carl put his hands on Raya's cheeks, kissing her lips. "Sorry, that came out wrong... I meant to say that many men love a big woman... Prefer a big woman. I'm one of those men."

She kissed him passionately. "Thank you, Carl."

"Don't worry about the girls... I have a feeling they're gonna do just fine around here."

Carl gently moved the hair away from her eye, then threw his head back in surprise. "Damn... She tore that eye up."

Raya looked up at him, unamused. "Goodbye, Carl." She turned and walked back to her desk.

Carl stood in the doorway, turning to speak, but quickly closed the door when Raya picked up an object off her desk. "We'll talk later," Carl shouted through the closed door.

# CHAPTER 11

The following day, Raya was getting ready for work when there was a knock at the door, and then it opened. "Just me, Jazzy!"

Ocean came running out of her room, her uniform tucked inside her school bag. "Okay, I'm ready to go now."

She kissed her mother on the cheek before shifting into a large calico panther. "Don't forget to ask your mom!" Jazzy reminded her as she shifted into her leopard form.

"Oh yeah, that's right!" Ocean turned and looked at her mom. "Mom, I'm doing an essay on military weapons and need information about the Dolls of Wrath," she roared.

Raya looked at her daughter and shrugged her shoulders. "Sweetie, they're just bedtime stories your grandfather used to tell."

"Please, Mom!" Ocean brushed against her mother's Human frame, her fur creating static electricity as she began to purr.

Raya smiled and quickly gave in to her daughter's plea. "All right, fine. I'll use the computer in my office and connect to the Uteakon archives and see what I can find."

"Thanks, Mom!"

Raya smiled as she watched Ocean and Jazzy head to school. She guzzled what was left of her coffee and then ran out the door.

Raya arrived at her office an hour early. She wanted enough time to collect what she needed for Ocean's homework. Carl opened the door and walked in, holding a breakfast tray with coffee and donuts.

"I knew I'd find you here." Carl smiled and handed her a cup of coffee and a powdered donut.

"Thank you, Carl."

Raya looked at the donut, raising her eyebrows in confusion.

"Carl, what is this?"

Carl looked at her and grinned. "It's called a donut. It goes great with coffee," he reassured her, smiling. "So what brings you in here so early?"

Carl smiled, admiring Raya's beauty as she blew into her cup.

"I'm helping Ocean with her homework. She needs information on the Dolls of Wrath."

Carl looked at her with an inquisitive grin. "Dolls of Wrath. What is that, a new rock band?"

Raya picked up the donut. "They were war dolls, weapons created by a race of beings called the Timeless Ones. The Timeless Ones are from the realm of shadows. Or what you would call the dark dimension, where light cannot penetrate, but life flourished there, just not as we know it."

Carl gave Raya a puzzled look. "So why did they create these dolls?"

"To fight against their enemy, but when the Shezón invaded, they proved to be too powerful. Desperate, the Timeless Ones created the four Dolls of Wrath, which were even more powerful than the previous dolls." Raya took a bite of her donut while Carl encouraged her to sip her coffee.

Raya followed Carl's suggestion and nodded in approval, her reddish-pink lips were covered in white powder. "Tell me more about these Dolls of Wrath," Carl said, chuckling at the powder on her lips.

Raya smiled. "Carl, they are just bedtime stories for kittens."

Unable to resist any longer, Carl leaned in and kissed Raya's powdered lips. "Call me a kitten at heart." He smiled.

"By the time the dolls were finished, the Shezón had conquered and devoured everything in the shadow universe; only a few survivors remained. They brought the dolls with them when they escaped into our universe."

Raya laughed, looking at Carl's lips. "Oh, you think that's funny, do you? Control, show mirrored image."

Raya looked at her image and then pushed the donut toward Carl.

"I don't want that anymore," she said with a pouting look.

Carl was laughing. "Come on, it's funny," he said, looking at the annoyance on her face.

Raya wiped the powder from her lips and then continued her story. "These dolls are a very destructive force."

"That's precisely what we need right now. I wish I had one of those dolls," Carl muttered half-jokingly.

Raya looked over at Carl. She had a concerned look on her face.

"I'd be careful what you wish for, Carl. These dolls cannot be controlled. Be glad they're just bedtime stories, Carl. One doll alone could take down the base...if they were real."

Carl began to have suspicions about 305 and its mysterious origins. 305 was technically the first Mud Dog candidate. Carl questioned the sanity of the top brass even more now.

Raya noticed Carl's silence and the concerned look on his face. "Carl, what's wrong? You look worried," she asked, touching his arm.

Carl looked at her with a pale complexion. "The first Mud Dog candidate has arrived."

"That's good news. Where is she? I can set up an interview with her," Raya replied.

"She's currently in an observation chamber in sector four," Carl whispered nervously.

Raya was confused, and her frustration was growing. "Carl, why is she in an observation chamber, and why are they treating her like this?"

"Because she's not Human, nobody seems to know what this thing is."

Raya gave Carl an angry look as she grabbed her badge and stormed past him.

"Raya, where you going?"

"To put a stop to this. I will not let the military treat these girls like this. They are here to be soldiers, not objects of curiosity!" she barked, reaching for the doorknob.

"Your father ordered it."

Raya stopped and turned around. "My dad ordered this?" She went silent, even more suspicious. "I want to see her right now, Carl!"

"Raya, that's not a good idea."

"Now, Carl!" she demanded.

Carl led her to sector four. They walked down a long corridor leading to 305's enclosure. The walls were made of steel and reflected the ceiling lights. At the end was a metallic door, above which read, "Behavior identification." Carl stepped onto the pad as the AI scanned him.

"Good morning, Captain Winfield. How are you doing?"

"I'm doing good. How are you doing?"

"I'm good as well. Please identify the following pictures."

He identified the first two pictures without hesitation, but when the AI showed him a picture of a puppy, he hesitated, and Raya noticed the fear in his eyes when he answered. "Dog."

The AI briefly stalled while it processed the information. "Identity confirmed." Carl opened the door with a loud click and gave her a nervous smile. "Come on in."

The room was enormous, and the lights were so bright it was impossible to cast shadows. Behind transparent steel was a fully staffed observation room that monitored whatever was behind the titanium curtains electronically.

"Carl, how big is she?" Raya asked, looking at him with a bewildered expression.

Carl placed his hand on the scanning plate. "Big, very big!" The light blinked green, and heavy metal rumbled as the metallic curtains slowly rose, revealing a slumbering beast. The creature's size and appearance were terrifying but familiar. Suddenly, it dawned on her it looked like the larvae of a Phoenix fly. They were harmless moth-like creatures, no bigger than her finger, from the shadow dimension. However, this one was on a much larger scale and looked anything but harmless. Raya felt the cold hand of fear steal what was left of her courage as her body trembled and her face paled.

Carl noticed the panicked look as she stared aimlessly at 305. "Raya, are you okay?"

She looked at him with shock and then headed for the door; he followed after her. "Raya, wait, please, tell me what's wrong," he pleaded, pulling her into his arms.

She looked up at him, trembling. "Carl, 305 is a Doll of Wrath!" She tore herself out of his arms and headed for her office.

He followed Raya. She was furious, and he didn't blame her; the military had put everyone in jeopardy having the doll on base. "Raya, can we talk?" Carl pleaded.

Raya gave him an angry look. "Yes. Come in," she said, trying not to take her anger out on him. "I don't like this, Carl; these dolls are very dangerous."

He tried to hold her; she looked him in the eyes and pushed him away. "Don't."

Carl ran a hand across his bald head. "I don't like this any more than you do. Raya, I've seen what the Shezón can do. We don't have the luxury of choosing our allies. When I was twelve, the Shezón made their first appearance; in less than one hour, the Mantis soldiers wiped out everything; the streets were covered in blood, and it was so strong it made me sick, and everywhere you looked, there were dead bodies, friends, family. Even people you hated. They were all dead; later in life, when I joined the military, I killed enough of them to realize that the Mantis soldiers that took down Fort Eagle were just workers collecting food." There was a cold, angry look in Carl's eyes.

"Carl?" Raya started to speak, but he interrupted her.

"There's a blood storm coming; I guarantee the true soldiers will be far worse than anything we've seen yet. You don't trust the military, I understand that. But right now, we're all the universe has. So if you have a better plan, I'm willing to listen," he said sternly.

Raya looked at him. She felt bad for panicking. "Carl, I'm sorry I panicked."

He hugged her. "I'm sorry, too. I shouldn't have snapped at you like that."

"It's okay; we're both under much stress right now," she said, resting her head on Carl's chest.

"Why don't you take the rest of the day off," he suggested.

"No, Carl, I'm fine now," she insisted.

"Raya, I want you to go home and relax. Tomorrow, we will start the interview."

"All right, Carl. See you tomorrow." She grabbed her handbag.

Carl walked with her. "I'll drive you home."

As Carl was driving Raya home, he couldn't shake the gut-wrenching feeling he had. Even before the cadets signed their names on the dotted line, the sword of Damocles was already swinging above their heads with the presence of 305; the blade just got lower. Worst-case scenario... If the Shezón didn't get them, then something much worse would. Carl stopped his thoughts as they drove up to Raya's apartment building.

Carl walked Raya to her apartment. "Would you like to come inside for a cup of coffee?" she asked, stepping onto the key mat. The apartment control unit scanned Raya. When the light blinked green, the apartment door unlocked and greeted her as she walked in, "Good afternoon, Raya. There are no messages at this time. Captain Winfield, your transport is still running. Shall I park it for you?"

"Yes, thank you," Carl responded.

Raya put her handbag on the kitchen table and made a fresh pot of coffee. As she set the cups on the table, she noticed Carl's hands were shaking, so she put her hand on his shoulder. "Carl, you're scared and have every right to be. But right now, we must communicate with her before she becomes angry."

Carl looked up at Raya. "You are right, I'm sorry. Stress."

Raya grabbed Carl by the hand. "Come on, let's go!" she said, leading him down the hallway.

"Where are we going?"

"Release stress," Raya responded sarcastically.

Carl chuckled and followed her into the bedroom.

Raya was resting her head on Carl's chest, deep in thought. "What are you thinking about?" Carl asked.

Raya ran a finger across his chest. "That I should be mad at you."

"Me, why?"

Her voice changed. It was low with a menacing overtone. "Because you hide things from me. I don't like that." She leaned over and gave him a peck on the lips before straddling him.

Carl gave her a guilty look. "I told you, I didn't know what it was until you told me."

"She, Carl. 305 is a girl, and I'm not talking about that."

"Then what do you mean?"

"When we mated, you never ask for the other pleasures men like. Why is that, Carl?" Raya asked, resisting the temptation to laugh as a guilty look suddenly swept across Carl's face.

"Other pleasures." Carl had a nervous grin on his face.

"Where did you learn that?"

"The Human females in the office. We heard them whispering about it."

"I wouldn't listen to that; guys don't go for it," Carl replied.

Raya enjoyed watching him think of an answer that wouldn't offend her. "You know, I don't like being lied to. Makes me believe you don't trust me."

Raya shifted forms as Carl's body stiffened. Her deep yellow eyes stared into his while the sun reflected off her large pearly whites.

Carl suddenly let out a scream as Raya's nose slowly made its way down his stomach while her deep, hollow growls echoed in his ears. "All right, all right, I just get nervous around women with big teeth, especially when they're longer than my fingers!" Carl admitted.

Raya shifted back, laughing as she continued straddling him. "What's wrong, Carl? Don't you trust me?" she asked, getting out of bed.

Carl got up and followed her. "I trust you; it's your jaws that make me nervous," he responded in defense.

Raya stopped and turned around. "Now, Carl. Why would I bite it off? That would be like shooting myself in the foot." She chuckled, heading for the bathroom.

Carl continued following her, defending what was left of his pride. "You know you're not half as funny as you think. Lucky I didn't drop something on your bedsheets."

"Your scream was," Raya responded, laughing as she turned on the shower.

Carl enjoyed hearing the laughter in her voice and seeing the smile on her face. The thought of putting her or anyone else in danger rubbed him the wrong way. He knew there was more to the Mud Dog program than what he was told. Carl began to have his suspicions. Three other girls in the program were on the same threat level as 305. Carl pulled Raya into his arms. "Raya, I feel the Army knows where the other three dolls are."

Raya wrapped her arms around Carl. "Two legs or four, I'll stand by your side." She paused momentarily and continued, "And when we go to war, I'll be the sword you wield."

"Thank you," Carl whispered, moving in for a kiss.

# CHAPTER 12

Carl walked into the kitchen to see Zoe and Tylee setting the table. "Dad, you're home. Good, dinner's almost ready," Tylee said, carrying plates.

"All right, I'm gonna change, and I'll be right down."

Carl grabbed his T-shirt from the drawer and noticed a family picture buried beneath a pile of shirts. Zoe was seven, and Tylee was five. It was the first time they had chili dogs. Carl laughed, thinking how cute they looked, their faces and hands covered in chili. Caroline decided to take a family picture. She was holding Zoe, and he was holding Tylee. A tear fell from Carl's eye and landed on Caroline's picture. It would be the last one they would take together as a family. He could feel that helplessness coming back. The Shezón had taken everything from him, and there was nothing he could do. Zoe and Tylee were all he had left in the universe; if he had to, he'd sell his soul to protect them.

"Dad, dinner's ready," Zoe hollered up the stairs.

"Coming!"

During dinner, Carl listened to his daughters talking about their day. Most of the time, their conversation was about school and the teachers they didn't care for, but tonight the hot topic was boys. He loved seeing them being typical teenagers, hearing them laugh, but all that came at a price, and now it was time to pay.

After dinner, Carl sat on the back porch watching the stars, wondering if the good outweighed the negative. It didn't matter whether he agreed or not. 305 was a part of the Mud Dogs and had the same rights as any other soldier. But his fear of her was clouding his judgment.

Carl felt as a leader it was his job to lead by example, and part of that was following the laws of the United Military Alliance. And under the agreement of the alliance, it was written in big, bold letters. *All soldiers shall be treated with respect and privileges given according to rank and shall be judged only by their performance as soldiers.*

Tylee walked onto the porch carrying a glass of iced tea.

"Here, Dad. I thought you might be thirsty," she said, putting the glass into his hand as she sat with her head resting on his shoulder.

Carl put his arm around her and kissed Tylee's forehead.

"Thank you, baby girl."

"Dad, you look worried. Is anything wrong?"

"No, I'm fine, just sitting here thinking about rules and regulations. What about you?"

"Nothing, just taking a break from homework," Tylee responded.

"That reminds me, your ballroom teacher sent me a performance report today. It said you're not doing as well as you should," Carl said in a soft, reprimanding tone.

"Dad, it's because I always get stuck with these short, dorky boys staring at my chest!" she responded defensively.

Carl laughed, remembering how he had been caught doing the same thing.

Tylee was upset and almost in tears.

"Dad, it's not funny, it's embarrassing, and the other kids are always laughing," she snapped back, her tears mixed with anger.

"I'm not laughing at you, baby girl. I used to do the same thing in my classes," Carl admitted shamefully.

"Why, Dad? You know how humiliating that is?" she scolded.

Carl hugged her and promised he would talk with the teacher. Tylee suddenly shot him a panicked look.

"No, Dad, please promise me you won't do that," Tylee begged.

Carl looked at her, puzzled and even a little hurt.

"Why not?"

"Because I don't want you getting angry and embarrassing me like you did last time."

Carl put up his hands and shrugged his shoulders.

"Baby girl, I told you I was trying to get him to shut up long enough so I could talk."

"Dad, your hand was around the teacher's throat," Tylee said, making her point.

"Fine, I'll send one of the ladies in the office to do the talking."

Tylee thanked him and kissed him on the cheek as she returned to finish her homework.

The following day, Carl was late getting to the office. Everyone greeted him as he walked through the door.

"Good morning, sir," they said in unison.

"Good morning, ladies." Carl smiled and nodded his head.

From the corner of his eye, he could see Grace sitting at her desk and remembered his promise to Tylee and decided to ask her if she would have a talk with Tylee's teacher. She was the wisest and the kindest of the ladies in the office and would get much better results than he would.

"Grace."

"Yes, sir?" She looked up with a warm smile.

He was about to ask her when it suddenly occurred to him Grace was from a planet where females were dominant and gave out harsh and sometimes fatal punishments to any male that got out of line. Carl gave her an awkward smile.

"I just wanted to tell you you're doing a great job. Thank you," Carl said, avoiding the question and his daughter's wrath.

He was walking to his office as Sergeant Epstein, the

receptionist, passed by. She was an older woman in her early thirties; she was polite, and her people skills were incredible.

"Sergeant, I have a favor to ask." He explained Tylee's situation, and she understood and agreed to take care of it immediately.

"Thank you, Sergeant. I appreciate this."

"Not a problem, sir." She smiled and headed for the door.

After about forty-five minutes, Carl became anxious about the results and decided to call.

"Control, send a connection request to Sergeant Epstein."

"Sending a request now," the control unit responded.

"Hello, sir. What can I do for you?"

"I was just calling to see how things are going."

"Not to worry, sir, I have a firm grip on the situation as we speak."

"All right, Sergeant. I'll see you when you get back to the office."

"Sounds good, sir," she said, severing their connection. She then turned back to the teacher to finish their conversation.

"Now, either you are not listening to me, or I failed to make myself clear. So let me just say this one more time," Sergeant Epstein explained as her hand clenched firmly to his balls. "If you put Tylee Winfield with any more short, dorky boys, I will come back here and make you one of the girls. Am I making myself clear now, sir?" she asked politely.

"Yes," he replied nervously, shaking his head.

Sergeant Epstein released her grip.

"See how much better it is when you're not acting like a prick?" She straightened his tie and then headed for the door.

"And by the way, if anyone finds out about our conversation, I will also come back and make you one of the girls. This time I'll bring a dress," she stated, walking out the door.

Carl was in his office when he got a message from his daughter. It had a smiling heart avatar blowing kisses and repeating the phrase, "Thanks, Dad. I love you."

Carl smiled, feeling a warm sensation in his heart. It was always good to know his daughters were happy and even better knowing he was the reason. Carl went to the receptionist's desk to thank Sergeant Epstein for his daughter's happiness.

"Sergeant, I want to thank you for everything you have done for me today. Your people skills are incredible. I could have never done it. Thank you."

"It is okay, sir. I'm happy to help. Besides, it's just a matter of reaching out and helping them understand, sir."

While going over 305's files, Carl noticed all the questions were marked as "NA." All that was known about 305 was that she was not Human and was potentially the most dangerous entity the military has faced. Carl's thoughts were suddenly interrupted as Raya opened his door and poked her head in. "Carl, are you ready?"

Carl took a deep, calming breath. "Ready as I'll ever be." He grabbed his badge, and they headed over to the sector four, where a young sergeant in his early twenties greeted them.

"Good morning!" He smiled and pushed the button on his desk. A pair of doors opened, and two guards in long white coats approached, one male and one female.

Raya became annoyed and deactivated her uniform badge. "As you can see, I have nothing to hide, so unless you plan on doing a cavity search, I have an appointment to keep."

The sergeant went wide-eyed, a blushing shade of red on his face, turning to Carl as if wondering what to do next.

Carl tried to keep a straight face. "Don't look at me, Sergeant. I'm not doing a cavity search."

The sergeant gave them an awkward smile as he allowed them to pass. Carl looked at Raya with disbelief. "I can't believe you just did that."

Raya looked up at Carl with a pouting face. "What is it with Humans and nudity? Uteakons don't wear clothes, and when our tails are in the air, everything is right there, in plain view, and no one cares. Except for Humans. Why is that?"

"No comment!" Carl responded, laughing as they headed for 305's containment unit.

———— ••◆•• ————

Carl stood at the door to her enclosure, activating the identification scan. When it was complete, they entered the room, looking nervously at one another. Carl knew the longer they kept her waiting, the worse it would get. His hand trembled as he reached for the keypad.

Suddenly, Raya called out his name. He turned to see her surrounded by red mist. Her hands were around her throat, gasping frantically for air. Carl felt his heart slamming against his ribs as adrenaline rushed through him. He tried frantically to get to Raya's side but was thrown back as he couldn't penetrate the red fog. He watched helplessly as she lost consciousness, shifting forms as she fell to the ground. Carl tried to get to his feet but couldn't as the deafening sound of heavy metal rumbled as the iron curtain rose, revealing the hellish beast. Even from a distance, he could feel the dark energy radiating from her scaly body as the red mist surrounded him, leaving him nowhere to go but to 305.

She was the essence of darkness, but what choice did they have? They were out of options and running out of luck. Without her, they would only be delaying the inevitable. Carl stood and cautiously approached her, trembling as he passed through the cold gray fog surrounding her. Suddenly, something whispered in his mind. "Tell me, boy, does my appearance frighten you?"

Everyone was covered in the red mist. Carl didn't know if

they were alive or dead. "Everything about you frightens me," he admitted. "And it's Captain Winfield, not boy."

Carl felt a sudden chill race through him as he recognized her giggle.

"And yet you stand before me willing to make a deal. Tell me, do you still want vengeance?"

Carl's head was pounding with confusion, realizing there was something all too familiar about her.

"Well, what are you waiting for?" she inquired impatiently.

Carl knew there was no turning back. Even if he wanted to, there was nowhere to run: the red mist was everywhere. 305 had previously tried to pull him in, but their connection was severed. However, this time, she made sure there would be no interference.

Despite his fear, Carl was able to muster a response. "What do I have to do?"

Carl suddenly found himself transported to a new and unknown universe brimming with endless planets and an array of dazzling stars and constellations. Shrouded in gray, a mysterious figure materialized out of the darkness as he stood frozen in fear. Immense power emanated from her as she ran a hand across his chest. Carl's screams echoed as cold, dark energy rushed through him.

"Open your mind to me. Show me your world." Carl fell silent as tranquility swept through him. She began pulling out pieces of his life from the depths of his mind, starting the day he was born. His mother was holding him, laughing as she watched the nurses trying to revive his father.

Carl burst into laughter, watching the events as if he were reliving his life. Gradually, the images began to speed up until it was nothing but a blur, as if his life were suddenly put into fast motion.

Without warning, everything came to a stop. Carl watched as an image of a boy standing behind bushes came into focus. He recognized the child. It was himself; he was ten years old, and they had just returned from church. Carl remembered that day as if it was yesterday. He was taking out the trash when he heard singing. Carl smiled as he remembered hiding in the bushes, listening to her angelic voice. Carl laughed until he cried. It was the first time they met.

Her name was Rebecca. She was General Raincheck's little sister. Everybody just called her Half-pint. She was standing in a gazebo with her back to him, singing an old nursery rhyme. She wore a pink dress that hung past her knees, and her long blonde hair was always tied with the blackest bow he had ever seen.

"So, are you just going to stand hiding in the bushes... like some creepy old man?" she responded without turning around.

Carl swallowed hard and stepped away from the bushes.

"I wasn't trying to be creepy... I was just curious, that's all."

"Well, you failed miserably at that...didn't you?" She turned, staring at him with her hazel eyes.

Before he could say anything, a guard came running down, grabbing him by the arm. Half-pint looked over at the guard. "Sergeant!" she barked loudly.

"Yes, ma'am," he responded nervously.

"Bring that boy here."

Carl would never forget how the guard's hand trembled as he walked him to the gazebo. Half-pint smiled at him, then turned her attention to the guard. "Get out of my sight," she barked as the sergeant turned pale before obeying her order and, returning to Carl, she asked, "What's your name?"

Carl never knew whether it was her beauty or her boldness that left him speechless. Either way, she was becoming impatient, waiting for an answer.

"Well, spit it out, boy."

Fixing her with a steady gaze, he declared firmly, "It's not boy. It's Carl! Carl Winfield."

With that, he reached out his hand toward her.

Half-pint held it while she ran her other hand up his arm. "You're lucky to have such beautiful black skin."

Carl looked at her, scrunching up his eyebrows. "Lucky? I'm blacker than midnight. Everybody teases me, even black people."

The smile on her face vanished as she still held his hand. Carl remembered the cold chill that ran through him as she stared into his eyes. "Why do you care what others think?"

Carl lowered his voice as he looked into her eyes. "I just want to be normal...like everyone else."

Her smile returned. "You should be proud to look the way you do."

"Why?"

Half-pint put a hand on his cheek, looking into his light brown eyes. "Because you're a pretty doll, just like me." She was silent for a moment. Her hazel eyes stared like a bird of prey as her good mood suddenly changed. "And the only reason I didn't let the guard throw your ass out of here."

That day, they explored the woods and discovered a small lagoon. The sand was as white as snow, and the water was crystal clear. He remembered they were looking at the water, debating whether they should go in when he questioned her about the guard, and he also remembered the chill that ran up his spine when she gave him his answer. "It's not me they're protecting. Now come on, let's go swimming!" She smiled and took off her shoes.

"I can't," he answered nervously.

"Why not? You afraid?" she asked, standing.

"No, I just don't have a swimming suit."

"Suit!" She looked at him with a grin. "You've got a birthday suit," she hinted while taking off her pink dress, laying it neatly next to her shoes.

Carl looked at her with a guilty grin, thinking about his answer. He didn't want to come across as a coward and certainly didn't want to get caught.

"What are you waiting for, me to take them off for you?" Half-pint barked.

"No, I can take off my own clothes!" Carl shot back in defense.

"Well, then hurry up and do it. Besides, I doubt my mom has anything to worry about," she added, removing the rest of her clothing.

Carl scrunched up his face. "What's that supposed to mean?" he inquired.

She walked over to him and put her face in his. "Time will give you that answer. Now hurry up."

Over the summer, Carl spent most of his time with her. He didn't care that she was different from other people. She never spoke down to him or teased him. Whenever she used words he didn't understand, he would scrunch up his face. She'd look at him and smile, then explain the term and its use. Sometimes he would make the face just to hear her laugh.

Carl suddenly stopped. "Please, no more... It hurts... It hurts!" He fell to his knees, sobbing heavily as she continued pulling the memories from his mind.

"Then I shall free you from the burden of pain. Make it my own," she whispered in his ear, sending more energy rushing through him.

Carl began thinking about the two years he'd spent with her and all the good times that followed. There was only one time they got into an argument. He was waiting in the school hallway for Half-pint when a girl named Tamika Jones began harassing him. Even though she was almost as dark-skinned as he was, she teased and even pushed him, knowing he would never push back; his father had always taught him never to hit a woman. "What are you gonna do, Winfield? Hit a girl?"

Before he could answer, Half-pint flew around the corner and grabbed Tamika by the hair.

"No, he won't, but I will!" Half-pint roared, pulling Tamika's head to the side as she continuously slammed her fist into Tamika's face until it was covered in blood. Half-pint let go of Tamika and grabbed Carl by the hand, leading him away from the crime scene.

"What's the matter with you, Carl? If she were a boy, you would've kicked her ass."

"My dad told me never hit a woman."

Half-pint stopped and stared into his eyes. "Really... Easy for him to say, he's not the one being pushed around... You better change your thinking real fast, because next time... She'll be going to the morgue." Half-pint walked away and didn't speak to him for the next two days.

Carl had two days to think about what she said but they were the loneliest days of his life and on the second night he called her, expecting her not to answer. It rang four times before she did. "What do you want, Carl?" she responded dis- appointedly.

"Just called to see what you're doing."

There was a moment of silence before she answered. "Just thinking."

"Yeah, me too..." he interrupted. "Look, I'm sorry about the other day. You're right. From now on, I won't let anyone push me around," he told her sternly.

"I'm sorry too... Are we still friends?" she whispered softly.

Carl threw back his head and scrunched up his eyebrows. "Now and forever!"

Half-pint burst into laughter. Together, they laughed and talked until the early morning.

But out of all her memories, the one that stood out the most was the promise.

Two years had passed since that day, and they were at recess. Half-pint looked up at him, smiling. "I've decided I want you to be mine." She blushed.

Carl put his hands on the top of his head, cringing as he watched his childhood self scrunch up his face, thinking about the question. "Don't say it, Carl...please don't say it," he pleaded desperately.

"What?"

The smile on her face vanished as she hit him on the arm so hard he felt it for the rest of the day. "Figure it out yourself, moron." She turned and stormed off in a huff.

"Okay, I will, I promise." That same day, the Shezón attacked, and his promise was never kept.

Carl dropped to his knees, crying over the emptiness he had felt all these years without her. In the last memory he had of her, they were running from a Mantis soldier. Carl remembered falling behind when it took flight. He would never forget the deafening sound its wings made as it zeroed in on him, or the sacrifice Half-pint made when she shielded him with her own body.

Neither he nor Alex remembered how they had survived that day. He only remembered reaching out and calling to Half-pint, but it was too late. The Mantis soldier was carrying her away.

Carl could feel himself growing stronger as the dark energy began feeding on his pain. "Child of Earth! I have seen your world, felt your pain, and now I shall make it my own, and when I arise, we shall bathe in the blood of our enemy. Indulge in the sweetest taste of crimson victory," she whispered passionately in his ear.

Suddenly, the figure vanished, followed by an eerie silence and then the sound of a heartbeat while the flow of rushing energy carried him back into his own dimension.

Carl awakened on a stretcher. Alex Raincheck was standing next to him. "You did it, old friend. You saved us."

Carl looked around the room. It was filled with medical staff rushing people out on stretchers. "Are they okay?"

Raincheck hesitated. "Everyone's fine. They'll just have a little headache," he spoke in a hushed tone.

Carl had a bad feeling. Alex Raincheck wasn't the kind of

man who'd encountered a situation he couldn't handle.

Carl grabbed Alex firmly by the arm and gritted his teeth. "Alex, I hope you know what you're doing... Because what we just unleashed into this universe...is far more terrifying than those bugs."

Raincheck placed his hand on Carl's shoulder. "You and the girls come over for dinner tonight. I'll inform Alice we're having company. Don't forget to bring your girlfriend. This involves her too," he said before closing the door.

Carl tried to get off the stretcher when the medic gently pushed him back down. "Sorry, sir, we need to follow protocol," she told him politely.

"Sergeant, I'm fine, really."

She looked at him with a sarcastic gaze and couldn't have been taller than Raya. "It's been a long day; my feet hurt, my body aches, and on top of it all, I'm getting my period."

Carl gave her an awkward grin and then laid back down. She patted him on the shoulder. "Thank you for understanding," she said, wheeling him off for medical attention.

Carl chuckled. "You're welcome, Sergeant."

Raincheck informed him dinner would be at seven. Carl arranged to pick up Raya and Ocean a little after six. As they drove up to the apartment building, Tylee put her arm out of the window, waving to Ocean. "I didn't know you knew Ocean," Carl stated.

Tylee looked at him, raising her eyebrows. "Everybody knows Ocean... She's one of the popular kids in school," she answered as Ocean got into the back.

Raya got into the front. He looked at her, smiling. She looked back, inquiring about it. "Just noticing how beautiful you look," he answered below a whisper, catching the passengers' attention in the back, followed by their own whispering and then little chuckles.

When they arrived at the house, Raincheck's wife Alice and the girls' aunt greeted them at the door. "Hello, Carl, it's good to see you again." She hugged him and gave him a taunting smile that always reminded him of that night when one mistake changed his life.

He smiled back at her and gave her a firm squeeze. "It's good to see you too, Alice," he said earnestly.

He walked away, thinking about that night of mistaken identity. He and Raincheck were in college. He had just started dating Caroline, Alice's twin sister. Although they sounded alike and their hair was the same length, they weren't identical and didn't have the same personality or hair color. Alice had long blonde hair, and her bust was quite noticeable, an attribute she was most proud of. They were like having credit she didn't have to pay back. Alice wasn't just beautiful, she was free-spirited and attracted to physically fit men, which she often pursued successfully, but in the morning, they were just another conquest, and it was on to the next. Now, seeing her graying hair and grandmotherly smile, you would never know that she was once wild and untamed.

That night, Caroline agreed to sneak him into her dorm and told him she would leave her window open, and he was supposed to climb through when it was lights out. She warned him several times not to climb into the first window, which was her sister's. Hers was the second. Carl had been training all day and wasn't thinking straight that night; he climbed into the wrong window. It was pitch-black, and she was lying asleep. Thinking it was Caroline, he removed his clothes and climbed in with her. "It's just me," he whispered, trying not to startle her.

She woke up. The tone of her voice sounded happy and seductive. "Well, this is a surprise."

Carl caressed her body. She began moaning as his hand went inside her silk panties, diverting any suspicions he had. He gently kissed and licked her stomach as he removed the only thing Alice was wearing. Her moaning became louder as his tongue made its way between her thighs. When the pleasure became too much, Alice's hips quivered as he tried to muffle her screams. She drew a heavy sigh of relief, then pushed him firmly on his back, returning the favor before mounting him. While her hands explored his body, her hips moved slowly, then gradually increased the more she massaged his overworked muscles. In the heat of passion, Carl reached up and squeezed her breasts, realizing he had entered the wrong room, but it was too late, and he couldn't stop himself.

They made love until they fell over, exhausted. In the morning, Carl woke up but wasn't surprised to see Alice. "What the hell are you doing here?" he said, trying to cover his guilt.

She looked at him angrily. "You climbed into my bed."

"Because I thought you were Caroline, and you knew it... Why didn't you tell me?"

She looked at him, surprised he'd be stupid enough to ask her that question. "If a beautiful woman snuck into your room in the middle of the night, willing to give you sex because she thought you were somebody else... Would you tell her?"

Carl was silent, looking at her. Before he could answer, she interrupted, "I didn't think so! Besides, I'm pretty sure when you were fondling my breasts, you knew damn well I wasn't Caroline, so don't hand me that shit, and don't slam the door on your way out," she muttered, heading for the bathroom.

When he got back to his dorm, he told Raincheck about climbing into the wrong window and mistaking Alice for Caroline and her reaction to it all. Raincheck was impressed and threw him a beer, making him tell everything.

The next day, Caroline came over to his dorm. She seemed as if she were unaware of what had happened. He knew then he didn't want to lose her, but she deserved to know the truth. Carl swallowed hard and then admitted his guilt. He was surprised she wasn't angry about it and even laughed over the irony. "I know, my sister told me." There were tears in her eyes.

He held her in his arms, apologizing. She looked at him and smiled. "They're tears of joy. You told me the truth. I wasn't sure if I could trust you. The last soldier I gave my heart to broke it." She cried in his arms.

"I would never intentionally hurt you, Caroline," he whispered softly.

"I know. That's why I love you." She kissed him passionately.

Raincheck grabbed a six-pack of beer from the refrigerator and headed for the door. "I can see you two want to be alone." He stopped and turned around, looking at Caroline. "Is your sister home?"

"I think so... Why?"

"No reason, just thought I'd stop and welcome her to the neighborhood," Raincheck said, grinning.

Carl stopped thinking about the memory as Raincheck was coming down the stairs. "Good, you're here." He walked past him, grabbing two beers out of the refrigerator. "Come on, I want to show you my new toy." Raincheck handed him a beer as they went out to the garage.

Inside was a land vehicle Carl had never seen before. It was a metallic orange and shined like polished glass.

Carl was impressed and a little jealous. "What is that?"

Raincheck looked at him with a boasting smile. "It's a 1972 Chevy Nova, an old earth transport. The engine has to be modified. It runs on some type of fossil fuel that hasn't been seen since mankind left Earth."

Carl was given a tour of the strange-looking transport. Afterward, they went back into the house to see Raya and Alice setting the table for dinner as the girls were upstairs talking with their cousin. Raincheck walked up to Alice, patting her behind as he kissed her lips. "I'll be on the patio, talking with Carl." He grabbed two more beers, and they stood outside looking at the backyard before Raincheck started to speak. "To answer your earlier question, no, I don't know if

I'm doing the right thing. We don't know anything about these entities." Raincheck chugged what was left of his beer and continued. "But it doesn't matter now. Three more of them arrived last night."

"Alex, this is way beyond insane!"

"You won't get any arguments out of me. I tried to reason with the last general." Raincheck paused. There was a look of fear in his eyes. "Right now, they are in sector four, and as soon as their Rebirth is complete, they're to be out of sector four and processed. She made it quite clear they're to be treated no differently than any other soldier."

Suddenly, Alice walked onto the patio, announcing dinner was ready. As they were walking to the door, Alice pulled Carl to the side and then turned to her husband. "Honey, will you give Raya a hand in the kitchen? I want to have a little talk with Carl," she asked, giving him a kiss.

Raincheck pulled her into his arms. "You got it, my love."

Alice turned and looked at Carl. Before she could say anything, Carl spoke first. "Alice, I know what you're gonna say, and we're just friends, nothing more," he tried to reassure her.

Alice laughed. "Carl, I'm glad you found somebody. She's a wonderful person, but she's not Caroline, nor is she a substitute. I love my sister, and not a day goes by when I don't miss her, but I've said my goodbyes, and so must you." Alice gave him a supportive hug. "I worry about you, Carl, and so do the girls."

Carl swallowed hard before he spoke. "I've gone up to the attic hundreds of times, telling myself I would donate her stuff." He lowered his head. "But each time, I couldn't do it. I'm not strong enough to say goodbye, Alice."

She looked up at him, her tears mixed with frustration. "That's why you have a family. You have me. I'm here for you, and so is Alex."

"I'm sorry, Alice. I just didn't want to burden anybody with my problems."

"It's not a burden when it's somebody you love."

"As soon as we get the Mud Dog program off the ground, I'll take a day and go through the attic."

Alice put her hands on Carl's shoulders and gave him a peck on the cheek. "This time I'll help you, and so will Alex."

He smiled at her and nodded his head. "Thank you, Alice."

She smiled back at him and shook her head. "I swear, between you and Alex, the two of you are going to put me in the insane asylum yet." Together, they went into the house to join the others.

After dinner, Raya and Alice were clearing the dinner table and the two men were in the living room talking when Ocean roared a loud battle cry, startling the women in the kitchen. Dishes fell to the floor while Carl and Alex burst into laughter as Raya hollered up the stairs, "Ocean, I've told you several times not to do that indoors!"

Raya apologized to Alice as they started to clean up the mess while the two men were still laughing hysterically. Alice was becoming annoyed. She grabbed the broom and dustpan and walked into the living room. "Since the two of you think it's so funny. You can clean up the mess. Raya and I are gonna take a break."

The two women walked onto the patio and then burst into laughter. "I wish I could have seen the look on our faces," Alice stated.

Raya apologized again about the dishes and offered to replace them. "No, don't worry. I would've paid anything to hear those two laugh again." She paused to take a deep breath. "It's been three years since I've heard Alex laugh."

Raya could hear the sadness in Alice's voice as she continued her story. "My husband was supposed to be the ambassador at the alliance banquet, but he and Carl were called away at the last moment. That morning, I said goodbye to my husband," her eyes watered, "and I've been waiting ever since." Alice choked up, gasping for air as her tears fell like heavy rain. Raya shifted forms, placing her large paws on Alice's shoulders, trying to comfort her the only way she knew how.

Alex walked onto the patio, freezing in his tracks when he saw his wife crying while Raya towered over Alice, trying to ease her pain.

He knew why those tears were there. He put them there three years ago when they found 305. Every night, she was forced to watch helplessly as dark energy surrounded her husband, pulling his conscience into a universe, along with the others she scanned that day they opened Pandora's box.

The dreams always started out the same. Trapped in the scene of endless people, all suspended and held captive in her universe of lost souls. It was almost as if she were feeding on their nightmares, growing stronger the more she took. Even in his waking hours, she lingered in his mind. Raincheck wiped the tears forming in his eyes. "I'm sorry, Alice," he whispered under his breath.

He had always felt as if the military had reached into the grab bag of the universe and pulled something from the darkness that should have been left alone, and now all they could do was hope that fate favored the foolish.

Raincheck watched nervously as Raya slowly approached. Her icy stare and how she sauntered told him she wasn't happy about the dolls. "Raya, we were only following orders." He paused for a moment, reluctant to finish his sentence. "We don't have a choice anymore."

Raya shifted, looking up at him. "I know. Carl already told me... And I'll stand by his side." She walked back into the house to join Carl.

After dropping off Raya and Ocean, Carl went home but couldn't sleep. He'd spent the last hour tossing and turning. He was still feeling the intoxicating power of 305.

Carl had always been fascinated with danger, and women were no exception. He realized that the first time he met Raya. She was somebody you didn't want to meet on the battlefield.

You were either dead or dying when you knew she was there. Raya appealed to his darker nature, the person he used to be before he met Caroline. But now, that part of himself was returning, and he was quickly coming to terms with it. But he'd have to bury the past and say goodbye to the ones he lost. He didn't want them looking down from heaven and seeing the person he was becoming.

Carl drew a deep breath and got out of bed. While reaching for his bathrobe, he realized time was running out. There was less than a month before the grand opening, and the Mud Dogs' quarters still weren't ready. Not to mention the Dolls of Wrath could awaken at any moment. A blood storm was coming, and his job was to turn the candidates into Mud Dogs. Carl shook his head, knowing two years wasn't enough time, but it was all he had, not a day more.

"Captain Winfield. You have a communications request from first Lieutenant Skyler," the AI announced.

"All right, I'll take it in the kitchen."

"Transferring now."

Carl walked into the kitchen. "Lieutenant, what can I do for you?"

"Well, sir. I've done everything I can... And well, we're going to need a new AI. The universal AI is obsolete."

Carl scrunched up his face. "Lieutenant, that's a brand-new unit."

"Not for blind tech, sir, but not to worry. I talked to my dad, and he's willing to send over a new unit that will suit the Mud Dogs."

Carl was silent, deep in thought. "Lieutenant, I know your dad. What's the catch?"

Skyler laughed. "I don't know, sir. With my dad, it's hard to tell sometimes."

Carl smiled. "Well, give your dad my thanks and tell him I owe him one. And Skyler. Go home and get some sleep. That's an order."

"Yes, sir, I will. Thank you, and have a good night."

After the connection was severed, Carl poured a glass of wine and then made a call to Raya. "Hello, Carl. What can I do for you?"

"Raya, sorry to call you so late. I hope I didn't wake you."

"No, I was just going to bed. Why, what's up?"

"I have to talk to somebody about replacing the AI unit, so I'll be late, and I was wondering if you could round up volunteers for the candidates' quarters."

"Sure, I'll do it first thing in the morning." Raya suddenly had a worried tone in her voice. "Carl... Is something wrong?"

"What if I'm wrong about 305?" Carl was silent, thinking about all the lives he had gambled with. And the bargain he made with something dark and sinister, but even in the darkness, there was still hope.

"What if you're right, Carl?" Raya interrupted. "And even if you're not, it's too late to worry about it now. There's a reason they're here. We just don't know what that reason is... yet."

———◆◆◆———

The following day, Carl drove to the maintenance building and was greeted by the receptionist. "Good morning, sir. What can I do for you?"

"I need to speak with somebody about replacing an AI unit."

"That would be Captain Wicks. Unfortunately, he just stepped out for a moment, but if you have a seat, he should be back any time."

"All right, thank you, Sergeant."

Carl didn't have to wait long before a tall, dark-skinned gentleman entered the lobby carrying a breakfast tray. "Here you go, Doris, coffee and a bear claw."

Doris looked up at him, smiling. "Thank you, sir. Oh, sir,

this gentleman would like to speak with you."

Wicks turned to Carl. "Captain, step this way." Carl followed Wicks into his office. "Please, have a seat."

Carl explained the AI situation and having to replace it. Wicks looked at him, confused. "That's a new unit. There should be nothing wrong with it."

"It's not compatible with blind tech, and Colonel Skyler has offered to give us a new unit."

"Sam Skyler! What's the catch?"

Carl chuckled. "According to his daughter, there is none."

"That's right! Lieutenant Skyler. She's an ABS soldier, isn't she?"

"Yeah."

Wicks shook his head. "Those are some scary-ass soldiers. You couldn't pay me enough to go up against one of them."

"You and me both," Carl added, grinning.

Wicks looked over at Carl. "Let me make a few calls, and I'll get back to you by the end of the day. To switch over to the new unit, the communication shields will have to be down for about ten seconds, which could compromise Project Orphan, and we can't afford that. Especially with the spider queen looking for these children; she's far worse than the Mantis soldiers."

Wicks shot Carl a serious glance. "I only met her once. I was working off base, trying to make a little pocket money at a bar called Spiders, a really fancy place, nothing but money." Wicks leaned over. His elbows rested on his desk as he finished his sentence. "And in walks this woman! Business type." Wicks grinned. "This woman was fine... Real fine, and she was turning lotta heads. But she didn't care about all that. All she wanted was a drink and a little privacy. But there are always guys who can't take a hint, and this dude was one of them. He was hitting on her hard, but she just kept ignoring him. Finally, she had had enough of it, looked over at this dude, says to him, 'Stop talking to me now, and you'll save yourself a lot of embarrassment.'"

Wicks shook his head in disbelief. "All that fool had to do was leave her alone like she wanted. But you know what they say. 'Deeper the pocket, the bigger the prick.' This man's pockets were so deep he did whatever he wanted, and no one said shit about it. I looked away for a split second... I hear this crash. I turn around. Glass everywhere, liquor bottles smashed. "She had thrown this fool across the bar counter. Another bouncer and I ran up on her." Wicks had a stunned look on his face. She took our asses back to school real quick! The other bouncer was bigger than me, and I'm six foot six. She took him down so fast that I didn't even see it happen, and I was behind him."

Carl drew back his head in surprise. "Damn, she did all that?"

"Oh yeah!" Wicks shook his head, and his eyes widened. "As a college graduate, you would think I would have better sense. But oh no, not me. I went at her, fists blazing. I swung with everything I had. I figure if she's gonna fight like a man, she's gonna go down like one... She caught my swing with one hand, and as she was crushing every bone in my fist, she looked me dead in the eyes and said, 'You're not man enough.' The next thing I knew, she threw my ass like a bad habit. It took me two years to learn how to walk again. Even today, I still feel like the luckiest man in the universe."

Carl shot him a puzzled look. "Lucky! How do you come to that conclusion?"

"The infantry platoon she ran into before us wasn't so lucky. They were covered in spiderwebs and drained of fluids."

His story had struck a nerve. Carl could feel himself getting angry. It was one more reason to make the Shezón pay. Carl pulled himself together and then stood up from his chair. "Thank you, Captain," he said, extending his hand.

Wicks stood up and shook it. "I'm not saying you can't have your unit. We must be cautious because we are no match for the spider queen. I'll get a hold of Colonel Skyler and set up something with him."

Carl was heading back to his office when he met up with Lieutenant Skyler. She was wearing her PT uniform, and in her hand was a light blue gym bag with the Marine emblem and the words "Death from the shadows" in big bloodred letters. "Lieutenant, are you busy at the moment?"

"No, sir. I was just on my way to the training room."

"About that, I noticed you haven't taken your combat remembrance test yet."

"Well, sir. I've been trying, but I can't find anybody to give me the test."

"Nobody!" Carl said, trying to sound surprised.

"No one, sir," she responded disappointedly.

Carl was familiar with the look in her eyes. It was the same look Tylee had when she discovered she couldn't join the Little League boxing team because she was a girl. He agreed to teach her how to box but didn't calculate her height when he told her to hit Daddy's stomach. Needless to say, she dropped him with one punch when she zeroed in on a new target.

Carl felt bad for Lieutenant Skyler. He knew it was because she was an ABS soldier. The one soldier you didn't want to go up against for any reason. And their motto, "Death from the shadows," did little to encourage people. Any second, his daddy instincts were about to kick in and say something he'd regret. "All right, Lieutenant, give me ten minutes, and I'll meet you in the testing room."

"Oh, sir, thank you so much," she said, kissing him on the cheek. He only hoped it wasn't the kiss of death.

Carl went to his office, grabbed his gym bag, and then poked his head into Raya's office to see her sitting at her desk. "I'll be in the testing room, giving Lieutenant Skyler her combat test."

"All right, Carl. Just be careful, don't say anything stupid," she responded, laughing.

"What's that supposed to mean?" Carl chuckled.

She looked up at him with a straight face. "You heard me."

Carl changed into his PT uniform and walked into the testing room to see Lieutenant Skyler practicing for the test. In her hand was a Marine battle saber, a weapon made to take down the Mantis soldiers. It was made of semi-transparent steel, and almost impossible to see it coming or avoid its vicious bite. He knew she'd have no problems passing, and he wanted her to take the test to see for himself how good ABS soldiers were. It almost brought tears to his eyes, watching her swing the saber as if it were a part of her body, hitting every digital target the AI threw at her. She wasn't just tough, she was Marine tough, and he was honored to have her.

He knew the Marines hadn't given her up easily, but they did, and he was grateful to them. With blind tech and Lieutenant Skyler on the team, the Mud Dogs' odds of survival just shot up. Carl gave Lieutenant Skyler applause, and she stopped and turned around. "Oh, hello, sir."

"Hello, Lieutenant, and congratulations. You just completed two of the requirements."

She had a confused look on her face. "Sir, I don't understand."

"The practice, Lieutenant... Told me everything I needed to know."

"Thank you, sir!"

"Don't thank me yet. We still have the hand-to-hand... That's going to be a tough one."

"Understand, sir."

Together, they walked over to the mat. "All right, lieutenant, your goal is to pin me to the mat... I'm not gonna go easy. Do you understand?"

"Yes, sir, I understand," she said nervously.

As they got into position, Carl looked over at the Lieutenant. "All right, Lieutenant, give me what you got." Before he knew it, she grabbed his arm and threw him over her shoulder. He landed so hard on his back it echoed in the room.

Lieutenant Skyler ran over to him in a panic. "Oh, sir, I'm so sorry!"

"Don't be. I got exactly what I asked for," he said, trying to laugh, but the pain in his back cut it short.

As he was walking back to his office, Raya was passing by. "Carl, the girls and I are going over to the Mud Dogs' quarters to clean up."

"Okay, tell them not to worry. I'll handle the extra load."

"It's all done. We finished it this morning... The office is complete and ready for operation."

Carl was pleasantly surprised. "Wow, that's great!" he said, reaching over to give her a pat on the shoulder when he felt a sharp pain in his back.

Raya looked at him with a suspicious smile. "So, what did you say?"

Carl gave her his best poker face. "What makes you think I said anything?"

She looked up at him. "Call it a hunch," she responded sarcastically as she playfully slapped him on the back.

Carl flinched and gave her a grumpy look. "I'm not talking to you anymore," he grumbled, walking back to his office.

Raya laughed, thinking how cute his grumpy face looked. "Goodbye, Carl!" she said lovingly.

━━━━•◆•━━━━

When Carl walked into the office the following day, everyone was gone, including the receptionist. There was a note on his desk from Raya. "Carl, everyone's at the Mud Dogs' quarters, waiting for the furniture to arrive."

Carl was returning from lunch when he got a communications request from Captain Boswell. "Captain! What can I do for you?"

"Winfield, my men are down there now trying to deliver the furniture you requested. Now, your girls won't let them through."

Carl was suspicious. "All right, Boswell, I'll meet you down there."

There was a moment of hesitation before he spoke. "All right, Winfield. Give me twenty minutes."

When Carl got there, there was a commotion going on. The ladies were on one side, and the movers on the other. In the middle was Sergeant Epstein, shouting obscenities at one of the movers who was towering over her with tears in his eyes. Carl was momentarily confused until he got closer and noticed her hand clenched tightly to the crotch of his pants. "Not so tough now, are you!"

Carl was shocked. Epstein was five foot three and very petite, while this guy was almost the same size as himself, and she had him in tears. Carl almost felt sympathy pains for the man who was unfortunate enough to see a side of Sergeant Epstein he didn't know she had. "Sergeant, care to tell me what's going on?" he asked, trying not to laugh.

Epstein calmed. "Well, sir, we told them they weren't bringing that old smelly furniture into the Mud Dogs' quarters." She was silent for a moment and then burst into anger, gritting her teeth. "Then this asshole comes over thinking he's going to kick my ass if I don't move. Who's the bitch now?" she hollered, squeezing and shaking her hand as the man screamed in agony.

Carl walked over, trying to calm her down while holding back his laughter. "All right, Sergeant, I'd say he's had enough."

"Yes, sir," she said meekly, then released the man, who fell to the ground in the fetal position, moaning in pain.

Carl followed Epstein over to the furniture. Carl was furious, seeing the condition it was in. It smelled of mildew and was covered in dust as if it had been stored in somebody's basement, forgotten for centuries.

Captain Boswell was coming onto the scene. He had a concerned look on his face. "Look, Winfield. There was a mix-up. This is just temporary until I can find out what happened." The look on his face and the tone of his voice was anything but convincing.

Carl felt his blood pressure rise while his hand slightly trembled, trying not to lose his temper. "I suggest you correct this little mishap real soon, or good luck getting past them," he told him, walking back to his transport.

"Come on, Winfield, gimme a break here."

"I am. That's why I'm walking away. Next time, you'll be dealing with me. I'm not as nice as they are."

━━━━━◆◆◆◆◆━━━━━

Carl looked at the timepiece on his desk; it was almost five o'clock, and he still had work to finish. He decided to call Tylee and let her know he was going to be late. "All right, Dad." There was silence, and then Tylee spoke. "Dad, I know it's not easy moving on with your life, but you are not alone. You have Ocean's mom now... So don't screw it up!" she chuckled.

Carl laughed until there were tears in his eyes. "All right, baby girl, you got my promise... I won't screw it up." Carl severed the connection and then opened the Mud Dog files.

Despite coming from different backgrounds, the candidates were all born with the NewGen parasite and had public infractions against them, such as aggressive behavior or disturbing the peace. People deemed them socially dysfunctional and treated them like second-class citizens. Carl had nothing but admiration for these girls. Even though they knew what they were getting into, they all agreed it was better to die on the battlefield than in the streets. At least on the battlefield, you were dying as somebody. All they wanted was a better way of life and a little respect, and the only way they could get it was in the Army, and he would make damn sure they did.

Everyone in the office had given their all to the program, and now it was time for him to do the same. He knew because of the parasite, the candidates were capable of so much more, but two years wasn't enough time. But like they say, "If there's a will, there's a way."

Carl had just completed the last of his work when there was a knock at the door. "Come in!"

"Oh good, you're here." Captain Wicks walked into the office. "I talked to Colonel Skyler. They're sending technicians to install the new AI sometime this Wednesday."

"Well, that's great... Did you find out why he's doing it?"

Wicks shook his head. "He never said... My guess is it's to protect his little girl."

"Yeah, but who's gonna protect us from her?"

Wicks looked at him, grinning. "You know from experience, do you?"

Carl told him about the remembrance test. The two men laughed. "You're a braver man than me, Winfield." They shook hands and parted ways.

Carl locked up the office and headed for the security desk.

"Good evening, sir." Sergeant Williams nodded his head, then held out the security pad.

Carl put his hand to it. "Good evening, Williams. How are you doing?"

Williams pulled the pad away. "I'm good, sir. What about you?"

"Better now!"

Williams smiled and opened the security doors. "Enjoy your night, sir."

"Oh, Williams, you know a lot about women, don't you?"

"My fair share! Why?"

"What's the best way to make them happy?"

Carl's jaw dropped when Williams suddenly stood up.

He had to have been eight feet or taller. "I don't know about Humans, but Evolutions like the simpler things, dinner, dancing, and even going for walks, but you gotta be careful with them."

"Why is that?" he asked, looking up at Williams.

"They're quick-tempered and unforgiving." There was a moment Williams's face had no expression, and then he smiled. "Have a good night, sir.

Carl thanked Williams and headed to his transport.

Carl was driving by the Mud Dogs' quarters when he noticed the lights were still on and decided to stop and see if he could help. Inside, it was quiet. "Hello, anyone here?"

"Just me! Carl," Raya responded, coming down the hallway.

He smiled like a schoolboy as the rhythm of his heartbeat changed when she came into view. Even with the smeared dirt on her cheeks and cleaning pails in her hands, she was just as beautiful, if not more. "I just came to see if I could help."

He pulled her into his arms and moved in for a kiss. "Carl, I'm afraid you're too late. Everybody's..." She lost her breath as Carl muffled her words. Raya dropped the buckets and wrapped her arms around Carl.

Their kiss lasted until they had to stop for air. "The night is still young. What do you say we take advantage of it?"

His voice was deep, sending warm shivers racing through her. "Okay, Carl, what did you have in mind?"

"I figured we could hang out at Bravo Six. You can show me your world."

"Quite the brave man, aren't you!" she responded playfully.

"With you by my side, how can I not?" He kissed her once again before they headed into the night.

They were walking down the street of Bravo Six when a woman from one of the shops called out to Raya. "Yes, Elder," Raya answered.

"Will you be a sweetheart and feed the elder race? I've been in Human form too long, and now it's getting the best of me." She chuckled.

Raya walked over to her and smiled. "Of course I will."

Despite her youthful appearance, she walked and spoke like an old woman. She handed Raya a fifty-pound bag of cat food, thanked her, and then shifted into a giant gray wolf. "I hope you feel better!" Raya called out as she disappeared down the street.

As they strolled down a narrow alley, Carl inquired about the Elder race.

Raya took a moment to reflect before answering. "What you refer to as house cats, we call the Elder race. They are the ancestors of all Uteakons, as we evolved from the cats that remained on Earth. These cats were scavengers, feeding on anything they could find, including the refuse from genetic labs. This altered their DNA; many cats died from genetic pollution. Those who survived passed on their strength to their offspring, eventually leading to the evolution of a new race."

Raya opened the bag and poured it into a giant metal dish in the center of the alley. As swarms of noisy cats appeared out of nowhere, Raya smiled. "Now you know where Uteakons come from."

"Uteakons are amazing people," Carl whispered as they headed for the center of town.

Carl felt like a schoolboy as they casually strolled down the street of Bravo Six, Raya's hand in his. Their fingers locked together while his emotions swirled around like a teenager on his first date, and when she kissed him, he would always blush as if it were his first. There were mixed couples everywhere he looked, all young and in love. There was even a lovers' spat. A tall Human girl was storming out of a building, fuming angrily, followed by her Newtopian boyfriend. "Babe, you know I'm not used to that Human stuff," he tried pleading with her.

She stopped and became even angrier. "I suggest you get used to it real fast... Otherwise, your nights are gonna get pretty damn cold!" She turned and walked away from him.

Carl chuckled as the tall Newtopian followed after her, pleading his case to deaf ears.

Carl couldn't believe how beautiful and strange Raya's world was. Everything from the restaurants to the shops sold things he had never heard of. The only thing familiar to him was the early nineteenth-century buildings that looked as if they were made of brick. The streets were dimly lit, and the sound of people echoed as Humans and Evolutions casually mingled.

"I feel like Humans have forgotten how to make places like this," he marveled, half to himself.

Beside him, Raya snickered. "There's much you've forgotten. While you fled your past for the stars, we picked up the pieces. Your art, your craft, your architecture, your music. We kept it all safe. We've been waiting for you to value it as we do."

Carl was getting hungry and suggested they find a place to eat. Raya looked at him with a smile. "Carl, they don't serve Human food here, and they don't serve meat."

"No meat, why?"

"Because meat taken off the hunting grounds is considered selfish; few Evolutions will eat it. Besides, we prefer it fresh."

Raya was silent, wondering about Carl. She loved being with him and welcomed the attention he gave her. But why? What did he see in her that Uteakon males didn't? An Uteakon male only paid attention to a female when she was in heat.

And even then, he'd break the ice with a wet, cold nose to her backside, hardly romantic. *The least they could do is show some kind of gratitude*, she was thinking to herself when Carl interrupted her silence.

"Well then, you can order for both of us," he responded with a kiss.

They stopped at a Newtopian deli. Raya ordered mushroom steak sandwiches to go. It was served on Rowbarry bread with a light coating of lemon pepper.

Carl was enjoying the city nightlife when Raya grabbed his arm as everybody suddenly started running into the buildings. "Come on, Carl, we gotta get out of the rain!"

He looked at her as if she were crazy. "Rain! What rain?"

No sooner had he asked the question than it began pouring as Raya burst into laughter. He had always believed the sexiest quality of a woman was her happiness and that warm feeling it left you with.

Raya suddenly interrupted his thoughts. "Carl, you're getting wet!"

He smiled and pulled her into his arms. "Now, we're getting wet."

Together, they laughed and then headed into the coffee and tea lounge.

The following day, Raya had half awakened to the sound of somebody pounding on her door. "All right, all right, I'm coming," she grumbled.

It was a little after 3 AM, and she was annoyed. Whoever was at the door was still pounding on it. "Stop pounding on the damn door!" she hollered.

Raya was becoming angry when the pounding got louder and more rapid. She quickened her pace, ready to give them a piece of her mind. She opened the door and fell silent as tears began streaming down her cheeks. "Hi, Mom," the visitor said with the biggest smile she had ever seen.

Raya jumped into her son's arms. "Remix!"

Ocean heard the noise and came out of her room, still in her birth form. "Mom, what's going on?" she roared.

Ocean turned the corner and burst into tears when she saw her brother standing at the door holding their sobbing mother. "Hey, squirt... It's good to see you again."

Raya suddenly found herself pinned between her children as Ocean's calico paws rested on Remix's shoulders, towering over them.

Remix looked up at Ocean. "I missed you, squirt."

Raya wanted to spend time with her son and sent Carl a text telling him she wouldn't be in the office today. She was surprised when Carl responded immediately. "That's fine. I was going to send everybody home. Nothing to do."

"Why are you up so early?" she texted.

Carl texted back, "Couldn't sleep, too much on my mind."

"Carl, why don't you come over and meet Remix? Spend some time with us. It might make you feel better."

"Okay, I have to take my daughters to school, and then I'll be over."

"Great, I'll see you then."

Ocean looked over at her mother with a big smile. "Was that Carl?"

"Yes, and I invited him over."

Remix looked at the both of them, curious as to whom they were talking about. "Who's Carl?"

Ocean looked at her brother, smiling. "Mom's boyfriend. He's Human, and she mated with him twice." Ocean giggled.

Raya blushed. "All right, little miss, tell everything. I'm sure your brother didn't come all this way to hear about that."

Remix looked over at his mother with a malevolent grin. "Mom...are you sure that's okay at your age?"

Raya kissed him on the cheek, smiling. "Careful... I brought you into this universe, and I'll take you out of it."

Remix could feel the tenseness in his body. He had been in Human form too long and was beginning to feel the stress.

Raya opened the closet and pulled out a hanger. "Sweetie, why don't you give me your clothes and get comfortable?"

"Okay, Mom," he said, doing as he was told.

Raya burst into tears when she saw the scars on his back. They were deep and looked as if they had just healed.

Remix turned and held her in his arms. His voice was soft and gentle. "Mom, please don't cry... I'm a lot stronger than I look...after all, I got your strength and your knowledge, and that's kept me going. Besides, you know what they say. Behind every great soldier, there's Mom."

She looked up at him with a teary smile. "They don't say that."

"They should." He hugged her and kissed her cheek.

Remix turned and shifted, letting out a loud, hollow growl. Remix had become a champion. He was almost the size of his grandfather, but more robust. Despite his sweet gesture, his size and strength came from his father, who was from the Highlands of Uteaka and had white fur with black markings that blended with the snowy tundra, but on the Backlands, his white coat worked against him. Remix quickly overcame his weakness. In his Human form, his black skin allowed him to move more easily through the shadows, sneaking up on prey that was usually too fast to catch. By the time they knew he was there, it was too late. He was already shifting forms as he was lunging for them. But even this was little comfort knowing he was going up against the Shezón.

Raya was enjoying the moment, watching her children sleep. It felt like old times. Remix was in the living room trying to sleep while his little sister curled up next to him with her cheek to his; his tail twitched out of protest. Eventually, he'd realize she wasn't going anywhere, his tail would stop twitching, and they would sleep like two peas in a pod.

Raya was in the kitchen making coffee when Carl knocked on the door. "Come in, Carl," she hollered.

Carl came around the corner with a guilty look on his face as Zoe and Tylee followed behind him. "They wanted to meet Ocean's brother."

Raya looked at the girls, smiling. "He's right behind you."

Tylee and Zoe gasped as they turned to see a majestic white feline with black markings on his side. Carl was just as speechless as his daughters, staring into his moon-blue eyes. His daughters got startled as Remix let out a loud roar, unaware they didn't speak feline. But their fear turned to smiles as Remix shifted forms. "I'm sorry, I didn't mean to scare you. I was just saying good morning," he said in a deep voice.

"That's okay!" Tylee and Zoe responded in unison as they shamelessly looked him up and down.

Carl was uneasy seeing his daughters follow Remix and Ocean into her bedroom. He also knew that Evolution males were very respectful toward females and wouldn't make any moves on them. His daughters, on the other hand, were not as refined. After a while, Remix came out of the room, and Zoe followed after him. He could tell by the look in her eyes and the way her smile radiated that she was on a mission.

Carl thanked Raya for the wonderful day and gathered his daughters. "Tomorrow, the new AI is going up, and all the computers will be down for a while, so you can stay home and spend time with Remix before he leaves. And then tomorrow night, if you want, we can go off base." He paused for a moment. "There's this place called Spiders I've always wanted to check out."

Raya looked at him with a blushing smile. "I would love that, Carl, thank you," she responded with a passionate kiss.

As they pulled up to the parking lot of Spiders, Carl was still puzzled about the Uteakan security guard's reaction when he saw Raya. The guard was about to say something to him when he suddenly changed his mind and told them to have a good night.

Carl smiled as he looked over at Raya. "We're here." He got out of the vehicle and opened her door for her. Together they walked toward the building. He was a little nervous as they approached the entrance. It was a fancy place, and more of a social lounge than a bar. He had heard about it through conversations but never thought to check it out. He was always unsure how they would react to his dark skin or his Evolution shifter companion.

Carl smiled and opened the door for Raya. "Beauty first."

He was relieved to see a mixture of people, Evolutions and Humans, socializing and dancing.

They were even greeted by a tall, beautiful, dark-skinned woman. "Good evening. Welcome to Spiders. My name is Lorraine, and I'll be your server tonight," she said, easing his nervousness.

Carl smiled as they followed Lorraine to a table near the dance floor. She seemed to be popular with the patrons, especially the men, who greeted her by name when she passed by. When they were seated, Lorraine smiled and took out her order pad. "And what can I get you good folks tonight?"

Carl decided to leave it up to Lorraine. "Surprise me!"

"Very well, sir," she responded pleasantly, then turned to Raya, "and you, ma'am?"

"I don't like surprises, so I'll take an Uteakon Lacour if you don't mind."

Carl looked at Raya. "Come on, where's your sense of adventure?"

"At home, next to my patience," she responded sarcastically.

Carl laughed and reached for her hand as the band played Boyz II Men. "Care to dance?"

"Carl, I don't know how to dance to this," she responded bashfully.

"Do you trust me?"

His deep voice sent shivers racing through her as she blushed. "Yes!"

He loved watching the smile on her face as she tried to keep up with the dance moves. Once or twice, she stumbled, but he always caught her. He wished moments like this would last forever, but in reality, forever never comes.

Carl began to notice that the two of them were attracting attention from one of the VIP tables. Three young men were staring at them. No doubt they were college students in their early twenties, with the arrogance of upper-class money. And money has the loudest voice, especially when drunk. Carl knew it wouldn't take much to light their fuse. It was clear that the big guy in the black leather suit wasn't happy to see him with Raya. The last thing he needed was a drunken scene to get Raya worked up.

Carl cursed his luck as he suddenly realized why the Uteakon guard at the entrance had looked nervous, seeing Raya sitting on the passenger side of his transport. The guard had tried to warn him, when Raya silenced him with a glance. Now Carl knew it was best to de-escalate the situation before it began.

"How about we give our old bones a rest," he suggested to Raya.

Raya reluctantly agreed. Carl felt terrible as they were walking back to their table, and the three jerks continued to leer. He knew she didn't deserve to be treated like that. "Raya, I'm sorry."

She looked at him and smiled. "Carl, it's okay!" Before he knew it, she was kissing his lips.

Suddenly, Carl heard a commotion at the VIP table. He turned just in time to see Leather Brute being held back by his two buddies, a tall, blonde-haired, scraggly-looking man and a short, stocky guy. "Hey, jungle boy, why don't you stick to your own women," Brute shouted.

The room fell silent. Carl was furious and wanted to confront him. But he knew if he did, it could jeopardize the Mud Dog program. "Come on, Raya. Just ignore them."

Raya had a confused look on her face. "Carl, what does he mean, stick to your own women? Are you gonna get in trouble for being with me?" Her hands trembled. "I don't wanna be here anymore."

Carl tried to calm her down. "Okay, okay, we'll just leave right now."

They were walking away and almost to the door when Leather Brute threw a bottle at him. "Hey, boy! Don't turn your back on me!" he shouted.

The words, quick-tempered and unforgiving, echoed in Carl's mind as Raya caught the bottle and snapped her attention toward the three men. Carl glanced over at the VIP table to see Leather Brute still being held back by his buddies. For a brief moment, he wished they'd let him go. Carl turned his attention back to Raya, holding her arm to gently restrain and calm her. "Just ignore them, please. They're just dumb kids who had too much to drink."

The expression on her face showed that she was beyond annoyed, and his words fell on deaf ears. Raya yanked her arm from his hand and gave him the bottle the drunk had thrown. The sudden calm look in her eyes and the playful tone in her voice sent a chill racing through him. "They're not kids. They're men. Rude and disrespectful, and I won't ignore it."

Carl watched nervously as she casually strolled over to their table. "What would you morons say if I told you I was black and more kitty than you can handle?" The tone of her voice was seductive. Without a smile or a hint of deception, like easy prey, the men were lured and blinded by beauty, unaware of the Huntress watching them.

Scraggly Man got up from his chair and slowly approached her, grinning from ear to ear. She watched him, undecided about what she found more irritating about the man: his sly, hungry look or how he strutted. "You're a feisty little one, ain't you!"

Raya locked his scent and the other things she didn't like about him into her memories. "So I've been told," she said, tempted to claw the grin off his face.

"So, who do you want first?"

Before Raya could answer, Leather Brute got up from his chair and rudely pushed Scraggly Man to the side. "Me, I'm going first." He looked her in the eyes with a cold, angry gaze. "So you decided you wanted a real man."

She knew by the tone of his voice that he wanted to punish her for being with Carl. Her father's voice had the same tone when he found out about her and the corporal. The very thought of it angered her even more. Like her father, the man had no right to make her decisions, and there was a vast difference between him and her father.

"We'll go in the back, and I'll let you prove it," he leered, grabbing his crotch with an angry smile.

Her eyes briefly followed his hand. "Why don't we prove it right here, or aren't you man enough?"

Carl walked over and tried to break it up. "Raya, let's just go somewhere else. I know a better place."

"Carl! We're not going anywhere. I'm a big girl and can handle myself!"

"I know. That's what I'm afraid of."

Raya put her hands on Carl's shoulders and looked into his eyes, angering Leather Brute even more. "Relax, Carl. We're just having fun," she reassured him with a calm, almost playful tone.

"Hey jungle boy, the lady's talking to me," the Brute shouted over her head.

Carl was tired of listening to him throwing racial slurs. Unaware she wasn't Human, these men only saw a beautiful white woman who looked young enough to be his daughter, and with the combination of ignorance and alcohol, they were asking for trouble. Carl shook his head and decided to leave the fool to his fate. "Enjoy." He grinned and walked back to the table.

By now, the whole lounge was engrossed in the drama as Brute turned his attention back to Raya. "Even your boyfriend knows who the real man is."

She hated the arrogant tone in his voice, and every part of her wanted to silence him, but instead, she watched curiously and with no expression as he proceeded to unzip his pants, exposing himself to her. "Now prove it," he demanded.

Raya looked up at him with a malevolent smile. "Gladly." Then she shifted into her feline form, flexed her claws, and let out a deafening roar.

The lounge exploded into laughter as the man's black leather pants fell to his ankles. His face turned pale when he felt her warm breath on his genitals. People were laughing so hard, there wasn't a dry eye in the house as the "real man" went screaming out the door, followed by his two cronies.

Raya shifted back to her Human form. "Well, that was fun." She smiled and walked to the table.

Carl looked at her, surprised. "Where'd you learn to talk like that?"

"From those romance movies."

Carl tried to keep a straight face. "I told you those aren't romance movies."

"It looked pretty romantic to me!" she responded with a confused look on her face.

Carl burst into laughter and put a hand on her cheek. "I really enjoy being with you," he whispered, followed by a kiss.

She looked at him with a blushing smile. "Are you falling in love with me?"

Carl looked at her calmly. "I don't know...maybe! It depends. Would it be a bad thing?"

"I can think of worse," she replied with a playful kiss. Then they embraced, laughed together, and finished their drinks.

Raya got up to use the restroom while Carl went for their transport. "I'll meet you outside then," he told her.

•••◆•••

Raya was standing outside Spiders, waiting for Carl to pull up with the transport, when a gunshot rang out, followed by a woman's scream. Her first thought was Carl. She followed the crowd as they ran to the parking lot to see a woman shouting hysterically and pointing toward the woods. "They ran that way!"

Fearing the worst, Raya ran toward where Carl's transport was parked. Her heart jumped when she saw him from afar, lying in a puddle of blood beside the vehicle. She ran to him in a panic. "Carl," Raya screamed, taking him in her arms, her tears falling on him as she tried to get her words out. "I'm sorry, Carl, I should have listened to you!" But Carl was unresponsive. "Carl, don't leave me... Please!"

Suddenly, a couple broke through the crowd and ran as fast as they could to Carl's side. "It's okay, I'm a doctor, and my wife is a nurse!"

She watched as the couple tore Carl's shirt open to see blood pouring from a bullet wound in his stomach. They worked frantically to keep Carl alive until the paramedics showed up.

Raya was distraught and in tears. *Why did they go after Carl,* she thought, *when I was the one who started it?* A woman from the crowd helped Raya to her feet, trying to give her as much comfort as she could. Then a man in a uniform spoke to her in a gentle but authoritative voice.

"Hello, ma'am, my name is Sergeant Kendelson. I'm with the military police," he said in a sympathetic tone. Then he took an ID scan and saw she was an Uteakan. From his experience with Evolutions, they were not violent by nature and weren't used to seeing this kind of crime. Raya stood silently, looking into his blue eyes as he read the scan results. "Ma'am," he asked, "do you know who did this?"

"They did this because of me, because I'm not Human." She told him about the three men in the bar, how they had called Carl "jungle boy," whatever that meant, but she knew it was an insult, how they seemed upset that she and Carl were together.

Kendelson tried to comfort her as best he could, but the only comfort he could give her was a few kind words. "Don't blame yourself for this... It's not your fault."

From what she told him, he knew it was a hate crime, but didn't know how to explain racial hatred among Humans. No matter how he worded it, the answer wouldn't make any more sense to her than it did to him. After all these centuries, the old Earth prejudices refused to die... So he didn't say anything about that, for fear that it would upset her even more than she already was. "Can I give you a ride somewhere?" he asked.

"No, thank you. I'll walk," she replied, turning toward the forest.

Raya was angry, and Kendelson didn't blame her, but he also knew why she was going into the woods. "Ma'am, I can't stop you from going after them, but I can tell you that killing those men would only make things worse between Humans and Evolutions."

"Then what am I supposed to do? Let them get away with what they did?" she hissed.

"Ma'am, I know how you feel, and I want nothing more than to bring these men to justice."

"Then why don't you?"

Kendelson was silent, thinking about his answer. "I'm sorry, I can't right now. It's mating season for the boar, and they prowl those woods at night. It'd be too dangerous for anyone out there."

Raya gave him a disappointed look. "Good night, then, Sergeant," she said, shifting form to feline and continuing toward the trees.

Kendelson thought about the crime scene as he walked back to his vehicle. He knew that during mating season, the chances of those men being killed by the boar were greater than at any other time of the year. He didn't want to see Raya do something that she would regret. Kendelson stopped and turned his head toward her. "Word of advice, ma'am, don't kill those men, lotta boar out there tonight... They have a strong taste for Human flesh," he said, putting the emphasis on Human. He hoped she would take the hint. Then he entered his vehicle and drove away.

Raya thought hard about his words as she entered the forest. Kendelson was right. If the boar were on the hunt, those men would not survive the night. But the image of Carl lying in a puddle of blood echoed in her mind. She wasn't going to let them get away with what they did.

The musky scent of boar in the woods was strong and made her stomach rumble, which always triggered her instinct to pursue and take down prey. But tonight she had bigger game to hunt, and her stomach would just have to rumble. Raya only hoped she had the self-control not to kill the men before the boar did. She knew the boar would flee the area if they picked up her scent or heard her growl. The only way her plan would be successful was to become invisible to the boar, who always kept a ten-mile distance from the base for fear of being hunted by the Evolutions.

Raya took out some masking spray from her handbag, becoming invisible to the boar's keen sense of smell as she covered herself with it. This was only a temporary fix, but if she was lucky, it would last long enough for her plan to succeed. She had to act quickly. If the men got within ten miles of the base, the boar wouldn't pursue them.

Raya hung her handbag on a tree branch, she had already been in feline form, and went on the hunt. It wasn't long before she picked up their scent. One of the men had urinated on the ground, and the other two had stepped in it, leaving an easy trail for her—and the boar—to track. To the boar, they were easy prey. It was only a matter of time before they picked up their scent. But their odds of survival for the men were greater with the three of them together. All that was about to change.

When she found the men, they were sitting on an old fallen log, boasting proudly of what they had done. She didn't understand the slang they were using, but there was something about how the words sounded that she didn't like. She remained silent among the trees, holding back her tears as she listened to them talk about Carl as if his life meant nothing.

"Look at that. Jungle boy bled all over my new suit," Brute whined while the other two laughed.

Raya's eyes filled with tears of heartbreak while the reality of losing Carl lingered in her soul. She had promised to protect him and failed, and now he was paying the price. Raya dried her tears, then continued listening and plotting. She planned to separate the men and then keep them in a state of panic, making it easy for her to lead them to the boar. She had learned from her veteran sisters that Humans have two weaknesses that slow them down: they have a poor sense of smell and can't see in the dark.

She gathered from their conversation that Leather Brute wasn't very bright. He was arrogant and underestimated the danger when it came to the nocturnal. She was okay with that because tonight she was going to teach them a lesson they'd never forget.

Raya was trying to decide which one to take first when Scraggly Man made her decision for her. He was jittery and looked around every time he heard a noise. "What was that?"

"What are you afraid of?" shouted the brutish man.

Scraggly Man stood up. "Boar; they eat Humans, you know."

"So we eat them, they eat us. Who cares?"

"I do! I don't want to be eaten," he responded angrily.

"Relax, you wuss. Everyone knows animals are afraid of Humans."

Scraggly Man walked over to Brute, looking him in the eyes. "Oh yeah, what about that cat chick? She wasn't...afraid of us."

Brute stood up and spoke with a cocky tone. "Her! What are you worried about her for? She's probably hiding in a closet, afraid the bad guys will get her."

Even though she wanted to rip them from limb to limb, Raya kept calm and focused, waiting for the right moment as the two men burst into laughter. Then Scraggly Man shook his head in disbelief as he walked away from them, questioning their intelligence. "I'm gonna take a leak," he muttered.

Raya followed ten feet behind him until he found a tree and began urinating on it. She shifted into Human form and began taunting him, stepping on dry leaves. "Brute, is that you?" he called out.

She remained silent, watching him through the shadows as she continued taunting.

Scraggly Man began to panic. "Come on, guys, stop messing around. This ain't funny!"

Raya casually sauntered out of the shadows. "I'm not laughing."

Even in the dark, she could see his complexion turning pale as he slowly turned around to see her staring at him. He had that familiar look of fear in his eyes, one she had seen many times in her prey, just before they panicked. He tried desperately to reason with her. "Look, you gotta believe me. I didn't kill the colored guy. Brute did. He doesn't like the colored."

She was becoming more angry, listening to his selfish desperation.

"I'll turn myself in... Tell the cops everything. Just don't hurt..."

"You're not going to live long enough for that," she interrupted.

As she predicted, Scraggly Man ran off in a panic, unaware

that the boar had already picked up his scent. She watched as he ran far enough away that the other two wouldn't find him, yet close enough that they could hear him screaming.

Raya shifted and took off after her frightened prey. Scraggly Man was faster than she had anticipated, which made the chase even more exciting. But it was short-lived as she caught his left leg, tearing it from the socket as she slammed him to the ground. His screams echoed as the blood poured from where his leg used to be. Raya turned and headed back to the fallen tree, listening to the scraggly man's screams as the boar ate him alive.

The other two men heard the screams and ran blindly toward the base. Raya listened to Stocky Guy trying desperately to keep up with Brute. "Wait, don't leave me," he begged, quickening his pace as Raya closed in on him. "Help! Something's after..." His words were replaced by screams as Raya caught him from behind, her claws tearing shirt and flesh off his back as she forced him to the ground. Within a split second, her jaws were locked on his arm, pulling and shaking until it severed from his shoulder. With Stocky Man screaming, the boar quickly closed in on him. Raya dropped the bloody arm to pursue the last man.

She had no problem picking up the scent of leather and blood. By the strength of the odor, she could tell Brute wasn't far away. But he had already crossed the ten-mile border, which meant the boar wouldn't pursue him. She would have to drag him back, preferably kicking and screaming.

Raya continued stalking him from the shadows, keeping only enough distance to let him know she was there. By the sound of his running, she knew the brutish man was getting tired and quickened her pace, wearing him down faster. Brute had exhausted his energy and couldn't run any further. He stopped and pulled out his gun. "Come on, let's see what you got," he hollered with a confident tone, firing at anything that moved.

Raya had an intense feeling of satisfaction toying with him, waiting for the right moment and sound. And then it came... Click, click. Brute was out of bullets and out of luck. Raya emerged from the shadows, her large yellow eyes staring him down as she cautiously approached him. Desperately, he threw the empty gun at her as he made his getaway, screaming at the top of his lungs for help. Raya watched as the weapon flew past her and continued her pursuit until he tripped. She stopped and shifted to Human. There were tears in his eyes as he recognized her and begged for his life.

"Please have mercy," he sobbed.

She looked at Brute with no expression. "Mercy? Mercy doesn't feed hungry kittens...and even if I had it, you'd be the last person to get it."

Raya shifted back to feline and sank her jaws deep into his right shoulder. His scream echoed through the woods as her jaws shattered bone, while his blood left a foul taste in her mouth. Shifting back to Human form, she grabbed him by the collar and dragged him back into the boar's territory, kicking and screaming.

By now, the boar was well aware of her presence. With their strong taste for human flesh, she knew they would become brave and willing to fight her for the prey. She smiled and let go of Brute's collar. "Bon appetit!" she hollered, walking away.

---

Raya had an overwhelming feeling of satisfaction as she returned to the parking lot. Sergeant Kendelson was standing beside his vehicle, waiting for her.

"Are you going to arrest me now?" Raya asked. She was willing to take responsibility for her actions, but no matter what they did to her, it wouldn't even come close to the fee Carl had paid for her pride.

Kendelson stood silently, looking at her thoughtfully before taking off his coat. "Even from here... I could hear those men screaming." He stood behind her, putting his coat over her shoulders. "On the one hand, we both know you didn't kill those men, and I can't arrest you for something you didn't do. But on the other hand, I can't let you just walk out of here as if nothing happened."

Raya turned to face him, her eyes filled with guilt as she held out her arms, expecting to be handcuffed. "I know."

He put her arms in the sleeves of his jacket and buttoned it up, covering the blood on her flesh. "We both know those men got exactly what they deserved. With the war going on and doing everything we can to survive, they probably would've gotten away with it." He opened the door of his transport, and Raya remained silent as she got in.

There was an awkward silence between them as Kendelson drove her to the hospital. He got out and held out his hand as he opened her door. Raya put her hand in his and offered to return his coat. "Just leave it at the front desk when you leave."

She thanked him for his kindness and then headed into the hospital.

⎯⎯⎯••◆••⎯⎯⎯

Raya approached the front desk, asking about Carl. The receptionist looked up at Raya. "Captain Winfield is stable and recovering in his room."

She removed the jacket, laid it on the front desk, and shifted. Raya followed his scent to a room at the end of the hallway and slowly approached him. He tried to get out of bed to comfort her. She stood on her hind legs, one paw resting on the edge of his bed, while the other gently pushed him back down, shaking her head.

"All right, I'll stay in bed," he told her, "but only if you lay next to me." He smiled, knowing she was too big in her current form.

Raya reluctantly shifted and lay beside him, sobbing heavily in his arms. Carl's heart broke seeing her sadness. He had only wanted to show her a good time. Let her see the joy of his world. But instead, she saw its ugly side. Carl continued holding her until they had fallen asleep.

He was awakened by a knock on the door and looked down to see Raya still sleeping, her arms wrapped around his waist as her head rested on his chest. The door opened, followed by a familiar voice. "Winfield. It's General Goleen!"

Carl's heart jumped as he quickly threw the blanket over Raya. "Come in, sir!" he said with a nervous chuckle.

Goleen came around the corner. "Captain, I'm glad to see you're okay. I was afraid I would never get the chance to thank you."

Carl looked at the general with confusion. "For what, sir?"

"The happiness you've given my daughter... Of course, I'm not thrilled that it's from a Human... I thought my daughter would have better taste, but your spirit...is stronger than anyone I've known...which puts you on the top of the candidates' list." Goleen gave Carl a stern look, and his voice deepened. "But if you break my daughter's heart... I'll tear yours out. Do you understand me?"

"Crystal clear, sir," he said nervously.

Goleen turned and headed for the door. "And Captain, tell my daughter good morning when she wakes up."

"Yes, sir."

Carl drew a deep sigh of relief when he heard the door shut and looked under the blanket to see Raya looking up at him. "You little coward, you were awake the whole time!" he said jokingly.

"Sorry, my dad can be scary at times," she responded bashfully.

Carl looked at her and laughed. "You're telling me. I think I just aged ten years," he responded, moving in for a kiss.

The next day, Alice and the girls were talking with the doctor in the lobby when Carl walked in. "Dad!" Tylee and Zoe shouted, greeting him with teary eyes as Alice followed them.

Alice hugged him. There was a worried tone as she tried to hold back her tears. "I talked to the doctor, and he said you can return to duty on Monday. Until then, you're not to do any heavy lifting, do you hear me?" She paused for a moment as she stared into his eyes. "I'm serious, Carl."

"All right, Alice, I promise. I'll take it easy."

"You better!" she scolded as they walked to the transport.

Alice was driving them home, explaining to Carl about the yard sale they were having for the Mud Dogs when she noticed the inquisitive look on his face as she was talking. "What! You don't think they deserve it," she said, her hands clenching tightly to the steering wheel as she let him have it with all guns blazing. "These girls have been treated like shit because of a parasite..."

He could almost picture the steam coming out of her ears. "You're right, Alice. I should have just kept my mouth shut... I don't know what I was thinking," Carl interrupted sarcastically.

"I'm sorry, Carl. I don't mean to take it out on you." Alice took a moment to calm down as they stopped at a red light. "These girls have nothing...no money...no civilian clothes... and now everybody expects them to save their asses." Alice took a deep breath and rolled her eyes in frustration. "We all know how important these girls are...and I feel it's time people start showing their gratitude." She apologized for her outburst and kept silent for the remainder of the trip as Tylee and Zoe sat quietly in the back seat, staring at their media pads.

When they pulled up to his driveway, Alice parked the transport as Carl looked at her. "Alice, I thought we should donate Caroline's stuff to the yard sale. I know it's what she would've wanted."

Tylee and Zoe agreed and even offered to help, while Alice gave him a concerned look. "Are you sure about this, Carl?" she responded, holding his hand.

Carl's body trembled at the thought of 305 and the uncertainty of his eternal soul. Even now, her dark energy slowly consumed him, stripping away layers of what was left of his humanity. He didn't blame her for it. She was feeding on scraps compared to what the Shezón took from him. But his humanity came at a price, and now it was time to collect. Carl gave Alice a reassuring smile. "Yes...time to move on... Let the dead rest in peace."

Alice reached over and gave him a hug and a peck on the cheek. "Then there's no time like the present. I'll call Alex, tell him to come over, and we'll all go for dinner afterward. My treat."

"All right, Alice, but you're helping me, so it'll be my treat." Alice agreed, and the two of them went into the house.

⸻ ••◆•• ⸻

It was Sunday morning, the day of the yard sale. Tylee and Zoe had gotten up early and loaded the transport with the donations. "Dad! Hurry up, we're ready to go," Tylee shouted up the stairs.

Carl was putting on his basketball shorts. "All right, give me five minutes." As he opened the drawer to get a pair of socks, he found a picture of Caroline he had forgotten to give to Alice.

She had just given birth to Tylee and was holding her for the first time. Carl started drifting down memory lane when Tylee interrupted his thoughts. "Dad, we're gonna be late!"

Carl smiled and put the picture in his pocket. "All right, I'm coming down now."

When they got to the Mud Dogs' quarters, Carl was warmly welcomed by the ladies in the office. "Oh, sir, how are you feeling?"

"Much better, thanks," Carl responded as Grace pulled him aside.

Grace looked up at him. He could tell she was concerned about something. "Sir, the dolls have completed their Rebirth and are now at the processing station with the rest of the Human candidates."

Carl felt his blood boiling. "Are they out of their minds?"

Grace held Carl's hand as she interrupted him. "You need not worry about the dolls, Captain. They're completely Human... For now." Grace turned and started walking away.

"Grace, what are you talking about?"

"To put it quite simply, sir. The dolls respond to growth. As your team grows stronger, so will the dolls."

"Grace, how do you know this?"

"Because they told me."

Carl watched her walk away. Like the dolls, Grace was very much a mystery. He never trusted people or things he didn't know and wasn't pushing the panic button on the dolls because he knew Alex Raincheck. Alex always kept an ace up his sleeve in dangerous situations; these dolls were no exception. Carl smiled. He felt there was more to Grace than met the eye and looked forward to working with her.

Carl turned his attention to Tylee and Zoe, who were unpacking the boxes, carefully hanging their mother's clothes on the rack while they talked about their memories of her. Carl smiled, picturing their mother looking down from heaven and seeing how fast her babies were growing. Zoe was more like her mother and even had her demeanor. As for Tylee, she was more like her father, sometimes too much, he thought to himself. But when it came to genetics, Tylee was like most women on her mother's side, or as Alice puts it, bosomy blessed.

Carl turned to see Raya and Ocean coming across the street. They carried two medium-sized boxes, one stacked on the other as they peeked over the side. When they got closer, he noticed the boxes were made of metal, and on the sides were marked hardcover books. "Those look heavy," Carl responded as they passed by.

They set the boxes next to one of the tables. "Heavy, Carl, they are only fifty-pound boxes!" Raya responded modestly as Ocean ran over to Tylee and Zoe.

Carl pulled her into his arms. "Silly me," he whispered, kissing her lips.

While the ladies helped customers carry the furniture to the transports, Carl was sitting at the cashier's table ringing up items and answering questions about the Mud Dogs and the firepower they would bring to the battle. Carl was proud but not surprised to see all the support the Mud Dogs were getting, especially from the infantry units. Behind their smiles were beaten-down soldiers, their spirits crushed but not broken. It was the one thing the Shezón couldn't take from them.

By midafternoon, the sun had taken its toll on everyone. People were exhausted and drenched in sweat. "All right, everyone, let's call it quits!" Epstein shouted as she took the cash box and called for a bank escort.

Carl was talking with Raya when Tylee and Zoe came up behind him, anxious and ready to go home. "Well, I better get going." He smiled and kissed her.

"All right, Carl. I'll see you tomorrow." She turned and headed back to the others.

When they got home, Zoe and Tylee headed into the kitchen to make dinner as he grabbed the broom and a dustpan and headed up to the attic. While sweeping the floor, Carl had mixed feelings seeing how empty it looked. Although not everything was gone, the girls wanted to keep a few of their mother's belongings, such as baby clothes and their mother's wedding dress.

Even though she wasn't in his life, he still had her memories and the feeling of closure seeing all the smiles on people's faces when they purchased her things. It was the same joyous smile Caroline had whenever she'd bring home something she had found at a yard sale or secondhand store. Carl chuckled, remembering her answer when he'd tell her it was junk. "It's not junk. It's cute," she'd debate, followed by a kiss that always melted his heart. Carl drew a deep breath and grinned. He was no longer afraid of life's changes or moving on. Now he could dedicate his time to the Mud Dogs. He didn't know how he would do it, but somehow, in the next two years, he had to make miracles happen. Zoe hollered up the stairs, informing him dinner was ready. Carl swept up the pile of dust and then headed downstairs to join his daughters.

——••◆••——

The day of the grand opening had arrived. Carl was in the kitchen reviewing his speech while waiting for the coffee to brew. Zoe and Tylee sat at the table, eating breakfast and staring at their media pads. Tylee looked up for a brief moment. "Oh, Dad. Some lady from the office called. She wants you to go in ASAP."

Carl grabbed his traveling mug and filled it with coffee. "All right, if they call back, tell them I'm on my way."

——••◆••——

Carl arrived at the government building and walked down the hallway to his office when he heard several loud, angry roars. He quickened his pace and opened the door to see total chaos. Sergeant Epstein held underwear and demanded they be put on while unhappy felines hissed and growled at her.

"Sergeant Epstein... What's going on here?"

"Oh, sir... Am I glad to see you!" Epstein looked up at him. "Apparently, some idiot in uniforms thought one-size-fits-all in bras... Then, on top of it, they were given thongs."

Carl scrunched up his face. "Thongs... What are those?"

"Very uncomfortable underwear... I got it squared away, and now they refuse to wear it."

Carl decided to relieve her from the stress. "All right, Sergeant. I'll talk to them."

"Thank you, sir." She gave him the underwear and then headed for the door.

Carl looked over at them. "Ladies, there was a mix-up in the uniform department. The problems have been fixed now. So please...try them on one more time." The women hesitated and then shifted into Human form.

Carl went into his office to practice his speech while the ladies changed. When they were finished, Raya knocked on his door. "Carl, we're ready."

He walked out of his office and was speechless, seeing how beautiful the ladies looked in their evening gowns, and before he could speak, one of the Newtopians walked up to him, her eyes filled with confusion. "Sir, do we have to wear the paint?"

"The what? Oh, the makeup... No, you look just beautiful without it." Carl smiled as he looked them in the eyes. "All of you do."

The women blushed. "Thank you, sir," they said in unison.

Raya could tell something was bothering Carl. "What's wrong? Are you nervous?"

Carl looked her in the eyes. "Yes, but not about the speech."

"Then what, Carl?" Raya wrapped her arms around his waist.

"These next two years. Not only do we have to get these girls trained... But now we have to protect them at all costs."

Raya was confused. "From who, Carl?"

"From people who don't want these girls to succeed."

"Why? That doesn't make any sense."

Carl kissed her lips and smiled. "Pride... People have walked all over these girls since the day they were born... Giving them labels such as crazy, out of control, or just a menace to society. And when these girls become Mud Dogs... It's gonna come back and bite the same people in the ass."

Grace sensed his fear and walked over to him. "Don't worry, sir, you won't fail... That much I know." Grace turned and headed out the door, followed by the rest of the women.

Sergeant Epstein came into the office. "Sir, they're ready for your speech."

"All right, thank you, Sergeant." He grabbed his work pad off the desk and headed out the door.

"Oh, sir. The Evolutions... They're not wearing underwear."

Carl laughed as he headed for the auditorium.

————— ••◆•• —————

It was the day of the candidates' arrival. Carl was still asleep when the central control unit woke him up. "Captain Winfield. You have an emergency connections request."

"Okay, I'll take it," Carl muttered, getting out of bed. "Captain Winfield speaking."

"Sergeant Bronx, sir. I'm sorry to bother you so early, sir, but I'm outside the Mud Dogs' quarters with the cadets."

Carl became concerned. "Sergeant, where are the others?"

"They were called away, sir... All the sergeants were." Bronx paused. "Last night, the Shezón invaded Uteaka."

Carl fell to his knees, imagining the pain Raya must be going through. "All right, Sergeant. I'm on my way."

————— ••◆•• —————

Sergeant Bronx had the girls standing at attention when he arrived at the Mud Dogs' quarters. "All right. Sir, they're all yours."

"Thank you, Sergeant."

"My pleasure, sir."

Carl contacted Sergeant Epstein and asked her to meet him at the quarters of the Mud Dogs. He then turned his attention to the twenty cadets. "My name is Captain Winfield. I want to thank all of you for joining. In the military, respect is earned, not given. And by putting your name on the dotted line, you have earned my respect. Now, it is my turn to earn yours. The next two years will be the hardest, and you will be pushed to your limits until you can no longer move. And then you will be pushed again and again. By the time we're done with your training, you'll be kicking ass and breaking hearts. Do you understand?"

"Yes, sir," they shouted loudly.

"I can't hear you!" he shouted back.

"Yes, sir," they screamed at the top of their lungs.

Sergeant Epstein came onto the scene. "I can take over now, sir."

"Thank you, Sergeant." Carl turned and began walking away.

"Sir, please give the Uteakons my condolences."

"I will, Sergeant. Thank you." Carl turned and headed for his transport.

The streets of Bravo Six were filled with sadness as the Evolution community came together to support each other. Carl could feel the dark energy of 305 taking over what was once his humanity as he watched people cry over their loss, which painfully reminded him of his own. He pressed his foot on the accelerator, hoping to see Raya one last time before he completely turned into a blood soldier. He wanted to see her as a Human, not the monster he was becoming.

Carl drove to Raya's apartment building and rushed up the stairs to her side. When Ocean opened the door, he saw that she had been crying. He offered his arms to her and said, "Ocean, I'm so sorry." She ran into his embrace, and Carl could feel her helplessness as she sobbed. All she could say was, "Why?"

At that moment, Raya entered the room and asked calmly, "Carl, what are you doing here?" Although Raya showed no emotion, Carl knew she was trying her best to be strong for him. He extended an arm to her while Ocean held onto the other. "You don't have to be strong for me. I know how you feel," he whispered.

Raya broke down and cried in Carl's arms. As Ocean cried, Carl could feel the dark energy becoming one with him. Tears fell from his eyes as he embraced them, knowing that these were the last tears he would shed before the darkness consumed him entirely. Suddenly, his voice took on a dark, malevolent tone. "If they want a blood storm, we'll give them one."

❖

Carl was awakened by the central control unit's alarm clock. "Captain Winfield. This is your wake-up call!"

Carl slowly opened his eyes. "Okay, thank you. Any reminders?"

"You have one. Don't forget about the Mud Dogs' one-month review."

"Thank you," Carl responded as he headed for the bathroom.

Carl was stepping out of the shower when Tylee knocked on the bathroom door, reminding him breakfast was almost ready.

"Okay, give me ten minutes," Carl shouted through the door. He wrapped a towel around his waist, picked up his media pad, and texted Raya, reminding her that the Mud Dogs' first evaluation was on Monday.

Carl was surprised by how fast the cadets had adapted to military life. There were some difficulties along the way, particularly between the Marines' Coddy Cadets and the Army's Mud Dogs. This rivalry often led to intense arguments, resulting in a chaotic brawl. When well-meaning bystanders attempted to intervene, the combatants turned on their would-be helpers.

Carl ran the electric razor across the two-day stubble on

his scalp, thinking about the ongoing rivalry between the old Mud Dogs and the Coddy Cadets.

The old Mud Dogs fiercely rivaled the Coddys, leading to an all-out brawl known as Dawgfight. But the real show started when people tried to break up the fight; the Mud Dogs and the Coddys would team up to make short work of the intruders and go back to fighting each other. Their fights were legendary among the students; Carl enjoyed listening to his grandmother's stories about the old Mud Dogs when she was in college. However, over time, some stories become forgotten, while others get revised and replaced with new characters that everyone looks forward to reading about.

For the new Mud Dogs, their story began the first day they stood in formation, ready for inspection, and Carl was proud to be a part of the new Mud Dogs history.

Carl was jolted out of his thoughts when Tylee knocked on the door. "Dad, your breakfast is getting cold... Comb your hair later!" Tylee joked as she and Zoe erupted in laughter.

Carl opened the door and kissed his comedic daughters on the cheek as he went to his room. "Five more minutes."

"Yeah, right, you said that five minutes ago," Zoe shot back, laughing as she went downstairs.

While getting dressed, Carl could vividly imagine the new cadets in their school uniforms standing outside the dorms, waiting nervously for their first day of school or training, as the Army called it. The Human cadets were on one side, while the Uteakon cadets were on the other.

Sergeant Albright stood by his side, holding the roster pad as rain sprinkled her cocoa-colored skin. Albright was petite and lovely to look at, but her beauty kept a 400-pound secret as a tan and black panther lurked within her. "All right, ladies, you will sound off when I call your name." Her thunderous voice echoed in the early morning.

He remembered surveying the new recruits, eagerly looking back at him as he deliberated which one would be the new leader of the Mud Dogs. Two of the Human girls stood out: Warrior and Bookworm. They were the most formidable girls and the obvious choices, but their personalities differed as night and day. Where beauty shines, the other hides hers behind a mask.

Albright suddenly broke the silence. "Captain Winfield, sir, everyone is accounted for and ready for inspection."

"All right, thank you, Sergeant."

Carl Walked over to Warrior, his first choice for captain. He stood tall and intimidating, staring into her bluish-green eyes while raindrops raced down her pale cheeks. "Good morning, cadet."

She was young and vibrant, not intimidated by an old man, he thought to himself. She spoke politely but with an element of defiance. "Good morning, sir...how are you doing?"

Carl's smile barely registered as he whispered, "I'm fine, cadet... Tell me, what motivated you to join the Army?" Carl watched the raindrops shimmering on her pretty face while she pondered her answer.

"Just looking to spread my horizons... Sir," she declared with a flirtatious whisper.

Oblivious to her joke, Carl corrected her, "I think you mean 'expand.'"

"That too!"

She smiled just as he suddenly caught the punchline while listening to the barely audible chuckles from the platoon. Her name was Elizabeth Blackheart. According to his daughter, she was popular on social media, and all the guys wanted her, while the girls admired and aspired to be like her, and understandably so.

She was the daughter of the president of the largest supplier of military equipment, the Red Phoenix Corporation, Marcus Blackheart. Like her father, her unwavering ruthlessness inspired others to strive for excellence and show no mercy to obstacles and adversaries. He smiled and moved on to his next choice, Jessica Stone, a.k.a. Bookworm.

Like her adversary, she was intelligent, with long blonde hair and a beautiful voice. But her personal life and appearance stayed hidden behind her mask. "Where you from, cadet?" he asked sternly.

"Planet Shield, sir," she answered confidently.

"The planet's controlled by the corporations. Isn't it?"

"Yes, sir."

Even though he knew he would regret it, he asked anyway. "Tell me, young lady, what do you hope to gain from the Mud Dogs?"

"Well, sir, if I had to choose, I'd say your tutelage and firm discipline. Sir." There was no mistaking the suggestive tone in her voice as the other girls snickered.

Albright, fed up with the girls' behavior, bellowed in a commanding voice, instructing them to stand at attention. "I want twenty laps around the building." She approached Warrior and Bookworm and stood just an inch away from their faces. "As for you two comedians, you will come to my office after school. We'll see how funny you really are...and for your own sake, you better hope I have a sense of humor," she snarled.

◆◆◆◆◆

Despite the mystery surrounding her, Bookworm stood out for her determination to achieve her goals, regardless of obstacles. Although it seemed like a perfect match, there was one significant issue. The tension between them was as thick as mud and as stable as nitroglycerin, which caused a divide between the Mud Dogs. This could have grave consequences on the battlefield, where quick thinking and courage as a team were constantly put to the test.

Carl knew from his own experience that there was no room for mistakes regarding the bugs. The Shezón weren't monsters; they were intelligent and lethal predators, particularly the Mantis soldiers, who were twice the size of Humans and possessed remarkable agility.

But hunting them was difficult, especially in the jungles, where their preferred method of attack was to wait in hiding, grab the enemy, and decapitate them with their powerful mandibles, and killing them was a different experience altogether. Their skeletal structure was like mirrored steel reflecting laser and armor-piercing ammo. It was like trying to destroy a tank with sticks and stones, but not impossible, just incredibly difficult. But thanks to those girls and the Tiny Wonder within them, the tables were about to turn.

Carl thought about the NewGen and the limited information military scientists had about the parasite. The NewGen was an advanced life form that served to maintain the health of its host for its own survival. The NewGen were biological engineers that altered the host's DNA during fetal development, bypassing the need for generational changes. At first glance, the girls appeared no different from others regarding their appearance and behavior. However, their unique internal composition set them apart.

He remembered reading an article suggesting that Humans infected with the parasite possessed lightning-fast reflexes and cat-like agility, with infected females just as strong as the average male.

However, this brought little comfort to the host. All these girls wanted was their share of a brighter future, and the only way to achieve it was to fight for it and protect the people who put them in their situation. It was like pouring salt on an open wound. Whether the NewGen was a blessing or a curse, the Human race wasn't the only species chosen as a host.

The NewGen appeared in Evolutions. The felines possessed a distinct feature of being taller and more robust than their typical counterparts. However, due to their perceived threat to fragile masculinity, some were even killed; although rare, male NewGens also existed, and due to their defensive nature, they can blend into society without attracting much attention.

When provoked, the hosts become aggressive, which is more tolerable in men than women. Whether the older generation liked it or not, the presence of the NewGen was one more link that brought man and beast closer together.

Carl reminisced about the Uteakon and Human conflict he had heard stories about. Soldiers were said to strip the carcasses of fallen Uteakons, taking everything from their hide to their claws. Even the meat was harvested. However, his girlfriend once pointed out that Uteakons weren't entirely innocent, especially the males, known to gorge themselves on Human soldiers. Carl grinned, recalling the disgusted look on her face after she had finished her story and the snide comment she made before walking away from him. "Must be some idiotic male rite of passage or something just as stupid." As for the younger generation, the war between man and beast was now just a part of forgotten history. Like the rest of the youth, the girls quickly adapted and adopted new cultural changes.

Not everyone was happy with the situation. Carl's daughters claimed that the Evolution girls weren't shy in pursuing a potential mate, especially if he had the right scent. Initially, this was not an issue for Human girls. However, as hygiene practices changed and boys began to learn about Evolutionary Biology, it became clear that females were more attracted to a man's smell than his physical appearance.

While this worked in favor of the guys, for the girls, Human or Evolution, their choice of boyfriends rattled the civilian population. People unfamiliar with Evolutions were worried for their children's safety, and the same applied to Evolutions.

As a father, Carl understood their concerns. His oldest daughter, Zoe, was dating an Evolution soldier named Remix. Whenever she looked at him, it was always with a twinkle in her eye, even though she was well aware that a five-hundred-pound white feline lurked beyond his dark skin and Human frame. But what really left him with an unforgettable first impression was the cold, silent stare of his moon-blue eyes and large jaws that looked as if they were made of steel and covered in fur.

But to Zoe, he was her gentle giant and first love. When Remix talked to her, it was with the utmost respect and always with the same twinkle Zoe exhibited.

From a father's perspective, Remix was the very definition of a gentleman and a positive representation of the Army and his mother, who happened to be his girlfriend. Ironically, her father shared the same concerns about him.

After slipping the media pad into his pocket, Carl joined his daughters for breakfast.

———••◆••———•

Carl became concerned when he noticed Zoe staring at her breakfast with a pale look, lost in thought. "Baby girl, are you okay?"

Zoe turned her attention to him. "Yeah, Dad... I'm fine."

He brushed the hair away from her eyes. "You look pale and haven't even touched your breakfast."

Zoe reassured him she was good. "I'm just having female problems, Dad." She excused herself from the table, kissed him on the cheek, then headed to her room.

There was an awkward silence between him and Tylee as Zoe walked away. "She's worried about Remix. His unit got shipped out last week, and she hasn't heard from him since," she whispered before turning her attention back to her media pad.

As Carl thought of Zoe, the dark energy within him pulsated and grew stronger as it fed on the emotional torment triggered by his memories. He pictured himself at Fort Leonard Wood, standing at the door of the house where he and Caroline had first lived as newlyweds. Zoe was three years old, and Tylee had just turned one.

He remembered pausing before opening the door, trying

to shake the guilt of being on the battlefield for so long. When his courage was gathered, he'd walked through the door with open arms and a smile. "Where's my favorite girl?" he'd shout as Zoe would drop what she was doing and run to him with open arms. "Daddy!"

He picked her up and kissed her cheek. "There's my baby girl!"

Caroline entered the room carrying Tylee, reminding Zoe it was bath time. Carl laughed and put Zoe down as she argued with her mother in Russian. "Do as your mom says... I'll still be here when you're done."

Zoe reluctantly agreed. "Okay, Daddy!"

Caroline turned and walked over to him. "And you...can spend time with your daughter." Carl was nervous, seeing how tiny and frail Tylee looked. Caroline smiled and gently put Tylee in his arms. "It's okay...she won't break." She kissed his lips and then escorted Zoe to the bathroom.

Carl was holding Tylee and watching her tiny lips form a smile when she suddenly blurted out a word that sounded much like "Cornel," or at least he thought he heard it. Carl's eyes widened as he shouted to Caroline, "Hey, she spoke! She spoke!"

"She didn't speak!" Caroline insisted.

"She did!"

"Okay, what did she say?"

"I think she said 'colonel,'" Carl answered confidently.

"That was gurgle, not 'colonel!'" Caroline asserted firmly and turned her attention back to Zoe.

Carl brought his thoughts back to the present, got up from the table, and poured another cup of coffee when Tylee suddenly asked about Fort Eagle.

As he contemplated the question, a sensation of dark energy reverberated and throbbed inside his mind. "I remember dead soldiers everywhere. The streets: painted in blood. I could hear women and children screaming as the Shezón carried them off." Carl sat silently, dwelling on all he had lost during the hour he spent in what he would never forget as hell.

Tylee sensed her father's pain, set her media pad on the table, walked over, and embraced him. "I'm sorry, Dad. I shouldn't have asked." Her eyes teared up.

Carl gave Tylee a warm smile and kissed her cheek. "It's okay, baby girl; you have every right to know."

Tylee sat in the chair next to him as he continued his story. "I was twelve when the Shezón appeared in the skies and unleashed hell on Fort Eagle. Your uncle and I were the only survivors. We were given the choice of getting adopted by a civilian family or remaining with the Army. We chose the latter and never looked back."

"What happened after that, Dad?"

"We were sent to an Army training academy. I was small for my age, so I had to train harder than others..."

Tylee suddenly burst into laughter. "I'm sorry, Dad. I just can't picture you as small."

"I used to be small when I was a kid. That's why your grandfather taught me how to fight. He always said, 'If you're going to be small, you better be mighty.'" Carl paused for a moment and became quiet. "After the Fort Eagle incident, I didn't think I would ever love again. Only because of your mother did I find love again."

"Didn't you meet Mom at college?"

"Yes, we were waiting in line to register for classes, and your mother was ahead of me, chatting with Alice. They were having a good time, and when your mother turned around, she said something in Russian to me. I didn't understand, so Alice translated for me, 'She said you should stop looking so serious and smile. You're scaring everyone.' Your mother laughed and told me it was all good fun. Over time, your mother helped me break down the walls I had built around myself when I made a promise to never love again."

Just then, there was a knock at the door. Tylee excused herself and went to answer it, leaving Carl to his own thoughts.

He could only imagine how disappointed Caroline would be seeing the intense animosity within him or the cold, dark void that lingered in his heart as if love and happiness had never existed. As Carl sipped his coffee, he felt a warm sensation inside him as the hot liquid ran down his throat. It reminded him of a time when the blood in his veins wasn't cold, and the light in his heart had shone its brightest. However, that changed the day they took his family and the only girl he thought he'd ever love—Alex Raincheck's little sister.

There was a pain in Carl's heart that even time could not heal, nor could it extinguish the hate within him. He learned that painful lesson when his wife was taken by the bugs.

Carl sipped his coffee, feeling the warmth spread through his body and easing the icy grip around his heart. All he had left in the universe was his daughters, and he was determined to do whatever it took to keep them safe.

They needed to do more than just eliminate a few soldiers. His objective was to enter their dimension, destroy the queen, and cut off the empire's ability to replenish its dwindling number of soldiers, slowly leading to the empire's destruction.

Defeating the queen was easier said than done; the Shezón traveled across dimensions as easily as going to the local market. Their technology was far more advanced than the Alliance's, so they wouldn't expect an invasion, giving the Mud Dogs an advantage. However, this advantage was only theoretical since the Alliance lacked the technology to cross dimensions...for now. Carl checked the clock on the wall and realized it was already 7:30 AM. He had agreed to meet the cadets on the training field. He got up from the table, grabbed his gym bag, and headed out the door.

When Carl arrived at the training field, the cadets were waiting for him in their PT uniforms. "Ladies, I apologize for keeping you waiting."

The girls were on the last stretch of their ten laps, and Carl had the bullhorn in his hand. He could tell that the cadets were tired and ready to give up. Carl decided to motivate them with some words of encouragement: "All right, soldiers, let's move it! Time to work the fat off those asses!" Suddenly, the girls found their second wind and started running toward him. As Carl ran for his life, he made a mental note to work on sensitivity issues with the Mud Dogs.

# ABOUT ATMOSPHERE PRESS

Founded in 2015, Atmosphere Press was built on the principles of Honesty, Transparency, Professionalism, Kindness, and Making Your Book Awesome. As an ethical and author-friendly hybrid press, we stay true to that founding mission today.

If you're a reader, enter our giveaway for a free book here:

SCAN TO ENTER
BOOK GIVEAWAY

If you're a writer, submit your manuscript for consideration here:

SCAN TO SUBMIT
MANUSCRIPT

And always feel free to visit Atmosphere Press and our authors online at atmospherepress.com. See you there soon!

# ABOUT THE AUTHOR

**CHRIS BACHE**, a single father raising three children, stepped back from full-time work to fulfill a lifelong dream by authoring his first book, *Children of Earth*. He considers this creative journey to have been enriching and sincerely hopes that readers worldwide will connect with it as deeply as he did while bringing it to life. He is profoundly thankful for his children, whose unwavering faith has constantly encouraged him throughout this endeavor. Chris is currently working on the second book of the series.

www.ingramcontent.com/pod-product-compliance
Lightning Source LLC
Chambersburg PA
CBHW020909160726
47993CB00005B/1894